BLOOD ROYAL

BLOOD DESTINY SERIES BOOK FIVE

CONNIE SUTTLE

To Walter, Joe, Larry, Lee, Dianne, Sarah and Mark.
Thank you.

ACKNOWLEDGMENTS

As always, this book is the result of collaboration. If it weren't for the support of my editor, my cover artist and my beta readers, it would be less than it is. All mistakes, as usual, are mine and no other's.

About the Author:
Connie Suttle lives in Oklahoma with her husband and a conglomerate of cats. They have finally banded together to make their demands, which has proven disconcerting to all humans involved.

You may find Connie in the following ways:
Facebook: Connie Suttle Author
Twitter: @subtledemon
Website and Blog: subtledemon.com

ALSO BY CONNIE SUTTLE

Blood Destiny Series:

Blood Wager

Blood Passage

Blood Sense

Blood Domination

Blood Royal

Blood Queen

Blood Rebellion

Blood War

Blood Redemption

Blood Reunion

Blood Destiny Series Boxed Set (Books 1-10)

Blood Recall

Blood Alliance*

Legend of the Ir'Indicti Series:

Bumble

Shadowed

Target

Vendetta

Destroyer

Legend of the Ir'Inditi Boxed Set

High Demon Series:
Demon Lost
Demon Revealed
Demon's King
Demon's Quest
Demon's Revenge
Demon's Dream

God Wars Series:
Blood Double
Blood Trouble
Blood Revolution
Blood Love
Blood Finale

Saa Thalarr Series:
Hope and Vengeance
Wyvern and Company
Observe and Protect*

First Ordinance Series:
Finder
Keeper
BlackWing
SpellBreaker
WhiteWing

R-D Series:
Cloud Dust
Cloud Invasion
Cloud Rebel

Latter Day Demons Series:
Hot Demon in the City
A Demon's Work is Never Done
A Demon's Due

Seattle Elementals Series:
Your Money's Worth
Worth Your While*

BlackWing Pirates Series
MindSighted
MindMage
MindRogue
MindMaster*

Black Rose Sorceress Series
The Rose Mark

Rose and Thorn

Black Rose Queen

Queen of Thorns and Roses

Future Wars Series

Buffer Zone

Black Zone*

Other Titles from SubtleDemon Publishing:

Malefactor

Transgressor

Underhanded*

by Joe Scholes

*Forthcoming

CHAPTER 1

I was alone in bed when I woke and I didn't expect that. Gavin's ring was back on my finger too, with a matching wedding band. He'd slipped the rings on my finger while I was still sleeping—the schmuck.

Yeah, I still wanted to smack him around for being presumptuous, along with Wlodek and every stinking member of the Council. Of course, that would put me right back on the rogue hit list, so I just slapped a hand over my eyes and growled.

"Nice growl. You're coming along very well." My hand slid off my face and I glared up at Tony.

"What the hell are you doing in my bedroom?" I did a little more growling. If Gavin knew he was here, Tony might be a dead man. Well, vampire now, I guess.

"Wlodek's downstairs having a big pow-wow with Gavin, René and the others so I sneaked in. You should have told me how great it is to be vampire. I love it." Tony's grin was huge as he stared down at me, and a lock of black hair threatened to fall into his clear, gray eyes. Tony looked younger—in his twenties younger—and a mischievous dimple showed in a very youthful-looking cheek. Anthony Hancock, newly turned vampire that he was, seemed to be enjoying his life away from the sun.

"Tony, stop being a shithead," I grumbled, slapping a hand across my eyes again.

"Hey, is that any way to talk to your new cousin?" he was still grinning; I opened a space between fingers just to check.

"Who told you that?" I asked tiredly.

"Well, René is Gavin's cousin—you said so yourself. And if I understand what René said, then Gavin managed to marry you while you were gone somewhere. We're cousins-in-law, I guess." Tony reflected on that for a moment. "Just how does that work, baby? They can marry you off like that? Doesn't sound fair to me."

"Welcome to the land of unfairness," I huffed, letting the hand slide off my face. "If you'll remove yourself from my bed," I made a motion with my hands (Tony had plopped down beside me and looked as if he were willing to stay there for a while), "I'll get up and get dressed." Tony ignored the hint and stayed where he was.

"Who is that Kifirin guy? Did I hear right? He's a High Lord or something? From where?" Tony was full of questions and in a talkative mood. I wanted to slap a hand over his mouth, just to shut him up.

"René is going to lock you up and throw away the key," I snapped. Unless he had the patience of a saint, that is.

"Come on, give me some answers, I'm dying over here," the dimple was back and mocking laughter shone in his eyes. "Oops, already did that."

"Tony, do not, and I repeat, do not start with the dead jokes."

That made him laugh. "So where were you for three weeks?" he demanded. Just like that, we were back to business. I sat up on the bed and glared at Tony. How was he up so early? I still felt sluggish and wished coffee had some effect on me; I'd be drinking it if it did.

"I was off-planet," I replied. "On Refizan."

"You were not," he frowned at me. "And there's no such place as Refizan."

"I was and there is," I denied his denial. "That's what the locals called the planet anyway; Karzac was from there."

"Karzac? Lissa, are you delusional? Did that fight last night injure you somehow?" He reached out to touch my forehead. I batted his hand away.

"Lissa is not injured," Karzac himself was suddenly in my room, causing Tony to jump. "I would know; I am a healer and physician for the Saa Thalarr," he informed Tony haughtily, a slight bit of anger showing in his green-gold eyes.

The curmudgeonly physician side of him was present and in hurricane force. At least Karzac's hair was combed neatly, so he hadn't been treating patients in the last half hour.

"I came by to let Lissa know that the six you managed to poison with her blood have now been healed; I and one of my associates have taken care of your little faux pas," Karzac glared accusingly at Tony. "I certainly hope you have learned something from this, young one."

I was off the bed and hugging Karzac in a nanosecond. I might have been crying too, if my sniffles were any indication. "Thank you, thank you, thank you," I may have kissed Karzac, I was so happy.

"Lissa, that is the least I can do; you saved Dragon and my planet," Karzac held me away from him.

"I don't care," I wiped tears off my face. "I felt so awful about those men."

"I know. I must go now." Karzac beamed and disappeared.

"That was Karzac," I made a face at Tony. "I have to dress. Go away."

"You really were off-planet?" Tony stood and followed me into my bathroom. I wasn't prepared to have a conversation about aliens with the former Director of the Joint NSA/Homeland Security Department. Mostly because I didn't really know anything.

"I really was off-planet. Now go away before Gavin catches you in here. I'm not looking forward to hearing about your death a second time." I pointed toward the bathroom door.

"You were upset about that, weren't you?" Tony was grinning again and not taking the hint. "Come on; admit it—you care about me."

"Tony, Gavin will remove your head. I don't want that to happen. Shoo. Go away. Go have breakfast or dinner or whatever."

"I already ate; you're the one who can't get up at the right time. Sunset was nearly an hour ago."

"So, doing your usual, huh? Coming in and making my rising miserable, just because you can?" I had hands on my hips. I thought to look down at how I was dressed and sure enough, my nipples were showing through my thin, stretchy pajama top. Tony hadn't failed to notice either.

"Do I have to throw you out? Is that what you're waiting for?" I was truly grumpy, now; he'd made no pretense about staring at my breasts. My cell phone rang; it was sitting on my bedside table so I stalked past Tony to snatch it up and answer. It was Winkler.

"What the hell is going on? I just heard from Weldon that Hancock is a vampire now." Winkler wasn't wasting time on formal greetings.

"News travels fast, I guess," I mumbled. Winkler heard—his hearing is as good as mine. "Do you want to talk to him?"

"He's there?" Winkler asked. I didn't bother with an answer; I handed the phone to Tony.

"Hancock here," Tony said. Honestly, that blunt Director of the Joint NSA/Homeland Security Department would never go away, even if he were a baby vamp.

"Holy shit, they weren't lying," Winkler muttered.

"No, not in the least," Tony acknowledged. "A vampire was helping Paul, Deryn and me with the terrorist investigation in Paris when my hotel was bombed. My femoral artery was severed and he knew I was dying. He saved me the only way he could."

"Do you have a name for this vampire?" Winkler asked.

"I'm not allowed to reveal the name of my sire. He has instructed me not to do so and I'll honor his wishes. If not for him, I'd be in a box headed back to the states."

I was learning something, just by listening to Tony talk with Winkler. No wonder the vampire laws stated that death must be imminent to make a turn—the newly turned vampire was grateful for the intervention. It also brought up the fact that I hadn't been a good candidate in the vampire community's eyes; I had been in good health at the time and was particularly ungrateful for my turning.

Leaving Tony to have his conversation with Winkler, I stalked into the bathroom, rounded the turn into my walk-in closet, grabbed some clothes and proceeded to dress quickly. While I combed my hair at the dressing table afterward, I noticed my face held a bit more color and my lips seemed a little rosier since returning from Refizan.

I looked like my mother now—she'd been beautiful when she was young, with strawberry blonde hair that curled just a bit, sky-blue eyes with thick lashes and creamy skin that didn't require make-up. My mother only wore make-up after Howard Graham hit her in the face—to cover bruises.

It was probably a good thing he was already dead. He wouldn't want to meet up with me after I'd become vampire. Sighing over the twists and turns in my life, I set the brush down and returned to my bedroom. Tony was still there, talking to Winkler.

"They put Jennings in charge?" Tony didn't sound surprised—in fact, he sounded relieved. He was talking about Agent Bill Jennings, who'd been strictly by the book when I first met him. He'd loosened up during our travels across the U.S.

"Yeah, he's already contacted me about the updates to the software." Uh-oh. I was being forced to hand Tony and Winkler some secret and obscure truths.

"Both of you listen carefully," I came to stand next to Tony. "Winkler, the reason Gavin hung around so long when I was working for you was because he was watching you at the same time. The vampires were terrified of your software. They thought it could be used to identify them and destroy the race."

That statement brought complete silence from Winkler. I think he may have stopped breathing for a moment. "When you made the announcement that it didn't work and sold it to Tony," I went on, "that's when all of them relaxed their sphincters and Gavin hauled me off to the Council. If you want to live, you'll keep that information to yourselves."

Winkler didn't speak for several seconds. Tony was shocked, I could tell. He might have been less surprised if I'd suddenly sprouted a second head. "Holy shit," Winkler muttered finally. Tony was wide-eyed and nodding at Winkler's assessment.

"On another note," I said, changing the subject, "how are those babies doing, Winkler?" I wasn't going to ask about Kellee; she'd tried to kill me, with a little help from her dear old dad. Well, dear old departed dad, now.

"They're coming along very well, a girl and a boy!" Winkler was as happy as could be over that. That little girl was already spoiled and she wasn't out of the womb yet. Kellee was six months along or better, I figured. Female werewolves weren't as rare as female vampires, but the males outnumbered them six to one, at least. That's how Gavin found us—Tony and me—talking to Winkler over the phone about his babies. They were due the end of October, according to Kellee's physician.

Gavin frowned at first, finding Tony in my bedroom. But after listening to the phone conversation and hearing Winkler going on about the preparations he was making for the twins' arrival, his frown disappeared. In fact, he was smiling. Gavin likes children. Go figure. Who would think an Assassin for the Vampire Council had a weak spot for kids? He came up behind me and draped his arms around my shoulders, listening in as Tony and I talked with Winkler.

"So Kellee isn't giving you any trouble?" I asked.

"She's fine. We don't talk much; she was never a stellar conversationalist to begin with," Winkler snorted. "Did you hear that her mother and Davis have moved in together?"

Holy crap. I'd almost forgotten Davis; I'd handed the Boise Pack off to him after killing Kellee's dad and inadvertently inheriting his Pack in the process. "She wanted to?" The idea of Karl Johnson's widow in a relationship with Davis was a bit shocking.

"Hell, yeah," Winkler laughed. "Kellee's dad didn't let her make any decisions for herself. Davis likes her a lot and listens to her. Her life has changed dramatically and I think she likes her new freedom."

"What does Kellee think about that?"

"She tried to make her mother feel guilty over it and they ended up yelling over the phone. They're still grumpy with one another right now." Winkler was grinning—I could hear it in his voice.

"How's the new Second?" A werewolf named Trajan had taken Davis's spot when Davis moved to Boise.

"Trajan is doing great," Winkler replied. "He wasn't sure he wanted the authority, but it suits him, I think."

"Tell him he'll do fine as long as he doesn't challenge you," I said. "And that goes for anybody else who might get that idea."

"Gee, Lissa, does this mean you'll come back and act as Second if somebody gets his underwear twisted?" Winkler teased.

"Oh, look, Mr. Fuzzy can't take care of himself?" I was teasing him right back and he knew it.

"Lissa, the house next door went up for sale," Winkler was serious, suddenly. "I'm buying it for you."

"Winkler, what the hell do you think you're doing? What am I going to do with a house between Denton and Dallas?"

"Come and visit, sometime? Play with the kids? I don't know, Lissa. I just want you to have it."

"Buy it for her," Gavin said. Winkler now knew that Gavin had come into the room; he hadn't said anything earlier. "I'll pay someone to keep it up for her in the interim. Just send the information and invoices to the postal address you have."

"Will do," Winkler was smiling again; I just knew it.

We talked a few minutes more with Winkler before hanging up. Gavin's arms were now wrapped around me. Tony took the hint and left. "René already cares for his newest," Gavin kissed my neck.

"I think it's mutual," I replied. Gavin was now nibbling on my earlobe and that always makes me melt into a puddle. "I realized after talking with Tony that being grateful for your life is part of the sire-child bond," I mumbled. Why is it so hard to make a coherent point when somebody is playing with your breasts?

"That plays a very large part in the bonding," Gavin was doing his best to remove my blouse. "The child realizes quickly that their sire wants them, when they are there to feed them the first time and reassure them."

"Aurelius was an amazing sire, wasn't he?" I watched Gavin's nimble fingers unbutton my top. After all, René was out for blood ever since he'd learned that Xenides and Saxom had arranged for Aurelius' death.

"Aurelius was my father. And René's. Our blood parents were never as caring as Aurelius was." I ran my fingers through Gavin's wealth of dark brown hair—he keeps it short and it looks good that way. His dark eyes narrowed in pleasure as he tasted the skin over my collarbone. I traced his jaw with a finger. He kissed my hand and placed it around his neck. Gavin had my blouse off shortly after that and rational speech stopped for a while.

~

"Greggy, what's up?" Greg was sitting on a barstool at the island while Franklin cleaned the kitchen when I finally made it downstairs. I went to put my arms around Greg. Gavin wasn't far behind me; we'd shared a pint of blood after doing the horizontal bebop.

"My mother used to call me that," Greg said, patting my arms. I gave him a kiss on the cheek before letting him go. Greg's face held more lines and wrinkles than I remembered, but I wasn't about to point that out. The disease was taking its toll—in more ways than one.

"Frank, do you want some help?" I asked. I hadn't seen Lena since I'd left for Refizan, and asked Franklin about her, too.

"I'm almost done," Franklin turned to smile at me. Greg wasn't the only one looking a bit older. Greg's disease was weighing heavily on Frank, too. "Merrill found another family for Lena to work for," he said soberly. "Those two vampires that Tony, Paul and Deryn killed tracked her down, somehow. We were worried that she might be in terrible danger if she kept doing this and going home every night. So Merrill found something else for her."

"Crap," I muttered. I didn't get to say good-bye.

"This happens, cara. Humans are placed in danger at times, because they associate with us. This is the way it has always been." Gavin came to stroke my hair before pulling me against him.

"Meanwhile, Merrill is looking for someone to live in," Franklin continued.

"Where will we find somebody, Frankie? We can get them all killed," I said, pulling away from Gavin. I was upset that I wouldn't see Lena again, too. "You can't do all this yourself," I swept a hand out. Frank had his own set of worries to deal with—Greg's health was only going to get worse. "We'll need somebody to help clean this behemoth, especially since there are so many people here, now. Where will Merrill find anyone who can help?"

"Your surrogate sire may curtail his search," Kifirin appeared as if he'd been called, and the two comesuli that I'd met before were with him. They shouted with delight when they saw me, and both came to give me a hug.

"Nexus Echo," Kifirin explained as I stared at him in shock. "It is a Larentii trick I have borrowed. They listen for key words—or names even—and they can follow up at a moment's notice if those words are spoken by certain people. It is quite handy, m'hala." He bent to give me a kiss. The comesuli were still attached to me like leeches, and they smiled their approval when Kifirin kissed me.

"This is Roff," Kifirin placed his hand on the dark-haired comesula's shoulder, "and this is his son, Giff," he did the same for the lighter-haired one. Gavin was staring speculatively at the way both were fawning over me.

"They'll fawn over you, as well," Kifirin smiled at Gavin. "You may only drink from them once every two weeks. Do not do this more often, even if they beg."

"You hear that?" I tapped Giff on the nose. He beamed excitedly at me.

"I hear that," he nodded.

"Hey, you can speak English!" I was very happy about that.

"The High Lord has done this for us. We begged him to bring us to you, and he says that your home needs help." Giff seemed ecstatic over housework. "We are very good at this, along with making oxberry wine. That is my father's trade. We can sell this and increase your wealth."

"If you sell anything, you can increase your own wealth," I said. "And we'll pay you. Fairly. What are oxberries?" I'd never heard of them.

"They are not native to this planet," Kifirin answered for him. "The closest you might come are blackberries, but that description does not do them justice. They are very sweet and make exceptional wine."

"We'll get blackberries for you, or any other kind of berries if you want to make wine," I said. "Roff, how have you been? I didn't realize when I first met you that you were Giff's father." I'd been too stunned, I think, to notice the related scents.

"There was no time for that information; you left us too quickly," Roff smiled, his honey brown eyes twinkling. "My second child, Toff, is still on Kifirin, helping my brother and his son with our business."

"Really? How old is he?" I asked.

"He has recently gained his adulthood," Roff was happy to talk about his child.

"That means forty in their culture," Kifirin supplied. "The comesuli live an average of six hundred years, and when they were near death on their homeworld of Le-Ath Veronis, the Vampire Queen and her inner circle would decide whether they should be made vampire."

Frank and Greg were listening to Kifirin's explanation, spellbound. "It was the next step in their lives, should they be selected," Kifirin continued. "As comesuli, they have no genitalia and only experience sex with the vampire's bite. If they were chosen and turned, they became male or female, as they were disposed. On Le-Ath Veronis, the numbers of males and females was nearly equal."

Giff and Roff's eyes were shining as they listened to Kifirin speak of their ancestry and the promise that a new day might come for their race. I could almost read their minds on this.

"Is this true?" Gavin was surprised, although he was doing his best not to show it.

"Yes. However, I was sleeping when the Ra'Ak came and the High Demons failed to wake me as they should," Kifirin said. "Le-Ath Veronis was the last of my Dark Worlds to fall; the Vampire Queen sacrificed much to get some of her people away. She sent as many comesuli to the High Demons as she could; they accepted them at least, although they would not accept her vampires." Kifirin sounded sad.

"My Bright brothers came for the vampires and the werewolves that still lived," Kifirin went on. "The Bright Lords sowed those two races across their worlds of light, asking them to remain hidden and to respect the life already there. Some have honored those rules, while others have not. The Vampire Queen died on Le-Ath Veronis, fighting off the Copper Ra'Ak." *Someday, you will take her place.* Kifirin sent mindspeech to me alone.

Those sound like big shoes to fill, I returned.

Her feet were small, like yours, he teased mentally.

"I have many things to do," Kifirin said aloud and disappeared.

"I wish I could do that," I sighed, staring at the empty space he'd occupied seconds earlier.

"You do well enough when you're mist," Merrill was now listening in the doorway. "Who have we here to take care of us?" He came to meet Roff and Giff.

"A King," Roff's voice was reverent as he bowed to Merrill.

Merrill's eyebrows rose sharply in surprise. "How do they know?" he asked, turning bright blue eyes in my direction. I shrugged. I could have bet everything I had that Merrill didn't want that information leaked.

"They knew I was a Queen the minute they met me," I replied. "They were kissing my feet, too, and they should never do that," I came to hold Giff's face in my hands. He gave me a lovely smile.

"That's more than we knew," Gavin's voice held sarcasm.

"You are my Queen's other mate?" Giff asked.

"I am her first mate," Gavin declared.

"That is a technicality," Roff informed him. Greg snickered; he couldn't help it.

"Come on you two, I'll show you around," Franklin was laughing with Greg as he rounded up Roff and Giff before they could get into an argument with Gavin.

"They truly have no genitalia?" Merrill whispered as Franklin led them away.

"Yeah. Their blood is sweet, too," I said. "Kifirin says they reproduce autonomously. They grow a pouch on their side with the baby inside that, and it drops off when they're ready to be born."

"You're joking?" Gavin lifted an eyebrow.

"That's what Kifirin says."

"I'll ask Wlodek to set up identification for them," Merrill sighed. "And we'll determine what to pay them. Do you think they might learn to drive?"

"You won't even let me drive," I grumbled.

"You may drive me around later," Gavin offered.

Paul and Deryn chose that moment to walk into the kitchen, both yawning. They'd been asleep all day, I could tell. Not that I blamed them; they'd fought hard beside Charles the night before.

"Let's take the wolves for a bite to eat," I suggested, "since we're out of live deer."

"How do you know about that?" Deryn asked. Tony and René walked into the kitchen, then. René was dressed more casually than Gavin, in a designer shirt and slacks, his slightly curly, dark blond hair styled neatly. He had a smile in his warm brown eyes as he caught sight of Gavin and me.

Gavin pulled me against him and wrapped his arms around me, probably to declare his ownership in René's presence. I chose to ignore it. With René, Tony, both werewolves and the comesuli in the house, Merrill's huge manor was filling up nicely. I just hoped they'd all get along.

"I spent some time with Winkler and Weldon, remember?" I said, answering Deryn's question. "I misted over several runs, just to make sure the Grand Master was safe."

"You watched them hunt?" Deryn didn't know what to think.

"The bear was the hardest; I think I turned away when they killed it," I said.

"I love bear meat," Paul sighed.

"I don't think it's on the menu here or at any of the restaurants in London," I replied. "You'll have to settle for domesticated bovine."

⁓

"This restaurant belongs to Adam Chessman," Merrill informed me quietly as we walked into a restaurant later. Franklin offered to prepare a meal at the house, but Merrill decided to take the werewolves and comesuli out to eat so Frank wouldn't have to cook. The maître d' of the upscale eatery recognized Merrill immediately. Consequently, we were seated right away.

Giff and Roff were excited that they could read the language on the menu and talked together about what they should order. Paul got into a conversation with them, pointing out what was good. They knew not to reveal either race and were quite circumspect. Gavin, René, Tony and I didn't eat; we merely had a glass of wine and talked with the others.

Tony gazed longingly at the steak his brother ordered, but he knew he wasn't hungry; René had seen to his feeding earlier. Merrill had a small meal, laughing and talking with René, Gavin and Tony. I was content to watch all of them, I think, although Greg and Franklin were teasing one another and then teasing me.

"I want you to sing karaoke with me again," Greg announced.

"Buy a piano and we can do it at home," I suggested.

"But we won't have as good an audience," Greg declared.

"Fine. We'll go right after we get done here," I said.

That's how we ended up at the same bar Greg, Franklin and I had gone to, shortly after my stint in the sun. I can tell you this; every man inside the bar drooled over Merrill, Gavin, René, and the others. There wasn't a slouch in the bunch. Even Giff and Roff were invited for drinks. They smiled and said they were with me. Greg signed both of us up for a song apiece.

Greg loves Judy Garland so he did *Over the Rainbow*. I didn't know what I was going to do until I got on the stage. I did *You Raise Me Up* just for Greg, and played the piano instead of using canned music.

Merrill was staring at Franklin when I finished to a nice round of applause.

"I will buy a piano," Gavin said when I sat down again. "How did you hide this from us?"

"There hasn't been a lot of time for this," I pointed out. "I turned down a music scholarship at an out-of-state college when I graduated from high school. I wanted to stay close and make sure my mother had some support against Howard Graham. He managed to kill her anyway, after I finished my first year at OU. It was difficult after that, because people would recognize my name in some of my classes. I dropped out of several because I couldn't handle the stares after a while." Gavin didn't say anything; he pulled me against him instead, and dropped a kiss on my forehead.

Greg was tiring, so we left shortly after that. I had no idea how much time he had left or what the disease was going to do to him before it took his life. I wondered, too, when Merrill might make his offer as he said he would.

We found a bedroom for Roff and Giff; Merrill offered them separate rooms, but they insisted on using the same one so an extra bed was brought in. Merrill and Franklin arranged to buy clothing and other necessities for them.

Gavin and I left the others and went to Merrill's roof. I hadn't sat on a roof since leaving Refizan, which made me think about Gabron. So many of his vampires had died the last night I was there, and I didn't even know their names to grieve for them properly. Here on Earth, we were into August already; time was moving so swiftly and there I was, thinking that as an immortal it should slow dramatically.

"How have you done this, Gavin?" I shook my head sadly. "How have you watched things change around you daily while you don't change? How have you watched people you love die in front of you? How do you handle that?" I was sitting beside him, his arms wrapped around my shoulders.

"You worry for Greg." His words were a statement and not a question.

"And Franklin," I nodded.

"You have had much pain in your life already," he sighed, ruffling my hair with his breath. "You do not look forward to the grief coming because of this." I nodded at his words. "You cannot choose for everyone, Lissa," he pointed out. "They must make their own decisions in this respect. Some do not desire this immortality. They do not want the restrictions this existence imposes. They know the pain is coming and they are preparing themselves for it. All we can do is support them in their decisions and be grateful for the time we have."

"Gavin, I want you to know now, and for you to let Merrill know, that if anyone ever tells you I've walked into the sun and am dying as a result, then they are lying," I said. I remembered how Aurelius had died—he'd been lured into a trap with the lie that one of his vampire children had been injured by the sun. "When I went to Refizan, they put something beneath the skin on the back of my neck," I explained as Gavin stared at me in confusion. "It's technology from another planet that shields me from the sun. It's supposed to last a hundred years."

"It will keep you from dying in the sun?" Dark brown eyes raked my face, searching for verification. He was shocked, I could tell.

"Yeah. You should see the Larentii who put it there," I said, smiling. I was thinking about Pheligar's sky-blue skin.

"Larentii?"

"He's eight and a half feet tall, has blue skin, blue eyes and hair the color of wheat," I said. "He placed the disc beneath my skin and I didn't even feel it."

"The idea of other worlds is not new," Gavin sighed as his arms tightened about me. "I was in the Council chamber four years ago when the female Saa Thalarr was brought in. That was the last time I saw Chessman; he was with her, as was Merrill." Gavin's gaze was now turned toward the night sky; it was mostly clear and I could see a few stars shining overhead.

"I met them," I said. "Adam and Kiarra have a child, now. His name is Justin." Gavin drew in a breath at my words. "What's wrong?" I asked.

"When Chessman was turned, he had a younger brother named

Justin. Long dead now, of course. The Council considered taking him after Adam was turned. Merrill prevented it."

"Adam lowered his shields and I got his scent," I said. "He has Bright Elemaiyan blood—I know that now."

"He was a mister," Gavin nodded.

"Gavin, Tony has Elemaiyan blood, too. That's why he can mindspeak," I added. "Does Wlodek know this?"

"René has informed him," Gavin shifted uncomfortably at the admission. "That is a part of what the meeting was about earlier. Wlodek has given permission for Tony's training to be accelerated because he has so much experience in security and law enforcement. Wlodek wants him groomed to take Sebastian's place."

"I thought that might happen," I said. Gavin and I sat in silence after that, until I saw three vans rolling up the long drive to the manor. "Are we expecting company?" I asked, standing up to get a better look.

"Wlodek, Charles and Rolfe are moving in until the threat Xenides presents has been eliminated," Gavin stood up and stretched beside me. "Merrill's property is warded for two miles in every direction. Merrill tells me that Griffin does this for him, and that none who mean harm can cross the boundary he has set. This is the only safe place for the Honored One to stay. Come, we will see to their comfort; they are taking over the basement."

Warded? The property was warded? What had Merrill done for Griffin, that he merited such preferential treatment? And Merrill had a basement? That was a surprise, though it shouldn't have been.

I misted off the roof; Gavin floated down. Not only were there three vehicles now parking on the wide drive in front of Merrill's manor, but each van was towing a trailer. Wlodek had been busy, looked like. Tons of records had to be moved, with all of Charles's computer equipment. It made me wonder what Wlodek had done with all his priceless antiques, in case Xenides and his remaining horde showed up again.

Merrill came out, as did Deryn and Paul, and we pitched in to unload trailers. Charles grinned at me; I realized he was looking forward to this. Russell and Radomir were there, too, helping.

Merrill had six bedrooms in his basement, complete with private baths. Color me stunned. A locked door was hidden inside the butler's pantry, and that's why I'd never seen it before. I hadn't gone in there very often and the doorway was located behind the last shelf of canned goods. That shelf was shoved aside, revealing the wide entrance downstairs.

Everything in the basement was clean; Franklin must have kept it that way. Charles and Wlodek were moved in and set up first, Rolfe was set up last. Rolfe was just as happy as Charles was with their change of venue. Wlodek had the usual, unreadable expression on his face, so I couldn't tell how he felt about the move.

"We have a Council meeting tomorrow evening," Charles informed me later as we were getting the last of his things put away and his computers connected. "Wlodek wants you there; we have two vampires you need to check."

"Are we giving baseball signals so he'll know what I find?" I was doing my best impression of a third base coach. Charles stared at me for a minute before bursting into laughter.

"If we bring Brock, he'll know exactly what you're doing," Charles snickered. "He's a huge baseball fan."

"You will touch your hair when each prisoner is led before me, to let me know if they are Saxom's," Wlodek appeared from nowhere, I think. I had to keep myself from jumping at his sudden appearance.

"All right," I nodded. I was about to get the hell out of the basement. Things just weren't that comfortable between Wlodek and me at the moment, and in all honesty, he still scared the bejeezus out of me.

"Charles, do you have all the paperwork copied?" Wlodek asked. One of the things carried into the basement earlier was a portable copy machine.

"All done, Honored One," Charles nodded. I turned to go; they had work to do.

CHAPTER 2

When I woke the following evening, I found Roff and Giff in bed with me. Roff was curled up at my back; Giff snuggled against my chest. Both of them were about five-five or so, with honey-brown eyes and thin builds. Both were still dressed, but they'd taken their shoes off to climb into bed with me.

"Were you here when Gavin woke?" I asked as Roff placed his arms around me, snuggling closer.

"No, my Queen. We waited until he left and then climbed in with you." Giff was talking now and nuzzling my chin.

"Is this what I think it is?" I asked.

"Oh, yes," Giff was doing his best to press against me.

"Lissa, you must rise soon, we have a Council meeting," Charles burst into the room, receiving a shock at finding Roff and Giff in my bed.

"Charles, have you eaten tonight?" I sat up in bed and smiled at Wlodek's assistant.

"Yes, earlier," he nodded, a puzzled look in his hazel eyes.

"Might you be peckish in the least?" I went on.

"Well," he shrugged.

"Which one of you would like to go to Charles?" I asked my two sleeping buddies.

"Is he kind?" Giff asked.

"I would imagine so," I nodded. "If he isn't, you should tell me." I smiled at Giff.

"Then I will go to him," Giff slid off the bed, going to Charles and leaning his head over, exposing his neck. Charles was shocked, I think, at so blatant an invitation.

"This is the only way they can have sex," I informed Charles. Charles pulled Giff against him, held his neck in his hands, breathed on Giff's skin and then sank his fangs into the comesula's throat to drink. Giff received a nice climax and hugged Charles before it was over.

"That's the best blood I've ever had," Charles complimented Giff when he let the comesula go.

"We can only drink from them every two weeks," I said. "Even if they beg." I handed Giff a stern look. He smiled at me.

"My turn," Roff was scooting under me on the bed.

"I'm not going to hurt you, okay?" I gave Roff a kiss.

"I like it very much when you kiss me," he said.

"That's good, honey," I said, kissing him again before leaning over his throat and taking my dinner. He was quite pleased with the result, moaning in my arms while his body writhed beneath mine.

"Now, both of you go drink some juice or find something to eat," I shooed them out of my bedroom. Charles was still standing there, a look of shocked wonder on his face.

"There was an entire planet of them?" he sighed happily.

"That's what Kifirin says," I nodded. "Give me two minutes to get dressed and brush my teeth. I'll be right down." Charles left me alone so I hurried through my dressing, then brushed my teeth and did my hair before misting downstairs.

~

"We are driving across my property and going out through a hidden side entrance," Merrill informed me when we were ready to leave for the Council meeting. "Lissa, will you ride with Radomir and the Honored One in case an attack comes anyway?" Merrill was worried we'd be seen if we exited the property at the gates.

"Of course I will," I said. I just needed to be prepared to go to mist and take the occupants of the car with me as mist if anything happened. I ended up in the back seat of an SUV with Wlodek; Radomir was driving and Gavin sat up front with him.

Wlodek spoke after a bit, surprising me. "Lissa, I hear you were involved in quite a fight when you were offworld." Uh-oh. Merrill must have spilled the beans. Wlodek was waiting as I hesitated before answering.

"I was," I admitted. "But there wasn't anything else I could do unless we wanted to hand the entire planet over to the Ra'Ak. Do you know what they are?" I watched Wlodek's face; he was attractive without a doubt; his olive skin was flawless, his nose straight and his dark eyes concealed centuries of secrets. He didn't seem to care that he was handsome and always dressed as if he were going to be photographed for a men's fashion magazine. He had impeccable taste—I don't think anyone else made his clothing choices for him.

"I know what the Ra'Ak are," he nodded. "One of those creatures came here, four years ago. Saxom made a deal with that devil and nearly killed us all."

"Oh, dear Lord," I whispered in shock. They'd come here? "Those things are awful, Wlodek. They eat people. Or send their spawn out to eat people and then create more spawn." I shuddered at the thought of Earth being destroyed by those monsters.

"I have never seen one myself, but Merrill has seen them twice and described it to me."

"Their eyes are their weakness," I informed the Head of the Council. "I blinded three of them and got one eye on a fourth, before it was over. We wouldn't have lived through it, otherwise." I sighed, thinking how close we'd come (Dragon and I, along with all the

Refizani vampires) to being killed. Kifirin helped, killing the last two Ra'Ak after I'd gotten injured.

"Lissa, why am I only now hearing of this?" Gavin leaned over the back of his seat, a frown tugging at his mouth.

"It wasn't supposed to be that way, Gavin. There was only supposed to be one Ra'Ak. They broke the rules; that's what Dragon said."

"Were you injured? And I would very much like the truth," Wlodek said. I knew he wanted to place compulsion, but he also knew better than to make the attempt.

"A little," I shrank down in my seat.

"Lissa, I can tell it was more than a little. I know those things hold a deadly poison." Wlodek wanted an answer and he wanted it to be the truth.

"I ran into the forehead of the last one I tried to blind," I said softly. "I got poisoned, but Karzac and the Larentii came and took care of it."

"Father, we're being followed." Radomir made the announcement; we'd bounced off Merrill's property earlier and were now on one of the country roads.

"Are you certain, child?" Wlodek leaned forward, turning to look behind him. I did, too, and there was a car behind us with no headlights on.

"I'll get it," I said and misted out of the car before Gavin could grab me.

The two vampires in the car behind us weren't Saxom's; I could tell by their scent. I misted out again and flew forward, dropping into Merrill's Range Rover. "Merrill," I said, flopping into René's lap; he was in the passenger seat, after all—Tony and Charles were seated in the back.

Thank goodness, Merrill remains calm most of the time. "What is it, Lissa?" he asked, never taking his eyes off the road.

"There's a car with two vampires in it following Wlodek, but I don't recognize them and they aren't Saxom's. I don't know whether they've had compulsion placed or not. One is about seven hundred years old; the other is less than that, maybe four hundred."

"If I stop the car, they will realize we know they are following,"
Merrill thought for a moment. "Why don't you take Gavin or René
with you?" He turned to me briefly before concentrating on his
driving. "Either should be able to place compulsion easily on these
two and discover why they are following us."

"All right," I nodded.

"I will come, little rose," René held me on his lap and seemed quite
content doing so.

"Fine, but René, if I see them doing something they shouldn't, I
may be picking you up again as mist and hauling you out of there."

"I understand," René smiled. He was looking forward to being mist
—I could see it in his eyes. Well, René was more of an adventurer than
Gavin, it seems.

"Be careful, Lissy," Tony shouted as René and I turned to mist.

I dropped René in the back seat of the pursuing car as gently and
noiselessly as I could, but both vampires realized we were there in a
blink, by the scent. "You will do as I say," René placed compulsion as
they turned with a hiss. The vampires were nodding quickly at René's
orders. "Pull over," René commanded. The driver pulled over.
Radomir stopped ahead of us and began backing his SUV in our
direction as René ordered the two vampires out of the car.

"They're not Saxom's," I informed Wlodek as he inspected the two,
walking around them and getting their scents. The two were terrified.

"What are your names?" Wlodek barked, causing both vampires
to jump.

"I am Thaddeus," one of them replied, his voice shaky. Wlodek
definitely had that effect on people. Vampires, too. I'd certainly
been there.

"Lorenzo," the other said.

"Why are you following us?" Merrill had come and was now asking
questions.

"We seek the Council's help," Lorenzo admitted. "Our brother,
Dominic, was taken by one calling himself Xenides. We have become
concerned, because our brother does not answer his calls and we are
afraid that Xenides may come for us as well."

"Why has Xenides taken Dominic?" Wlodek demanded.

"Dominic has mindspeech," Thaddeus hung his head. "Our sire, Maxwell, always told us that Dominic would be taken by the Council, should this be revealed. Therefore, we kept it secret. Now, Xenides has taken him instead."

"How long ago?" Merrill asked.

"Ten days," Lorenzo admitted.

"Have you been placed under compulsion? Are you doing this at Xenides' bidding? Or one of his minions? Answer truthfully," Merrill's voice held *The Command.*

"No. We swear, we only want our brother back," Thaddeus begged. Lorenzo agreed with his sibling. They weren't true brothers, but they did have the same vampire sire and they certainly looked enough alike to be brothers, with brown hair and green eyes. They just hadn't been related as humans.

"Maxwell has been dead for more than fifty years," Wlodek observed.

"We know. We do not wish to lose Dominic as well." Lorenzo was clearly upset.

"How did you know where to find us?" Wlodek asked, pacing down the narrow lane between vehicles.

"We were looking for the one called Merrill," Lorenzo admitted. "Our sire told us that if there was ever trouble to find him—he might be willing to help those with difficulties and gave us a general location where he might be found. We have been searching the area for three days. We hoped Merrill could take us to the Council."

"I am Merrill," Merrill identified himself. "We will discuss your troubles presently. Gavin, will you drive their vehicle and bring them?"

Gavin nodded. Tony had been busy searching their car while the others talked, declaring it free of weapons and explosives. I guess it was good to have him around after all.

That's how we ended up at the Council meeting a few minutes late, with two extra vampires who had to be blindfolded before being led inside the cave.

The first prisoner brought forward was a vampire named Bartholomew, and he was definitely Saxom's turn. I touched my hair when Wlodek turned his eyes toward me. I got the idea that Wlodek already knew Bartholomew was Saxom's turn, but chose to test me and my ability.

Well, he knew now that I wasn't under Merrill's compulsion, so he had to make sure of things. Lovely. Regardless, Wlodek questioned Bartholomew accordingly. "Why are you listed as Jeremiah's child when Saxom sired you?" Compulsion was heavy in Wlodek's voice.

"My sire told me long ago that the Council would never discover the truth," Bartholomew insisted. Gavin, Merrill and I, along with Tony and René, were all in our usual spot along the cave wall to Wlodek's right, watching while Bartholomew was questioned.

"He held us in contempt, did he not?" Wlodek asked.

"Of course he did," Bartholomew snapped. "He finds you weak and ineffective." Well, that's something I wouldn't have bothered to tell Wlodek to his face, especially if I stood where Bartholomew did— facing that same ineffective Council.

"Why did he send you after Lissa's records in the U.S.?" Wlodek went on. This was news to me; I hadn't been informed of this.

"He wanted to discover if she had sisters, brothers or any living relatives." I only had cousins and they weren't close. Then it hit me. They were looking for others with my talents. I drew in a shaky breath. Gavin must have known, somehow; he moved his hand slightly, attempting to calm me down.

"And what did you determine from these records?" Wlodek was relentless.

"That Howard Graham was not Lissa's father. The DNA tests proved it. Xenides was quite upset when he discovered this and became infuriated when we could not find information on her real father."

I was numb. Completely numb. I had no feeling in my legs or my hands and would have given anything at that moment to slide down the cave wall and curl up in a ball on the stone floor.

Lissy, don't let him hurt you, baby. That was from Tony, of course, who never moved a muscle as he sent mindspeech. All those meetings with the president and heads of state were paying off for him big time. He already had the vampire non-expression thing and didn't need to learn it as I did.

"What did Xenides intend to do with this information?" Wlodek asked.

"He wanted Lissa's talents. Needed her talents, he said. He was very impressed with what he observed in Washington."

"And when he failed to find any sisters or brothers?" Wlodek continued.

"He wants to capture her and use her," Bartholomew replied.

"And how does he propose to do this?"

"He says he only has to find someone she cares for and take them. She will come and he will place compulsion and have her for himself." Xenides had already tried that tactic once—and succeeded—when he bombed Tony's hotel. If Jovana had been the stronger one when I found her, I'd have been placed in Xenides' clutches. The question was; could he keep me there if he succeeded?

It was bad enough, learning the truth about my parentage. Now Xenides was threatening those I cared for. Whom would he go after? Gavin? Franklin or Greg? Charles? Winkler or Weldon? The list was longer than that. I felt cold and shivered.

Wlodek questioned Bartholomew for a very long time, asking him about the murder of the legal secretary in Oklahoma—I'd seen her inside the courtroom years ago; she'd been helping the attorney defending Howard Graham. Now I knew for sure he wasn't my father; he'd been right about that all along. Howard Graham hadn't handled the truth very well and had taken his hate and anger out on my mother and me. I still wanted to curl up in a ball and whimper.

A few Council members were now casting speculative glances my way. I couldn't flinch or allow them to see any weakness. Who knew what they'd do to me if they saw that? And Xenides? I wanted to kill him. Just go out immediately and track him down. Take the head off this snake, to see if the body would die with it. He was threatening me and everyone else I knew. *The fucker.*

The vote was taken eventually, with all Council members turning in guilty verdicts. Gavin did the beheading and I didn't have any argument with that. Then another vampire was led forward. His name was Llewellyn and he wasn't Saxom's get. I did know who made him, however. Wlodek saw that I didn't touch my hair and looked away. I did my best to send mindspeech to him, just so he'd know.

Nyles Abernathy made him, I sent as strongly as I could. Wlodek fumbled the gold pen he was toying with but recovered quickly. I think he heard me. Gavin and I had faced off against Nyles in Florida shortly after I'd been brought before the Council myself.

Nyles had been Edward Desmarais' sire—the vampire who'd made the bet with my own vampire sire, Sergio Velenci. That's how I'd been turned. Nyles had taught his children everything he knew about playing with humans.

"So," Wlodek turned the pen in his hands for a moment, his dark eyes narrow and unrevealing, "I have been informed that Nyles Abernathy was your sire." As bombshells go, that one dropped pretty well. I even heard a gasp or two around the cave.

"Who gave you that information?" Llewellyn demanded. "Only my sire and I knew of this!"

"I have sources you cannot imagine," Wlodek answered calmly. "Did Nyles teach you to play with humans, just as he taught your sibling Edward Desmarais?"

"We enjoyed our games, father and I," Llewellyn snorted. "What should it matter if a few humans die? They are nothing but cattle to us. We are superior to those weaklings."

"Yet you were once of that race, were you not?" Wlodek's eyes were hooded as he watched Llewellyn.

"Only for twenty-two years. I have been vampire for fifteen hundred, now."

"Explain your dealings with Xenides."

"Xenides wishes to take the planet away from you and the humans and allow select vampires to rule." I was still trying to calm down; still quaking after learning that Howard Graham wasn't my father. Even so, it wasn't hard to find Llewellyn contemptible.

"So, you intended to assist Xenides in his takeover?"

"Obviously. I want humans to serve us. This is the only way it should be."

"Do you know where Xenides is, or plans to go?" Wlodek was hammering away at this guy, but Jovana had already said Xenides might be heading for the U.S. That worried me. He could be after Winkler, Weldon or Thomas Williams and his family; I was a member of the Sacramento Pack, after all.

"He talked of traveling to the United States, but worried that he might not be able to pass the borders again," Llewellyn stated. "Many are actively searching for him, and he has learned that his image has been recorded and handed to the authorities."

"Whom will he target and what are his plans should he go to the U.S.?" Wlodek asked.

"He would not tell me this," Llewellyn grumped. "Although I asked many times."

The guilty verdict was unanimous on Llewellyn and Gavin, as the only Assassin present, performed the execution. I wondered if he ever got tired of doing that. Things wrapped up quickly afterward; Thaddeus and Lorenzo had gotten an eyeful, I think; they'd watched the entire meeting in amazement. Afterward, they were blindfolded and led from the cave as protocol dictated; they weren't allowed to see again until we'd arrived at Merrill's manor.

Merrill placed the usual compulsion not to harm anyone inside the house or give its location away, before finding them a bedroom on the third floor opposite Paul and Deryn's rooms. I was still shaky, to be honest, and as soon as Lorenzo and Thaddeus were dealt with (Merrill promised we'd consider their dilemma later), Merrill, Gavin, Wlodek, Charles, René and Tony all crowded into Merrill's study with me. Gavin held me on his lap, his arms wrapped tightly around me while Charles read back the notes he'd taken from Llewellyn regarding Xenides' plans.

"Lissa, I am sorry this information came at such a time; we were unsure how to present the knowledge to you concerning Howard Graham. We realized it would upset you when you were given the truth." Wlodek did have a bit of sympathy in his dark eyes.

"Honored One, it did upset me, but what upsets me more is that Xenides is planning to take someone I care for in an effort to trap me."

"That is an old ploy," Merrill interrupted, his piercing blue eyes scanning my face. He saw the fear there and attempted to defuse it. "Xenides likely realizes that we will not allow you to search for him if he manages to do this. He still believes you susceptible to compulsion, and understands that we would place compulsion not to go seeking him or your revenge. I can only imagine he was toying with Llewellyn, convincing him that he had a legitimate way of taking you from us." I wasn't about to point out to Merrill that Xenides had already achieved his goal once; he'd just failed to capture me through Jovana.

"Then what is he going to do?" My voice shook. "Merrill, Weldon has a new grandchild. Winkler's wife is six months pregnant. He could hit any member of Thomas Williams' family in Sacramento."

"Does talent run in families? I heard that Xenides was looking for Lissa's sisters and brothers, if she had any," Tony said.

"It does," Wlodek picked up Merrill's letter opener—it was the replica of a Roman sword that I'd given him. Wlodek found it fascinating. "Lissa, please do not be offended when I tell you that we went looking for the same thing. We found nothing, just as Xenides did."

"I'm not surprised," I muttered, staring at my hands. Gavin gave me a squeeze.

"So, if Lissa's real father had other children," Tony wasn't allowed to finish his statement, René hushed him. Tony shrugged.

"Do you think that's possible?" I drew in a shaky breath. "That my real father might have had another family? I'm assuming he's dead now, since I'm as old as I am."

"Your father could be quite old now, but still alive," Wlodek said quietly.

"You think he could be a target?" That opened up new and horrible possibilities for me. I wondered who he was and why my mother had her fling with him. I assumed that's what it was; a chance meeting, followed by a brief affair. Had my father even known he'd fathered a child?

I'd read a short story once, about a child who imagined he'd been fathered by someone more important than his own father. I couldn't imagine that my mother had any aspirations in that area. She was mostly realistic; dealing with what she had and not what might have been. Perhaps Howard Graham had been sterile, too, and that's why I never had any sisters or brothers.

"I would hope that Xenides never learns who your father is," Merrill snorted. "I find it unlikely, actually. I feel he would need greater resources than he now has to obtain this information." Merrill turned away from me as he made the statement.

"I hope so," I mumbled. "I don't think I'd like to lose another parent to violence, although I don't know who he is or anything about him. My mother never said a word; she just let me believe I belonged to Howard Graham, though he claimed to the last I wasn't his. Turns out he was right."

"That did not give him the right to murder your mother and to nearly kill you, too," Gavin pulled me against him. "No man has that right and no vampire has that right. It is a death sentence if a vampire kills his mate or companion."

"A stroke killed Howard Graham. He's buried in the prison cemetery; nobody went to see him before he died, either." I said. "He had a brother who walked away from him when he killed my mom. Travis lived in Ohio at the time. I don't know if he's still alive."

"Travis Graham's safety should not be an issue since we know his brother was not your natural father," Wlodek said. "What about aunts and uncles on your mother's side?" He was still toying with Merrill's letter opener, focusing on it and not looking at me.

"Mom had an older brother who died in World War II; he died of peritonitis on the battlefield—they couldn't get treatment for him fast enough," I said. Merrill nodded; I'd told him this when Franklin had appendicitis. "He's buried in France, at Colleville-Sur-Mer, I think."

"His name?" Wlodek picked up a pen to write.

"Cecil Hart," I replied.

"Very well, we will investigate this." The pen scratched across paper on Merrill's desk. "Do you know if he was married or had any children?"

"Mom never said anything." Had he? I never thought to ask. Mom always cried when she talked about him, so I didn't ask any questions. There wasn't much information on him either, when I cleaned out the house before Don and the lawyer helped me sell it. It held too many awful memories for me to keep it and I'd used the money from that plus the life insurance policy to buy the house that Don and I lived in for twenty-three years.

"Charles," Wlodek said, handing over the scrap of paper.

"I'll search the records right away," Charles was already tapping on his computer. That man—or vampire—could do six things at once.

"How close were you with your husband's relatives?" Wlodek asked next. Uh-oh. I hadn't even thought about them; I'd been too concerned about my side of the family. I was going to have to push my brain in all directions.

"We weren't; Don and I only had holiday dinners and birthdays with his brother and his wife, though they lived about twenty miles away from us. David and Sara were at social functions more often than they were at home, sometimes. They had one son, but Danny got killed in Desert Storm."

"What about the son—was he married or did he have children?"

"None as far as I know. He was twenty-two when he died."

"Human wars have not been kind to your family," René murmured.

"They were doing their best to weed out the Workmans and the Harts," I agreed. "Don's father was a Korean war casualty. David went to Viet Nam. He was proud when Danny signed up with the Marines right out of high school. Don had heart disease, so he couldn't serve."

"Anyone else in your family?"

"Not on my mother's side, or my husband's, except for two cousins

of Don's and David's; their parents are gone. The cousins live in
Kansas; anyway, that's where they were when Don passed."

"We know about those," Wlodek nodded. He was still playing with
Merrill's letter opener; he seemed to like it. I wondered what kind of
sword the Greeks carried and what Wlodek's profession had been
before he became vampire. It also made me wonder about his sire. I
was probably not destined to find out about that.

"Now, Lissa," Wlodek went on, "while I realize that you can do as
you like, I hope you understand that it will be a mistake for you to go
anywhere alone. If Gavin is not available, then someone else will be
assigned to accompany you, should you leave Merrill's estate. I beg
you not to ignore me on this." Dark eyes bored into mine, compelling
me to listen.

"That's fine, I guess," I grumbled. I could probably take care of
myself, but backup was always a good idea.

"I am working out a deal with Paul and Deryn; I am tripling their
salary to stay and watch over Franklin and Greg if they venture out
during the day. They also will go with Giff and Roff should they
need to leave the grounds," Merrill said. "The vampires will not be
awake to attack while the sun is up, but they may have human
servants. The Werewolves will work out nicely as day guards." We
really were going to have a full house, especially if René and Tony
stayed.

The meeting was finally over and Gavin herded me toward my
bed. He had a few things on his mind besides sleeping, and that's why
we were going early.

"Did she seem upset that she might have a living father somewhere?"
Griffin landed in Merrill's kitchen while Merrill poured out a glass of
wine for himself and Wlodek. Merrill pulled out another wineglass
for Griffin and poured for him, too.

"I think she was worried that her father might be in danger if he
still lived," Wlodek sipped his wine and nodded at Merrill. Merrill

kept the best wine cellar and the door into it was next to Wlodek's bedroom.

"She was worried about me?" Griffin was beginning to feel hopeful.

"Yes. I believe she thinks her mother's affair was a fleeting one and now thinks her father probably wasn't aware of her existence," Wlodek went on.

"I knew Harriet was pregnant when I left her; there was only the once with her before Thorsten found out and hid her from me," Griffin grumbled.

"Your old war with Thorsten has not gone unnoticed," Merrill tapped his wineglass, encouraging Griffin to drink. Griffin lifted his glass and toasted his friend.

"Amara wants to come for a visit, and I understand your two new employees are adept at making wine. Might you be interested in a guest house a few yards away, where additional visitors might stay and where Roff and Giff might ply their trade as time allows?"

"I have no problem with that," Merrill smiled. Rolfe came in then; it was nearing dawn and Wlodek poured out a glass of wine for his bodyguard.

"You are the little Queen's sire?" Rolfe studied Griffin.

"How do you know this?" Griffin looked up at the tall vampire.

"The shape of her face is yours," Rolfe said. "And I overhear many things. It cannot be helped."

"My daughter looks like me?" Griffin seemed very happy with that information. "She has her mother's beauty," he added.

"Her willfulness has not gone unnoticed, either," Merrill observed dryly. "I believe she comes by that through you."

"You call it willfulness," Griffin took another swallow of his wine. "Do you know how much courage it takes for her to do that? It would be so much easier for her to sit and do as she's told—and so much worse for those around her. One of your misters would be dead without her. I have *Looked*, my friend. Without her help in New Mexico, five more vampires would have died, along with eleven werewolves and four humans. Is that what you wanted?"

Wlodek moved uncomfortably on his seat; he'd wondered about it but it hadn't changed the Council's decision or Lissa's punishment afterward. Flavio had been avoiding her; he felt responsible for Lissa's attempted suicide.

"When will the guest house go up?" Merrill asked, changing the subject.

"This morning," Griffin grinned. Rolfe was the only one whose eyebrows rose.

CHAPTER 3

was dreaming, and that was impossible; I hadn't dreamed since becoming vampire. My mother was standing in our old kitchen, wearing her favorite apron over old jeans and a T-shirt I'd given her for Mother's Day. Afternoon light was shining through the kitchen window, just as it always did when I got home from school. "Hi, baby," my mother said, giving me a smile.

"Mom?" I stared at her—she looked so young.

"Lissy, I always meant to tell you some things, but we never had any time," she said. The light pouring through the window bathed her in a glow as we talked—she truly was beautiful—that's why Howard Graham wanted her in the beginning and why he was never willing to let her go. Other men envied what he had; he'd just never appreciated it properly.

"What things, mom?" I was holding back from going to her—was she prepared to tell me about her affair, now? She turned away from me to swipe the kitchen counter with a cloth in her hand. It made me think of the times she did that before—to hide the bruises made by Howard Graham's fists.

"I was adopted, honey," she admitted, scrubbing at a spot on the counter. "Your Uncle Cecil wasn't, and my mother always wanted a girl. Somebody abandoned me when I was a baby, and my parents adopted me."

"Why didn't you say that before?" I wasn't sure how to take this information, and somewhere in my mind, I reminded myself it was only a dream.

"Don't be angry with your father, Lissy." She turned back to me, squeezing the cleaning rag in her hands. Mom always called me Lissy, just as Tony did. I never told him that—it would have made my heart seize up if it still worked.

"He killed you. I'll be mad at him if I want," I retorted. I was acting fourteen again for some reason, talking back to my mother.

"Not the one who killed me," Mom said. She reached out a hand to me, but couldn't touch, for some reason. "Your real father. He couldn't help it, hon." Sky-blue eyes pleaded with me to understand. I didn't.

"Couldn't help what?" I was reaching out to her, but she was sliding away from me as the kitchen disappeared. "Mom!" I was shouting and running after her, but I never got any closer. "Mom!" I yelled again, when a blinding light pushed me back, making me wake with a start.

I was sitting up in bed, whimpering and breathing hard, failing to notice for several seconds that darkness hadn't fallen—it was daylight outside. The muted light in the bedroom was strange and hazy to my eyes as I stared in shock at the clock on my bedside table. It was three in the afternoon. What was I doing awake? Vampires didn't wake during the day. Did they? The dream unsettled me, and that shouldn't be, either. I had no idea what was going on and my feet slid over the side of the bed automatically. I truly was awake during the day. I glanced back over the bed; Gavin was still asleep and not breathing (as was the norm), locked in the rejuvenating slumber that we all went through. I was just out of it, somehow.

Curious now, in addition to still being shaken (I hadn't dreamed of my mother in years), I walked out of my bedroom and then down the stairs leading to the first floor. My destination was Franklin's kitchen, but the light streaming through the windows there caused a bit of disorientation. Franklin was putting a grocery list together and Greg was standing next to him, his arms around his mate.

"Frank?" My one-word sentence caused Franklin and Greg to turn and gasp.

"Lissa, darling, what are you doing out of bed?" Greg was at my side as quickly as he could get there.

I rubbed my forehead with shaking fingers, "I had a terrible dream," I said. "I dreamed about my mother and that hasn't happened for years. I think it was because they were asking questions about my family last night."

"Come on, sit down," Greg steered me toward a barstool.

"Can I have some water?" I asked. I felt extremely thirsty. Franklin was worried, I could tell, but went to get a glass of water anyway, handing it off to me.

"Are you sure you don't want blood instead, little girl?" he asked. I was slurping water as if I did it every day and it wasn't coming back up—at least not yet.

"No, this is good," I said. "Is that sunlight?" I pointed to the window that usually showed darkness beyond. I rose and walked unsteadily toward it, so I could take a look. My eyes were mere slits and I shaded them with a hand when I made it to the window, but I gazed at a lawn that had been mowed recently, and flowerbeds neatly planted and tended. I wiped tears away as I saw a color of green that never came through at night.

"Why aren't you frying?" Greg whispered.

"They put a shielding disc under the skin at the back of my neck," I explained absently, staring at Merrill's expansive grounds.

"That still doesn't explain how she broke out of the rejuvenating sleep," Franklin muttered.

"I can hear you, Frank," I said, turning away from the light. It was still making my eyes water or I was crying, one of the two. Giff and Roff were now in the kitchen and Roff was leading me away from the window while the others followed along behind.

"Raona, you should go back to sleep," Roff reprimanded gently, his honey-brown eyes displaying concern and alarm. "What are you doing out of bed?"

"I had a bad dream," I said, pulling away from him and sitting down at the kitchen island; I was beginning to feel dizzy.

"No, Raona," Roff admonished, taking my hand again. "Come to bed."

"I'll carry her up," Franklin offered.

"No, I will do this," Roff waved Franklin off. "We were made to work with the vampires and defend them if necessary. We are stronger than we seem." Roff lifted me as if I weighed nothing, and with Giff trailing him, carried me up the stairs. Once there, Giff left us and Roff climbed into bed with me, holding me against him. He laid my head on his shoulder, put his arms around me and told me to sleep. I closed my eyes and slept.

"She was up? In the middle of the day?" Gavin ran a hand through his hair in a gesture of frustration. Wlodek and Merrill were both listening to Franklin's account of Lissa's brief journey downstairs in daylight.

"She said she had a bad dream," Franklin looked at Merrill. Gavin snorted. "I'm only repeating what she said," Franklin tossed up a hand.

"I'll talk this over with Griffin; He'll be here tomorrow with Amara," Merrill sighed.

The guesthouse was up and located fifty yards from the manor. It fit with the manor's architecture and was two stories high, with the lower story set up for Roff and Giff to make wine. They'd already looked at the space and were quite happy. Griffin had two adoring comesuli, now. The Saa Thalarr, when free to use their considerable power and talent, could make amazing things happen. Only the Larentii were more powerful.

"What's going on?" Gavin turned quickly, looking a bit guilty. I was yawning as I walked into the kitchen; I still felt sleepy, which wasn't surprising since I'd been awake earlier.

"Sweetheart, Franklin says you were out of bed earlier," Merrill came to me and held my face in his hands, his bright blue eyes narrowed in concern.

"I was. I dreamed about my mother and I haven't done that in years," I yawned again. "I think it was because we were talking about my family last night."

"Do you often dream?" Wlodek was standing beside Merrill, now, examining me carefully. Gavin wanted to move Merrill aside so he could get his hands on me, but Merrill wasn't moving.

"No, this is the first time since I was turned," I told him. "Now I feel tired."

"Did you feed?" Wlodek asked.

"Yes, honey," I said without thinking. Wlodek chuckled, then turned his head and laughed.

"Where is this disc that Gavin and Franklin are telling me about," Merrill asked, smiling. Wlodek now had himself back in hand.

"Back here somewhere," I lifted what little hair I had; it covered my nape now and I was happy about that. Merrill came around to study the back of my neck.

"Lissa, is that what these four puncture marks are?" Merrill leaned around to look at me.

"No, those are Kifirin's claiming marks."

"Claiming marks?" Merrill blinked at Gavin, who was staring at Wlodek.

"It's something he and the High Demons do," I shrugged. "They put their teeth in their mate's neck. Get him to explain it next time; I don't know much about it."

"The claiming is terrible when the High Demons do it," Roff came in, carrying a large container of blackberries. "They turn to their smaller Thifilathi and sink their canine teeth into the back of their mate's neck. The female is gravely ill for days afterward. Sex with the linking follows, when the female recovers. The claiming is never a pleasant experience for her."

"Is that what he did?" Gavin demanded.

"I wasn't sick, he just put his teeth in my neck," I felt embarrassed at the admission. "My neck was a little sore after, but that's all. The, uh, other stuff came later, and well, it was okay," I amended. "Dragon said we had a M'fiyah, Kifirin and I," I went on. "That's why I didn't fend him off after a while." I shrugged and went to help Roff wash blackberries.

"Mate recognition," Merrill informed Gavin, who must have worn a puzzled frown, still. I had my back to him at the time.

"I think I had it with Gavin, too. He smelled so good when I met him and no other vampire has smelled like that to me." I turned to look at Merrill and Wlodek, who were regarding me with confusion. "Of course he ended up being a big schmuck," I said, turning back to the sink. Roff and I were dumping washed blackberries into a large, wire colander.

"Am I still a schmuck?" Gavin came over to stand behind me.

"At times. You can't help it. It's a damn good thing I love you." Roff took his blackberries and headed toward the door into the garage. "Where are you going with those?" I asked. Roff seemed to have some purpose for dragging clean blackberries out the door.

"We, ah, have a new guesthouse," Merrill explained. Gavin pulled me against him and was now nuzzling my neck.

"Merrill, how can we have a new guesthouse? We didn't have anything yesterday," I said, trying to convince Gavin to stop nipping my neck. I mean, Wlodek was right there, after all, as was Merrill.

"Come, I will show you," Gavin picked me up and hauled me out the door. One of the garage bay doors was open; we went out that way and there it was; a huge, two-story guesthouse that had magically appeared in the last few hours, emerging like a mushroom that pops up overnight.

"Did somebody pour water on that to get instant extra space?" I asked as Gavin set me down outside it. I went to touch a stone wall with my hand; it was solid, all right, and looked as it had been there for months instead of hours.

"Merrill says Griffin completed this in very little time," Gavin informed me. "I had my doubts too, but here it is. Want to go inside?"

"Of course I do," I sniffed and walked through the door that Roff left open.

Roff and Giff were inside, crushing blackberries. They had buckets, bottles, bags of sugar and yeast plus many other winemaking things handy.

"Griffin provided everything we need," Giff was happy with what he was doing, mashing blackberries with his hands. "And a Larentii came to help build this," he waved a hand at our surroundings. "We knew of Larentii, but we have only seen them once before," he went on, smiling brightly before going back to crushing berries.

"Are you going to have purple hands?" I asked, watching Giff mash blackberries. I wasn't surprised that a Larentii came to help Griffin build a guesthouse—I'd seen Pheligar's talents before. Nothing would surprise me where he was concerned, and I wondered if he were the Larentii in question.

"I do not care if this is so," Giff replied, giving me a big smile and wiggling purple fingers at me. "Oxberries stain hands, too." Gavin pulled me away from Giff and led me toward the stairs that connected to the second floor. We walked up and found a beautiful space. It even had paintings on the walls, handmade rugs on wood floors, a full kitchen, an expansive living space, nice windows with views all around and a hall that led to a very large bedroom with its own bath.

"Wow, this is nicer than the one I have," I said. The bathroom was definitely larger; I knew that much.

"René has suggested that I allow you to renovate my apartment in London," Gavin's fingers stroked my neck.

"I think we have other things to do first," I said.

"And those things would be?" he was kissing my neck, now.

"I want to get Xenides out of the way. And his little hand puppet, Rahim Alif. Then we can talk about the outdated color on your walls.

Gavin, that bedroom of yours is a cave; anyway, it was the time I saw it. I've only been there once, if you remember."

"Then you will have to decide how to make it not a cave," Gavin said.

"Honey, this is somebody else's bedroom, not ours," I reminded him, as he attempted to lift my top.

"Then take us elsewhere," he mumbled. I took us into our bedroom by turning to mist and going through walls.

I got a lesson in vampire etiquette and protocol while we sat in the hot tub later, after taking a dip in the pool. I tried to put my one-piece suit on; Gavin wanted the bikini. I hadn't worn it before. He got the bikini.

"If you are meeting a vampire for the first time, the older vampire, if you know he is older, will dictate whether you touch or not," Gavin instructed. "He will turn his right hand slightly while it hangs at his side, to indicate that he is willing to shake hands with you."

"That might have come in handy in the past," I said. "Does this go for female vampires, too?"

"A few very old vampires will kiss a companion's hand if she is human," Gavin said. "Most male vampires will not allow their female vampire mates to touch another vampire. We all know not to offer."

"The only female vampires I've seen have been the two on the Council and Jovana, who turned out to be a real bitch." She had been; I could feel Saxom's taint radiating off her when I carried her as mist.

"I have seen a handful of the others, over the years," Gavin said. "They do not come out often and none attended the annual meeting last year. That is why you did not see any of them."

"Sounds like they're locked in the seraglio," I teased. The faint grimace on Gavin's face stopped me in my tracks. I would have been locked away, too, if I'd been susceptible to compulsion as they all thought. "So, there are thirteen female vampires, all of whom may be locked up and not allowed to go anywhere." I was about to climb out of the hot tub and leave Gavin sitting there. He grabbed me and settled me beside him again.

"I do not believe it is that bad," he sighed.

"They're all more than seven hundred years old, I figured that out for myself," I grumped. "So it's possible they've been locked up or placed under compulsion. For a very long time."

"Lissa, a female vampire is the rarest of jewels," Gavin said, wrapping his arms around me. "You do not leave your precious rubies and emeralds lying on the streets, you keep them safe. Otherwise, someone will come along and take them."

"We're talking females here, not chunks of rock," I muttered.

"The marriage bond must be renewed with the Council every hundred years," Gavin informed me. "If both parties do not agree to continue, the marriage is automatically dissolved."

"Do you think those guys are just going to let their jewels walk away? I've seen that hoarded stash your cousin has—he's not letting any of that go," I said. "You didn't see him when I took those tiaras; he was out for blood, Gavin, no pun intended. That's why I was so afraid of him."

"Lissa, let us talk of something else," Gavin begged.

"Fine, O vampire who wants to dance around the hot topics," I complained.

"Tell me about this dream you had," he said, wrapping his arms around me tighter and smoothly changing the subject.

"I dreamed about my mother, Gavin," I sighed, leaning my head against his shoulder. "She was telling me not to be mad at my father. She said he couldn't help it, whatever that means." I wasn't going into the adoption thing—I had no idea whether that was truth or not and had no desire to speculate. I pulled one of Gavin's hands out of the water and examined it for wrinkles—it didn't have any. "How come you're not all pruney?" I asked.

"That has never happened to me," he chuckled.

"Uh-huh. Not even when you were human? Those Romans were awfully fond of their baths, from what I hear."

"We had large pools available with heated water," he sighed, recalling it. "The marble and tile work was exquisite, you know. There were cold pools too, to refresh you after spending time in the hot baths."

"Yeah, and that was roughing it, I'm sure," I said.

"Are you teasing me?" he asked, his eyes crinkling just a little at the corners. He was amused, for some reason.

"Yeah," I replied with a shrug. Gavin leaned down to kiss me; probably just to shut me up.

Rolfe and Charles came in to join us after a while. "It's good to see you getting to relax," I told them.

"This is nice; the Honored One hasn't considered installing a hot tub," Charles sighed, sinking into the hot water. He and Rolfe wore swimsuits, but I wondered if they'd go in naked if I wasn't there. I wasn't about to ask, though. I was the only woman in the house and wasn't prepared for a bunch of men wandering around in the nude, should they be so inclined.

Within five minutes, we were joined by Franklin and Greg, then René and Tony, and then the two werewolves showed up. Deryn and Paul both grinned at me as they slipped into the hot water. Now I knew why Merrill had built the hot tub to hold fifteen people or so. Franklin and Greg seemed to like their bodyguards quite a bit; the two werewolves settled in near them. I was completely shocked, however, when Merrill and Wlodek showed up. Before then, I don't believe I could have pictured Wlodek in a swimsuit. He was well put together, I'll give him that, but then most vampires weren't hard to look at.

"I was going to call a meeting, but as everyone was together already, it was easier to merely join in," Wlodek announced. Well, I'd heard that politics and other things were often discussed in the Roman baths. This probably wasn't anything new to Gavin and René.

Gavin took my hand under the water, lacing his fingers with mine. I leaned my cheek against his arm and watched Wlodek, curious as to why he wanted to hold a meeting.

"I have received several messages from the new Director of the Joint NSA/Homeland Security Department," Wlodek began. "He wants to continue working with us to capture Alif and take down Xenides. I returned his call earlier in the evening and spoke with him at length about this." Wlodek's countenance was inscrutable, as usual.

"Merrill was with me while I placed this call, as was René, as this will involve him and his newest child," Wlodek continued. "I informed Mr. Jennings that Anthony was made vampire when he was found dying in the bombed hotel. Mr. Jennings was quite relieved and asked immediately to work with him on this matter that concerns both our races." Wlodek's gaze touched on Gavin and me as he paused for a moment.

"René has agreed to this as Anthony's sire, on the condition that he be allowed to go along and continue teaching his child as time permits. I am also requesting that you and Gavin join them, Lissa. Xenides has been seen in the U.S. in the past two days, according to Director Jennings. We believe he is making his way toward the central portion of the country, and as yet have not determined whether he is traveling to Oklahoma or Texas."

"Crap," I muttered. "He really does want to find some of my friends or relatives, doesn't he?"

"We are afraid this may be true," Wlodek agreed.

"When will we leave?" Gavin asked.

"You will leave in two nights," Wlodek replied. "Merrill will remain here for now, in case any of Xenides' spawn are instructed to cause trouble in Europe or in the event that Xenides returns without your knowledge. You will meet with Director Jennings in Dallas and travel from there as Xenides' movements dictate."

I glanced across the hot tub at Tony, who was grinning. He winked at me slightly. I stuck my tongue out just as slightly. His grin widened. He was back in the game, looked like, only as a vampire this time. *Settle down*, I sent to him.

We're going to get him this time, I know it, Tony returned.

"Will anyone else be joining us?" Gavin asked.

"Dalroy and Rhett will be available, should assistance be needed," Wlodek replied. "I have already spoken with them, and Weldon Harper and William Winkler have offered to provide help. If we have support from the werewolf community, it may work out well in this respect; Rahim Alif is still human and likely has other humans at his beck and call. Werewolves will certainly be helpful in guarding you during the day."

"Was Rahim seen with Xenides?" I asked.

"Not yet, but that does not mean he is not nearby," Wlodek informed me. "Alif has not been seen since the bombing in Paris."

"What about Thaddeus and Lorenzo?" I asked. I hadn't seen them since they'd come back with us from the Council meeting.

"They are with Russell and Radomir," Wlodek replied. "They are searching for their sibling, Dominic, and are questioning humans and others where he was last seen."

I thought Dominic might be in the U.S. with Xenides and ventured to say so. "Honored One, Xenides has mindspeech. Might he not have taken Dominic with him, just for that reason alone?"

"Xenides has mindspeech?" Wlodek quirked an eyebrow. Yeah, I was probably in trouble, but wasn't I always?

"He was sending out a blanket message when I killed the vampire holding the First Lady," I said. "But so many other things happened that it slipped my mind."

Wlodek gave a sigh of exasperation, something that I hadn't seen from him before. "Lissa, come over here," he demanded. I shrank down in the hot tub instead, the hot water nearly to my nose. It was as far down as I could comfortably go.

"Lissa, the Honored One has issued a command," Gavin hissed.

"Lissa, come," even Merrill was telling me to go. I wanted to whimper and mist away. Gavin pulled me up and set me on my feet and I had to force myself to take three steps to the other side of the hot tub. Merrill, who was sitting two feet away from Wlodek, grabbed my arm and pulled me down to sit between him and the Head of the Council. Yeah, I was shaking. I was wishing for my one-piece suit right then; it covered more of me than the bikini did.

"Lissa, you must tell me things like this," Wlodek gripped my face in his hand. I was so terrified my teeth were chattering and I could barely nod at his words. Everybody in the hot tub was holding their breath, I think. I was still blinking, my gazed locked with Wlodek's dark eyes.

"You must tell me," he went on, "no matter when you remember it. It could be very important, as I may have information you do not possess. Do you understand?" I couldn't help it; a half sob came, though I desperately tried to hold it back. "Moro mou." I was crushed against Wlodek so fast I didn't know what was happening, and he was crooning to me in Greek, begging me to stop shaking. I couldn't help it, my entire body was trembling, I was so scared.

"He will not harm you," Kifirin was there suddenly, standing before Wlodek in the hot tub, stroking hair back from my forehead. "Avilepha, relax or I will be forced to place you in a healing sleep." Kifirin sat down on Wlodek's other side. "Tell her," he said to Wlodek. Wlodek nodded. I had no idea what they were talking about and I was desperately trying to control my shaking.

"I performed the second turning to bring you back after you tried to give yourself to the sun," Wlodek whispered. "You have my blood and are now listed as my half-child in the records. Half-children are rare; they generally do not survive their bout with the sun. Nevertheless, there are a few and their new sire is listed along with their old one. If both sires live, they share custody. I chose not to reveal this to you before, as there was too much between us and you were not in a charitable mood toward me. That is my fault; I should have asked for better records."

Well, as shocks go, that was a big one. What did this mean? Was Radomir my brother, now, along with Flavio and Merrill? Was Charles my nephew? That was really weird. Those absurd thoughts skittered across my brain as I attempted to keep my hands from shaking and the rest of me from shivering in Wlodek's embrace. He pulled my head against his chest and placed a kiss on top of my head. Kifirin was chuckling.

"She's wondering if Charles is her nephew now," he said.

Charles found that amusing and laughed out loud. "I'll settle for brother or cousin," he said.

"I th-think the information c-could go b-both ways," my voice was still wobbly and I stuttered getting the words out. Why hadn't somebody told me this before? I was listed as Wlodek's half-child?

What did that mean, exactly? I had two sires to answer to, in addition to two mates?

"You have three sires, but I'm the most important one," Griffin slipped into the hot tub; Kifirin had moved aside to let Griffin have his space. Wlodek's arms tightened about me, perhaps in the hopes of keeping me there. Honestly, I was too shocked to move.

CHAPTER 4

"$\mathcal{I}$ have a story to tell you, baby girl," Griffin said, watching me closely as Wlodek held me in strong arms. I was afraid to move from Wlodek's grip, blinking at Griffin stupidly from the jolt I'd received. Merrill reached over and stroked my cheek.

"I knew the vampire and werewolf races were dying on this world," Griffin began, an unreadable expression in his hazel eyes. "As you've already determined, I was vampire before the Powers That Be and the Nameless Ones chose me to become the first Saa Thalarr. They made me what I am now, but before that, I was a quarter Bright Elemaiya and a King Vampire. I had mindspeech and foresight. Those were my gifts. As Saa Thalarr, I have the ability to *Look*; that is reaching out and obtaining needed information simply by searching for it with my mind. Combined with the foresight I already had, it made my talent in that area formidable. Those two abilities enable me to see many things. I saw you, Lissa. My daughter. You are the answer to so many things that were troubling me. I had to go *Looking* for your mother. I intended to keep her safe; keep you both safe. Unfortunately, I didn't *Look* for what might happen in the meantime, I was so happy just to have seen you in the future."

My mouth must have been hanging open, I was so shocked. This was my real father? How in hell had that happened? I had no idea what to do. I mean, I liked Griffin, but this—how do you react to this?

"When your mother became pregnant, my immediate supervisor punished me," Griffin went on. He was watching my face closely, I could tell. His hazel eyes held concern; it was almost tangible. "Saa Thalarr are not permitted to interfere with any race or world; which is why I was being punished. Your mother and you were hidden from me; I could not find you—the information was blocked. I would have willingly sacrificed myself, just to make sure you were both safe. I would have come to you if I could have, Lissa. I promise you that."

"Saa Thalarr cannot lie," Merrill whispered next to my ear. "It is impossible for them to do so. Everything Griffin tells you will be truth." I sniffled and nodded my head at Merrill's words.

"Your mother was also a quarter Bright Elemaiya," Griffin said. "We could mindspeak one another and that's what encouraged her to come to me. To make a child with me. She was adopted, baby, she just never had time to tell you. And I was never allowed to see her again after you were conceived. The punishment was placed. I only learned of you once more when you were dropped in Merrill's lap as his adopted child. That was extremely encouraging; it led me to believe that there were other forces at work, helping me to find you again." My dream was unfolding before my eyes and proving true—my mother had been adopted. I moved uncomfortably in Wlodek's grip.

"Merrill and I have been as close as brothers for fifteen hundred years; since he gave invaluable assistance to me when I came to defend this world against the Ra'Ak back then," Griffin went on. "When I convinced my supervisor that you could help Dragon on Refizan, he reluctantly agreed. His superior, one of the Nameless Ones, discovered that Kifirin had claimed you there." Griffin was smiling, now.

"Kifirin is brother to the Nameless Ones from long ago," Griffin continued. "He agreed to balance the worlds of light by creating the Dark Realm. When the Nameless One learned that Kifirin had found his mate, and that we'd taken her to Refizan to help one of the Saa Thalarr, he wanted an explanation. That is when I informed him you were my daughter. He made a judgment, determining that fathering a child is not in itself interfering. My punishment was lifted. I could claim my daughter. Therefore, I am here. I am your father. Wlodek is your only living vampire sire, Merrill is your surrogate sire. That will not change. However," Griffin turned to the others, a warning in his eyes, "should any of you decide to punish her in future, I expect to be notified and the final decision will be mine to make. If I am not informed, I may consider punishment of my own and I will not be merciful."

"I will know as well," a curl of smoke floated from Kifirin's nostrils. "You do not wish to stand before me if you have harmed her."

Tony had been listening to the entire exchange in disbelief. "You are fortunate, young one," Kifirin leveled a warning glare in Tony's direction. "Had I claimed Lissa before you took from her, you would not be enjoying life at the moment. She has forgiven you, I think. You are safe because of her charitable nature."

"I've learned my lesson," Tony held up both hands. "And my sire has threatened me if I mistreat Lissa in any way."

"You are doubly fortunate that Karzac wished to repay Lissa in some way by healing those six you infected with vampire blood and ash," Griffin said. "The one who did the research will not fare as well as you have out of this."

"How do you know this?" Tony demanded. "Larry was fine the last I saw of him."

"Don't question Griffin, he knows what he's talking about," Merrill snapped.

"Lissa, I have also come to give you other information," Griffin said. "While I am your father and will protect you as well as I can, I have not been given permission to interfere with any of Saxom's turns or their turns. This seems to be your mission, along with Merrill and the others, here."

"I also will not interfere unless there is no other way; this is a matter for the worlds of light to deal with," Kifirin added.

I looked from one to the other. "Well, then," I said. "I think it's just about time somebody told me who Saxom was."

Griffin looked at Merrill and then Merrill glanced at Wlodek. Wlodek sighed over my head and settled me between Griffin and himself. Griffin placed an arm around me. I blinked up at him, still a bit dazed. I had a father. A real one. No idea how that was going to affect anything, though.

"We must start at the beginning," Griffin said, squeezing me in an effort to comfort. "Saxom was from Orpali, a world far from this one. There, his name was Saxom Melitu, which he later changed to Meletius. It fit the language here; the other name did not."

"He truly came from another world?" René asked.

"Yes. He was chosen as a healer for one of the Saa Thalarr," Griffin nodded. "Lisster served more than thirty thousand years before requesting retirement. Saxom did not wish to go into retirement with him. He asked to stay with the Saa Thalarr in his healer capacity. This request was granted. At first, he served me, since the Ra'Ak had killed my healer. This was before I found Amara."

Merrill stirred uncomfortably at Griffin's explanation. "Then," Griffin continued, "Kiarra was chosen as Lisster's replacement and she inherited Saxom as her healer. They did not get along very well and as First at the time, I was not paying attention to this. I imagined that things would probably work out—that the two of them only needed to become used to each other. I was wrong. Saxom developed an unhealthy obsession with Kiarra and I failed to see it. He asked her to mate with him and she refused. Her refusal sent him down a dark path. He went looking for the Ra'Ak in order to get what he wanted."

"He was a healer for the Saa Thalarr?" that was alarming news. This sounded like their fuck-up, and now all of us were paying the price.

"You may well be correct, sweetheart," Griffin smiled sadly after reading my thoughts. "We all ignored Saxom. He was only a healer, after all. We had other things on our minds and I never bothered to delve into the matter. Saxom made a deal with the Ra'Ak and three of those monsters were sent for Kiarra, after Saxom promised to deliver her to them. Of course, he intended to get what he wanted from this, somehow." Griffin sighed, his eyes a bit unfocused at the memory.

"Kiarra managed to kill those that came for her—they never intended her or Saxom to survive. The Powers That Be punished Saxom afterward, but did not require his life—they did this because of the many years of service he'd provided the Saa Thalarr. Instead, they removed his immortality and set him upon the Earth to live out a normal lifespan. Unfortunately, Saxom found a way to become immortal once again—he convinced a vampire to turn him and then made another deal with the enemy when the Ra'Ak came four years ago."

"Is that what Shirley Walker was talking about?" I asked, recalling a conversation with the Corpus Christi Packmaster. "She said something about Unicorns, or something. I saw Dragon become a Dragon. Is Kiarra a Unicorn?" I was almost holding my breath.

"Kiarra is The Unicorn," Merrill smiled at a memory. Okay, that was part of the reason he had the hots for her; I just knew it. Griffin laughed out loud.

"Is that why they call you Griffin?" I looked up at my newly discovered father, ignoring the fact that he'd just read my thoughts.

"It is why they call me Griffin," he nodded, still smiling. "I don't change much anymore—Chessman wanted the Gryphon form and I didn't argue. His is solid black; mine was brown and gold."

"You weren't one of the Elemaiya that could shapeshift?" I asked.

"I never tried," Griffin said. "I was raised by my half-Elemaiyan mother in the Queen's camp. She forced me out when I was sixteen."

"That's what Gabron said about his mother," I offered. "He said she never got over it." I realized then that as a quarter blood, my mother had been culled as an infant. I shook my head to clear away those thoughts.

"They aren't kind about abandoning their children," Kifirin muttered angrily. "Perhaps they should show some sense. A day will come when they will greatly regret the laws they created regarding the dilution of the race."

"I have seen that as well," Griffin agreed. "The Ka'Mirai will not come to them as a result." Kifirin nodded and laughed humorlessly at Griffin's words.

"The Ka'Mirai?" I was curious about that word.

"A legend to the Elemaiya race," Griffin said. "One who can reverse time or events for them—the term means True Mirror. In a mirror's reflection, your left appears to be your right, and vice-versa. One day, the Elemaiya will greatly desire something to be changed, but it will be withheld because the Ka'Mirai will also be a quarter blood. I have seen it." I stared at Griffin's eyes as he made that pronouncement—the well of knowledge within was fathomless and the hazel color had gone pale. It was frightening.

"You should take one of the comesuli with you on your mission, avilepha," Kifirin said, breaking Griffin's spell. As if they'd been summoned, both Roff and Giff walked in.

"Which one of you wants to go?" I twisted around to look at them.

"Are Charles and Rolfe going?" Giff asked brightly.

"No, honey," I said. "I think they're staying here with the Honored One."

"Then I will stay, too," Giff declared. He'd already made friends with Charles and Rolfe, looked like.

"I desire to come, Raona," Roff informed me, bowing his head in my direction. He'd gotten a haircut, as had Giff—Greg and Franklin had probably seen to that when they'd taken both shopping for clothes. Roff's dark hair was now styled neatly, and a smile lit his face.

"Then I guess it's you and me, then," I said. "I think we can find a bag or two so you can pack."

It was getting late, so Franklin and Greg climbed out of the hot tub first, closely followed by the werewolves. Merrill placed compulsion on the wolves not to reveal anything they'd heard. They nodded and went toward their beds.

"Tony, is your father still alive?" I asked, leaning around Griffin to look at him. Kifirin was smiling at me when I asked.

"He is, we just don't talk much," Tony shrugged.

"You got that mindspeech from somebody that was Bright Elemaiya," I said. "I don't think it was your werewolf mother, dude."

"Holy shit," Tony muttered. "Do you think anybody else might know that?"

"I didn't tell anybody, you did," I pointed a finger at Tony. "You told Bill and Dusty and Arthur, at least." He had—he'd blithely announced to those three that his mother was werewolf.

"Larry Frazier knows, too," Tony rubbed his forehead—I could tell he regretted letting that information out. René was suddenly concerned for his newest turn.

"Him again," I snorted. "I should have just dropped him in the ocean and let him drown." That comment forced me to tell Wlodek what happened on the Arabian Sea; he was giving me the look—the one that was silently saying *you haven't told me something*.

"You should have seen her fight Karl Johnson's Second; that was epic," Tony was back to himself quickly.

"Like you'd know," I huffed. "You weren't there."

"I had somebody hooked up with a camera."

"You are a piece of work, you know that?" I glared at Tony, then turned to René who'd been sitting quietly by, listening to everything and not saying anything. "René, what will you do if I kick his ass?" I jerked my head toward Tony.

"Nothing, as long as you do not inflict permanent harm," René smiled.

I got up to go after Tony, but Wlodek hauled me back.

"We will not allow a brawl between our two youngest," he declared and settled me back in my seat. "Now, Anthony, where may we find your father and does he have other children?"

I'd gone to the kitchen with Griffin, after climbing out of the hot tub and shrugging into a wrap; Merrill followed us in and went to the wine fridge, pulling out a bottle of chardonnay. He uncorked it and poured three glasses. Wlodek and Charles had gone back to work in the basement and Rolfe had gone with them. René herded Tony toward Merrill's study to give him another crash course in vampire 101. Gavin had gone with them; René asked Gavin to help teach Tony how to take blood properly from a donor. Tony was about to be bitten by Gavin and I didn't know how that was going to go.

"Lissa, would you like for me to tell you why you were susceptible to compulsion for a year?" Griffin asked unexpectedly.

"Is it going to get me in trouble?" I asked, searching his face. Like Wlodek's, it could be shuttered and unrevealing at times. This wasn't one of those times.

"No, baby. Sergio Velenci placed compulsion to obey him and every other vampire for a year as your heart stopped beating. That is compulsion placed by your sire. The vampires on my home world called that PC—Preliminary Conditioning. It's an old secret, actually. It is also the ultimate compulsion—something a new vampire has to obey for the rest of his life. Your original sire did that to you, Lissa. The moment the year was up, the compulsion dropped away." Griffin paused to sip his wine, giving a nod to Merrill at the vintage.

"Sergio Velenci never expected you to live that long, of course, so he was toying with you just as he'd done with the others he'd turned," Griffin said. "This way, both he and Edward could command the ones they turned. Nyles taught them, I'm sure. Sergio wasn't intelligent enough to tell you to stay put and wait for him instead. Preliminary Conditioning must be placed quickly, in that brief moment before the change begins from human to vampire. Generally, it is only one sentence—that is all the time you have. It makes me grateful that Saxom failed to place it with Jovana, or she might have caused more trouble than she did."

I blinked at Griffin in astonishment. "You mean that if Saxom told her to kill everybody at just the right moment, she'd have carried on after he died?"

"Sadly, it is true, even with a King or Queen Vampire." Merrill lifted his usual eyebrow in alarm at Griffin's statement. "Most vampires do not know of this, and many who do refuse to attempt it. More than once, it has backfired, with disastrous results. Some vampires have been forced to destroy their vampire children, because of misplaced commands."

"Did you ever turn anyone? While you were vampire?" I stared at Griffin. I was still having trouble recognizing him as my father.

"That will come in time," he said softly. "And the answer is no. I did not turn anyone then. Someday, perhaps, I will tell you about my homeworld and what happened there. Someday. Meanwhile, Amara wishes to meet you."

"Amara? Your healer?"

"My mate as well as my healer. Your stepmother. We don't feel jealousy—we can't. She isn't upset with your mother. She only wants to meet the child she could never have herself."

I was beginning to feel shaky again. "Sweetheart, she already loves you," Griffin came over and pulled me into his arms. "She just wants to hug you and tell you that you have somebody in your corner, now. Somebody that isn't male."

"Lissa, don't ever be afraid of me." Her voice was musical and she was there, standing beside Griffin when he let me go. She was beautiful, too; one of those women who would always be beautiful— one of those who made me feel as if I were clumsy and gauche beside them, with almond-shaped dark eyes and black hair that hung in a shining river down her back.

"Oh, now, have you looked in a mirror?" Amara touched my cheek lightly and smiled. She read my thoughts as easily as Griffin did.

"I don't think she has," Griffin said.

"Your hair is growing nicely; Brenten said it was," Amara reassured me.

"Brenten?" I blinked at Griffin.

"My given name," he offered a crooked grin. "Even the other Saa Thalarr don't know it."

"She's your daughter, she ought to know," Amara teased Griffin gently. Merrill came over and gave Amara a squeeze. They were old friends, I could tell. I didn't have any old friends. Not anymore.

"A sad side effect of being vampire," Griffin nodded. "You'll have to settle for new old friends. And new old parents."

"Come to the guesthouse, we'll have wine and talk," Amara invited Merrill and me. Griffin must have moved us; we were in Griffin's guesthouse sitting room in a blink. Roff came in and sat on the sofa beside me, putting an arm around my shoulders.

"Raona, how much do you think I should pack?" he asked.

"Pack for two weeks at least; I hope we can do laundry sometime," I said. He pulled my face around and gave me a light kiss. Griffin passed out glasses of wine and Roff accepted his with a dip of his head.

"This is quite good," he said after tasting it expertly.

"How long have you been making wine?" Amara asked him.

"More than three hundred years," he said. "I am three hundred thirteen and my father began teaching me when I was ten. I was crushing berries and grapes before that, even."

"So winemaking is your family trade?" I leaned against his shoulder; he was very happy with me there.

"Yes. My family has been making wine for generations. My father always insisted that our ancestors were making it for the Queen before Le-Ath Veronis fell."

"You were on the High Demon world?" Amara asked. "How did you like that?"

Roff cleared his throat. Kifirin showed up as if he'd been called. Nexus Echo. Again.

"He will not say because I brought him from the future," Kifirin smiled, showing his beautiful, white teeth. If he were human, I'd have guessed him to be from India or ancient Persia—his skin was darker and quite beautiful. His smile widened at my thoughts and his dark eyes laughed at me. I swear, there's nothing on him that isn't gorgeous and when he smiles, he can create widespread swooning.

"My life for the past forty years has been good," Roff declared, breaking Kifirin's spell.

"Yes, it has," Kifirin acknowledged. "Before that, things were not so good. They call the comesuli common demons on my planet," Kifirin explained. "Many of the High Demons became corrupt and they mistreated the comesuli, though the comesuli tended the crops and herds and made sure the High Demons did not starve."

"They became lovers of themselves," Roff huffed.

"Roff, don't ever think you're a common anything," I said, leaning forward and giving him a smile. He smiled widely back and gave me another kiss before settling me on his shoulder again.

"Roff and his family are most certainly not common," Kifirin said. "They are one of two families that are winged Infilathi. They were always selected to become vampire because they developed wings with the turn. The winged ones were honorable and much admired."

"You have wings?" I sat up and stared at Roff in amazement.

"If I am turned," he nodded solemnly. "My ancestors were all winged vampires and much respected." I was duly impressed. I wanted to see a winged vampire, I think.

"When the High Demons called the comesuli common demons," Kifirin said, "it was an attempt to make the comesuli a part of themselves, when nothing could be farther from the truth. Comesuli are and always have been the young of the vampire race. Unfortunately, it is necessary for a mature vampire to turn them at the proper time in order for them to gain their true majority."

"Tonight has certainly been educational," I said. Roff pulled me back to his shoulder. I was comfortable there. So was he.

Sixty-nine-year-old Everett Hancock hit the mute button on his television remote; someone was ringing the doorbell of his small, two-bedroom home in Youngstown, Ohio. He wondered if it were his neighbor again, dropping by to ask more questions about his son Anthony and about Tony's death in France. He'd already talked to Corinne, Tony's mother, shortly after the bombing; the government had declared his son dead. Killed in the line of duty, the vice president said when he called.

Everett had been in the military in his younger days; was retired Army, actually. He'd seen Viet Nam and a few other places. Tony had gone with his mother when they'd divorced; Everett couldn't handle her disappearing one night a month and going off to run with who knew what. Everett had been home on leave when Tony was conceived—Corinne had written to let him know a few months after he'd gone back to Germany where he was stationed. Tony was born while he was away, too, and was four months old when Everett came home.

He and Corinne had done nothing but fight after he gotten home; she'd accused him of ignoring her to stay an extra three months in Germany, and he'd shouted about her stupid werewolf habits. Corinne packed her bags after the last blow-up, taking herself and Tony right out the door. Ran right off and married one of those damned wolves. Everett snorted at the memory as he opened the door.

"What the hell do you want?" Everett didn't recognize the two men who stood there. They were dressed in nice suits and ties, though. Probably from the church, wanting him to accept salvation or something.

"I am Christopher Townsend," one of the visitors said. "You will come with us." Everett opened his storm door and followed Mr. Townsend right out to a waiting car. The other man, who'd been standing next to Christopher Townsend, slipped inside the house, grabbed Everett's keys and locked the door behind him as he left. He followed his partner out to the car, where Everett was already sitting in the back seat. Special Agent White was dialing his cell phone as Special Agent Townsend put the car in gear and drove away. The phone rang on the other end and was answered.

"We have him," Special Agent Kenneth White said and hung up.

~

Everett looked around curiously, as he was led into a basement—Mr. Townsend and Mr. White had driven him to Pittsburgh and stopped at a house there. Everett still didn't understand why he'd willingly come with them and hadn't attempted to object. It just seemed that whenever Mr. Townsend told Everett to do something, Everett thought it was a good idea.

"Are you hungry, Mr. Hancock?" Mr. White asked. Everett looked

at the other man. He and Mr. Townsend looked young to him—
younger than his son, who'd been thirty-six when he'd died.

"I could eat," Everett nodded.

"What would you like?"

"Oh, a piece of chicken, maybe a sandwich." Everett didn't care.
The doctor was always on him to lower his cholesterol. Nowadays
Everett ignored that warning and ate what he wanted. Nobody was
going to live forever, after all.

"A chicken sandwich, maybe?" Mr. Townsend asked.

"Yeah. With fries." Mr. White went back upstairs.

"You will stay here, Mr. Hancock," Mr. Townsend showed Everett a
bedroom. "There is a bathroom there, too, if you need to go." Chris
Townsend showed Everett where the bath and shower were inside his
bedroom. "You will not attempt to leave and you will do what Mr.
White and I tell you." Everett nodded.

~

"Albert, they have him at the safe house in Pittsburgh," Charles spoke
quietly into his cell. "Wlodek wants you to check to see if he has
mindspeech."

"I can be there tomorrow; I'm in New York now," Albert replied.

"Let us know as soon as you can so we can make a decision,"
Charles said.

"Of course," Albert agreed and hung up.

~

"Take one or two nice outfits; the rest can be clothes you wouldn't
mind working in. Just everyday stuff," I sat on Roff's bed as he
folded clothing and placed it in his borrowed suitcase. Franklin
and Greg had bought jeans, shirts, shoes and other necessary items
for Roff and Giff. Both were quite happy with their new
wardrobe.

"Where will we be staying?" Roff asked, folding a pullover shirt.

60

"I don't know yet. Maybe hotels or safe houses," I said. "Do you have pajamas or something to sleep in?"

"I have pajamas, but prefer to only wear the lower half," he informed me.

"That's not unusual," I told him. I helped him pack shampoo and the soap he liked.

"It was not this complicated to make the pilgrimage to Baetrah," Roff muttered, zipping his suitcase.

"What is Baetrah?" I asked.

"Baetrah is the volcano on Kifirin's planet. The comesuli go there and ask Kifirin to take us back to Le-Ath Veronis."

"You can ask him in person," I smiled at Roff.

"You think we have not done this? He was not always available, you know. Only recently did he come to me and my family, offering us a place with you, along with the promise that if we worked hard, Le-Ath Veronis would again be inhabited by vampires and comesuli."

"So the volcano is the place to go if you want to ask Kifirin for something?" That made me chuckle. Honestly, I wondered about the volcanic scent I smelled around him at times.

"The Dragon's Teeth are nearby, too. That is the way for the High Demons to ask Kifirin for something. They should have asked long ago for him to wake and control the copper Ra'Ak. They did not."

"So, how did he wake, then?"

"Someone finally remembered how to wake Kifirin when it was nearly too late. The Dragon's teeth require blood. The blood given was almost too dear."

"That seems a little drastic," I said.

"It was," Roff nodded.

"It sounds like you've had a tough time," I gave him a quick hug.

"I would endure it all again if it would mean I could come to you," he sighed.

"Roff, you need to stop, you're going to make me think I'm more important than I am," I said. "And we don't need that." I patted his shoulder and walked toward the door. "Do you need help carrying anything downstairs?"

"No, Raona. I can get this easily."

"Merrill wants us downstairs in fifteen minutes. I'm going to grab my things. I'll meet you there." I trotted down the hallway. I'd left Gavin in his bedroom, packing his bags. At least he could do that for himself.

Gavin hadn't just packed his things; he'd carried all our bags down to the garage. He and René were making Tony load up the back of the Range Rover. Poor Tony—he was the rookie, looked like. Tony didn't seem to give a damn; he was having fun flinging heavy bags around as if they were throw pillows.

Griffin and Amara came to see me off; Griffin told me they might drop in on us now and then, just to say hello. I nodded. Amara hugged me. Griffin got a hug and a kiss before letting me go. Franklin and Greg got big hugs too. I was worried about Greg but afraid to say anything—his blood scent was far from normal. Roff appeared, carrying his bags easily; he truly was stronger than he looked. He and Tony got the last bags loaded in and we were ready to go.

The Council's jet was flying us to Dallas, and we were packed to the roof inside the Range Rover. Gavin held me on his lap, which was against the law since I wasn't wearing a seat belt. Roff was scrunched between Tony and René in the back seat.

Merrill drove us to the airport and we were loaded on the jet in very little time. I recalled that I hadn't flown with Gavin since our trip back from Florida. This time I sat next to him, while Roff sat across the aisle. This was old habit for Tony; I figured his hands were itching to send emails or something as he and René found seats. Roff was excited; he'd never done anything like this before.

We were in the air for nine hours, stopping once to refuel and landing in Dallas around midnight local time due to the time difference. Winkler, Rhett and Dalroy were waiting there to meet us. Winkler provided two of his company-owned SUVs, so we were loaded up and hauled off to Winkler's home outside Denton.

"Are you sure this is safe?" I asked as Winkler stole a hug while Gavin stood by, frowning. I didn't want to put him or his unborn children in danger by staying with him.

"It'll be all right," Winkler grinned at me. "I'm putting all of you in the guesthouse. We haven't closed on your house next door or I'd let you stay there." So many things had happened; I'd forgotten he was buying it for me.

In the meantime, I was no stranger to the guesthouse. Gavin, Roff and I got the top floor for old times' sake; René and Tony took the bottom floor. The only difference was that this time Gavin and I shared a bed; Roff slept in the second bedroom.

"Do you know how many times I wanted to come in and climb in bed with you?" Gavin asked as I hefted a suitcase on the king-size bed and unpacked a few things. Winkler had renovated since we'd stayed before—the bath had new tile and granite counters, the bedroom had new carpet, drapes and blinds. He'd spared no expense, I noticed.

"Hmmph," I grumbled at Gavin's question. "You didn't stop yourself from coming in and undressing me before digging around in my shoulder for that bullet."

"Cara, the feel of your skin under my hands almost drove me wild," Gavin came to nuzzle my neck. "I had to force myself to focus on the task instead."

"Uh-huh," I said. "Don't go down that road, Gavin. You know what happened not long after that." He'd placed compulsion and hauled me off to the Council. That still pissed me off every time I thought about it.

"Cara, put that out of your mind, I beg you," Gavin said, turning me in his arms. "This is our first time traveling when we are truly together. I do not wish to ruin this."

"You know what I remember?" I said. "I remember dancing with you at the wedding reception that we crashed. You had your eyes closed on the last dance, Gavin. I always wondered what it was you were thinking about."

"You wish to know this?" He blinked at me before lowering his head to steal a kiss. I shrugged when he pulled away. "For just a moment, I pretended that you were mine," he admitted. "That there was nothing standing between us and that you loved me. I wanted to take you to my home and keep you, cara. That is what I was thinking."

I let my forehead droop against his chest and he wrapped his arms around me. "I love you, cara mia. More than I have ever loved anything. You have to forgive my desire to lock you away at times; I only wish to keep you safe."

"What would you have done if the vote had gone the other way?" I leaned away from him and studied his eyes—they were a beautiful, deep brown. I stroked fingers through his thick, close-cropped brown hair before trailing a finger down his cheek. "You were set to kill me, Gavin. What would you have done afterward?" My fingers traced the line of his jaw. It was strong, that jaw, his lips fine and well-shaped. He quirked a dark brow and a corner of his mouth lifted slightly at my touch.

"Probably what I did anyway," he replied, kissing my fingers. "I drove straight to El Diablo and proceeded to get as drunk as I could. Flavio had to haul me away; I spent the day in his townhome afterward. I was terrified that you could never bring yourself to speak with me or care for me."

"Flavio," I huffed, moving away from Gavin. "He couldn't wait to tell Wlodek how I'd misbehaved in New Mexico."

"Cara, he was only doing his duty."

"Yeah? If they were discussing a beating for you, do you think I'd just let them do it? They'd get an earful, I think. There would be no doubt in their minds as to what I thought of all of them, too."

"And that would mean a beating for you as well, cara."

"Then they could do both of us at once. Two for the price of one, don't you think?" I walked away from him. "Fucking Council," I grumbled.

"You have not had many good experiences with them," Gavin nodded. "Perhaps if you give them some time, they will win you over."

"That'll be the day," I snapped. "I don't even know their names— except for Flavio and Oluwa. I know those two. That's it."

"Then introduce yourself at the Annual Meeting this year," Gavin came to stand next to me, trying to coax me back into his arms. "They cannot refuse the introduction."

"Maybe I shouldn't know their names," I moved away from him again. "Do you like any of them?"

"I like a few, I think. The others I tolerate."

"That dark-haired female is a problem, Gavin. Trust me on that. Someday, Wlodek may have her standing in front of him." Gavin lifted an eyebrow at my statement, but didn't say anything. I didn't expect anything else—I was used to nobody listening to me. I sighed. "It sucks being a new vampire," I said, picking up my shampoo and soap and carrying them into the bathroom.

"Cara, the first five years are mandatory," Gavin came in to stand behind me. "While your first years seem to be more troubled than others, you have many important vampires watching you. You are extraordinary, Lissa. A Queen. Wlodek is holding off informing the full Council because of Xenides—you understand why he must continue to think your weakness is compulsion. When the Council and the race as a whole are informed there is a Queen again, that will be cause for celebration."

"Celebration my ass," I muttered. I didn't want a celebration. I just wanted to make decisions for myself.

"Don't you want others to recognize you for what you are?" Gavin sounded puzzled.

"Sheesh. No," I replied, tossing a hand helplessly. Honestly, whenever Kifirin started talking of rebuilding Le-Ath Veronis, I got chills, and not in a good way.

"Lissy?" Tony's voice sounded through the upper floor guesthouse. I guess he didn't want to surprise us in case we were in a compromising position.

"Tony, what do you want?" I headed toward the bedroom door. René was right behind Tony; Dalroy, Rhett, Winkler and newly appointed Director Bill Jennings were right behind René in our small sitting area.

"Lissa, Director Jennings has unfortunate news," René said. Gavin stepped up behind me and placed his hands on my shoulders.

"What is it?" I was suddenly terrified. Tony looked gray. Bill's face had lost most of its color.

"This was sent to the OSBI," Bill held out a photograph. OSBI—Oklahoma State Bureau of Investigation. My fingers shook as I took the photograph from Bill's hand. Gavin's arm around my waist was what kept me standing; the photograph was of Don's brother, David. He'd been killed; multiple stab wounds covered his torso and he'd been dumped on top of Don's grave, his neck bent at an unnatural angle as it rested against Don's headstone.

"Oh, dear God," I muttered, my hand covering my mouth. "Where's Sara?"

"We don't know," Bill said. "We received a typewritten note with this photograph. It says *come to me or there will be more of the same.*"

"Lissa, the authorities don't have any leads. There weren't any fingerprints on the photograph or the note. Not even the envelope or the stamps." Tony had already discussed this with Bill, I could tell.

"Where was it mailed?" I was doing my best to keep from crying. David's body had been tossed carelessly onto Don's grave, his stab wounds likely from a vampire's claws. "How long has he been dead?" The photograph shook as I handed it back to Bill.

"He was killed somewhere nearby and thrown on the grave. We couldn't find shoe prints or other evidence," Bill said softly. "This happened two nights ago."

"Don's grave is at least twenty feet from the nearest road that runs through that cemetery," I wiped my cheeks. "Those fucking vampires threw him from the road so they wouldn't leave prints behind."

"We think that too; the coroner is certain that all broken bones were postmortem."

"Raona," Roff walked in the room. He'd been wandering outside; I smelled freshly mown grass and flowers about him. Roff had been exploring Winkler's four acres surrounding the house. He came straight to me now, wiping stubborn tears from my face.

"We're keeping this away from the media for now," Bill went on. "Of course, it was all done at night and nobody saw anything."

"Do you have surveillance cameras around the cemetery now?" Tony asked.

"Yes, but as you know, they probably won't go back there."

"Then how the hell am I supposed to come to them if I don't know where they are?" I was getting angry, now. If I had any idea where Xenides was, he would be a very dead vampire as soon as I could make him so.

"Lissa, you will get that thought out of your head immediately," Gavin growled. "You will not be going to any of them. We will track them down and take care of this."

"Then why did you bring me?" I considered misting away from him.

"Because you're good at this, Lissy," Tony said. "You make intuitive leaps sometimes. Look what you did about those child killers in England."

"Uh-huh." I attempted to wiggle out of Gavin's arms.

"Raona, come with me," Roff took my arm and Gavin let me go. Roff led me to the bedroom and shut the door behind us.

"Don't join up with them," I pulled away from Roff.

"I know you are upset and they are not allowing you your full potential," Roff said. "A Queen protects her people. I think they are too afraid of losing you."

"Honey, I think I love you," I said, giving him a hug.

Bill motioned the others out the door and pulled them down the steps leading away from the guesthouse. "Mr. Hancock asked me not to give additional information to Lissa," Bill said, once they were inside Winkler's mansion. Winkler led them quietly into the kitchen, glad that Kellee was asleep. Trajan was now living with him, and he'd kept James and Leon on as bodyguards.

"We didn't give you the full contents of the note," Bill said, once they'd settled around the huge island. "They want Lissa to come to them in Kansas City. They've given a date and time; otherwise, they'll go after her cousins who live in the state. We have our doubts as to whether Sara Workman is still alive since they're threatening the cousins, now."

Bill was thrown into a difficult situation immediately—there hadn't been an opportunity for him to ease into the job. His forehead was creased with worry; Rahim Alif could very well be with Xenides. In his experience, where one of them was in the past, the other hadn't been far away.

"What is the location?" Tony asked.

"They only gave coordinates. Latitude and longitude," Bill answered. "We've checked; that particular spot is a wooded area near Parkville, Missouri, located slightly north and west of Kansas City."

"Anything near there?" Winkler got in on the questioning.

"There's an underground business park nearby," Bill said. "They may be using that as a base; we're checking it now."

"You need to get Lissa up there, along with the rest of us to see if we can sniff any of them out," Gavin said. "What's the date?"

"They're being generous, they're giving us a month," Bill said, sounding puzzled.

"If we wrap this up quickly, we'll have time to return to France for the Annual Meeting," René observed. The meeting was to be held in France and scheduled for the beginning of October.

"René, you have always been fonder of those gatherings than I," Gavin said.

"You work them, cousin," René reminded his only living relative. "I go to enjoy myself." He didn't bring Gavin's attention to the fact that he'd put in a bid for Lissa during the last meeting. Had Gavin not intervened, Lissa might be wed to him instead. Gavin would not appreciate the reminder; René was sure of that.

Albert sent a mental message to Everett Hancock. *Can you hear me?* he asked Anthony Hancock's father. Everett blinked at him instead.

"You must answer if you hear my mindspeech," Albert laid compulsion. Everett nodded. Albert tried again. *Now do you hear me?*

Everett sat there, unsure what Albert wanted him to do. Ken white was watching the one-sided exchange, feeling a bit bored. Albert was trying desperately to get Everett Hancock to answer. They'd held hope that the elder Hancock could hear Albert's mindspeech. The unfortunate truth, however, was that Everett Hancock seemed to be—as far as mindspeech was concerned, anyway—deaf as a post.

"We have tried for the past hour and he is unable to hear Albert's mindspeech," Chris Townsend relayed the message to Charles, who would pass it along to Wlodek. Wlodek was actually listening to the conversation. He took the phone from Charles.

"Take him to Oklahoma City," Wlodek instructed. "Introduce him to Lissa. She will have a message for me afterward." Wlodek handed the phone back to Charles. Charles gave the address of the safe house where Lissa could be found in Oklahoma before terminating the call.

Chris put the phone back in his pocket. "Looks like we're going to Oklahoma City," he sighed.

We were driving north on I-35 about nine in the evening, two days after I'd learned that Don's brother was dead. It was Thursday, August twenty-sixth; Gavin had bought Roff a nice watch with date and time displays, and taught Roff about telling time and using a calendar.

Roff was happy with Gavin's instruction and was quite taken with the watch, reminding me in the mornings what day it was. I considered smacking Gavin and hiding the watch. Unfortunately, Roff never took it off—it was waterproof, too.

"There is a three-bedroom safe house reserved for us in Oklahoma City," Gavin informed me; he was driving the van Winkler lent us. It could seat up to nine people with room in the back for luggage. Tony and René sat behind us, with Roff in the back row. He didn't seem to mind.

Bill had flown into Oklahoma City several hours ahead of us to continue his investigation. Winkler would be joining us in two days; he had business to see to before following us to Oklahoma. Dalroy and Rhett were planning to come with him as added protection. My cell phone rang as Gavin drove.

"Lissa?" Charles was on the other end.

"Hi, Charles, what's up?" I asked. I was glad to hear from him; I hadn't brought my laptop since Gavin had his. I could use it to send email—if I could get past his frown whenever I asked to borrow it, that is.

He and Wlodek both forbade the use of my cell phone as a means to do email, saying it was much easier to lose a cell and they didn't want my contacts handed over to someone who'd managed to get their hands on my phone. They'd also discouraged me from taking my laptop. Therefore, I was forced to use Gavin's laptop as a means of electronic communication.

"The Honored One has instructed Chris Townsend and Ken White to catch up with you in Oklahoma City tomorrow evening," Charles informed me. "They are bringing someone with them. Wlodek wants to know whether you detect a kinship between this person and anyone else you may know."

"Oh. Okay, I can do that," I agreed. "Can you tell me who it is?"

"No. Wlodek doesn't want you to know," he said.

Gavin was listening to the conversation, as were Tony and René. "Chris will come for you and Gavin and take you to this person," Charles continued. "But Wlodek only wants the two of you to go. Understand?" Gavin was nodding, so I said that was fine. Charles had to go so we hung up.

"Wonder what that's all about," I muttered, putting my cell away.

"You will find out tomorrow," Gavin said and kept driving.

CHAPTER 5

"We have to find a grocery store and get something for Roff to eat at the safe house," I told Gavin when we reached the outskirts of Oklahoma City. "Where is the safe house?"

Gavin rattled off an address in the northwestern portion of the city. "There's a grocery store not far from there," I said. "I can take Roff after you guys get settled in."

"No!" Gavin, Tony and René all said at once. That's how four vampires and a comesula ended up in a grocery store that stayed open late, walking down aisles while Roff and I discussed what he wanted to cook. René hadn't been inside a grocery store ever, I think. There hadn't been a reason for him to go, so this was a new experience.

Tony was staring at a display of snacks, a look of longing on his face. I just went to him and rubbed his back. I knew that feeling. The memory of what the food tasted like was still fresh in his mind. I also knew that René hadn't had time for the food lesson, yet. Poor Tony. That was a difficult experience for me, when Merrill forced me to hold onto the food until I was in a safe place to get rid of it. Vampire bodies and solid food don't mix very well.

We only bought enough food for a few days, since we didn't know how long we were going to be at this particular safe house. Roff and I packed groceries away in the upper level of the house—it had a full kitchen, just as the basement did. Gavin, Tony and René unloaded suitcases and carried them downstairs. Roff's things were dropped in the upper level—he would sleep upstairs; he didn't have a problem with daylight as the others did.

"We're going to meet Bill at David Workman's residence," Gavin announced, once we got everything settled in. Bill was working late hours—it was two in the morning. Roff checked his watch and informed me of the time. We climbed back in the van and drove to Edmond, leaving Roff behind.

Don's brother, David, worked as an accountant for a large energy firm in Oklahoma City; Sara was a manager for a local restaurant chain. Both made good money and had a nice house in southeast Edmond.

Bill arranged to meet us outside the house, along with two human agents, neither of whom I knew. Xenides' scent hit me the moment we walked through the front door. Well, Bill could hear my mindspeech; he just couldn't reciprocate.

Xenides was here, I sent to him. He nodded to acknowledge the sending. *Another vampire was with him—a sibling to two others I met recently*, I added. It had to be Dominic—the same scent surrounded Thaddeus and Lorenzo. Bill didn't blink at my revelation. I then sent the same information to Tony, Gavin and René—I didn't want Bill's two agents to get the information. Better that they didn't know anything at all about us.

I walked through Sara's kitchen and got a whiff of the scents there. "Sara's dead," I blurted, beginning to shake. I smelled her death. I wasn't sure it had been violent; there wasn't any scent of blood. However, a heart attack or a broken neck could also be the cause. I wondered how her health had been before the vampires came to call.

"You're sure?" Bill stepped across the tiled floor, stopping beside me. The other two agents stared at me, wondering how I'd come to that conclusion.

"She's sure," Tony walked up beside me. *Send your agents to the car*, I sent to Bill. Bill ordered the two men out of the house.

"I don't smell her blood, I just smell her death," I said after the two agents had gone out to Bill's car in the driveway. "Has the backyard been checked?"

"We looked it over but we didn't bring any dogs—we didn't want to confuse the scents," Bill said. At least he'd known to do that much.

Let's go out, then." Bill led us through the house and out the patio door.

The scent that hit me when we walked into the backyard was overwhelming in its stench—wild animal mixed with Saxom's taint and Dark Elemaiya. I grabbed Bill's arm and barely had time to toss him inside the house, slamming the French doors in his face before they were on us.

Our three attackers resembled grizzly bears with the heads of giant cats—all had huge canines, reminding me of drawings I'd seen of saber tooth tigers. One was doing his best to savage Tony; he'd been closest to the creatures and they'd jumped him first.

René wanted to help Tony, but had a creature of his own to battle. I misted after Tony's attacker, coming up behind him as he clawed Tony to the ground, preparing to bite him in half.

The growls and screams from those creatures were deafening as they leapt at their intended prey, tearing up huge clumps of earth with enormous, clawed feet. If David had still been alive, he'd have had an aneurysm. He'd been rabidly meticulous about his lawn.

Since I'd turned to mist as soon as we were attacked, I allowed my hands and claws to materialize, severing the thick spine at the neck of Tony's monster. The animal roared in agony before falling over and turning to ash.

The noise of battle had brought Bill's agents rushing into the backyard. Both began firing at the animal Gavin was fighting. Neither Gavin nor his opponent was making any headway; it looked to be a standoff between them.

"Stop shooting!" Bill shouted as he forced his way past the jammed French door—I'd slammed it pretty hard.

René was having the same luck that Gavin was having; he'd gotten a slash down his arm but the creature hadn't been able to do better than that against him. One of the agents got in a final shot as I removed the head of René's attacker, and the bullet managed to lodge in my exposed forearm. I shrieked mentally as the bullet slammed into my flesh; I think everyone there heard it.

There wasn't time to deal with the injury, however. I went to help Gavin, who still hadn't been touched. That battle was like a tornado, with both of them attacking and retreating so swiftly I had difficulty getting in to kill Gavin's monster. When I finally got his attacker down and flaking, I rematerialized, causing both human agents to jump.

Tony was right there, injured as he was, placing compulsion. René was beside him, helping in seconds. Gavin gripped my arm and began to examine my bullet wound.

"Hold still, cara, I can see it," he said, and forming a claw on an index finger, he carefully dug inside the wound, flipping the bullet out in no time while I clenched my teeth to keep from whimpering.

"What the hell were those things?" Bill had waited patiently for Gavin to finish performing minor surgery before demanding answers. I let my head droop against Gavin's chest. I knew what they were and hoped there weren't any more of them.

"Vampire shapeshifters," I mumbled against Gavin's shirt. Gavin drew in a sharp breath. So did Director Bill Jennings.

We were sitting inside the house later; it was too late to contact Wlodek so I left a message for him on Charles's cell before calling Merrill and doing the same for him. I carefully explained as best I could what we'd fought.

Xenides was probably hoping to take out my guards so he could either take me or track me. I'm sure one of the shapeshifters would have been happy to grab me if he could and haul me off to Xenides.

How they planned to do that, however, was a mystery. Even Xenides knew how fast I could go to mist; he'd seen it himself. They must have been relying on compulsion to do the job.

Gavin helped Tony with his wounds while I made my calls; Tony wasn't thrilled to have his slashes washed out thoroughly with soap and water, but Gavin was giving him a lesson on the fact that anything caught inside the cuts and not washed out would heal right over, trapping the debris inside.

Tony had three deep rakes across his chest where he'd been clawed, along with a slash down his left arm when he'd held it up to protect his face. Gavin and René cleaned out all of Tony's wounds.

René submitted to his subsequent cleaning with stoic acceptance, grunting his thanks to Gavin when it was done. Bill, of course, was watching everything with fascination. He'd sent the two human agents back to the car, but only after Gavin checked the yard and surrounding area—it looked as if we'd gotten what was there to attack us.

~

"My lord, our three bears are dead." Angelo hid the smile behind his sly joke. He was a shapeshifter, just as the others were, but his shape was that of a bird—a blackbird, actually.

If any of the vampires had been able to hear over the noise of the growls and the heat of battle, they might have heard the rush of his wings as he'd taken flight, making slow circles overhead as he watched the last of the three shapeshifters go down. They'd all died at the hands of the little female; he'd seen her claws form to take heads. Xenides truly would love to have her, he knew, but the task of taking her seemed quite difficult.

Xenides cursed angrily before asking Angelo for details. Angelo gave them. Xenides had new respect for his little princess, now. He couldn't wait to have her under his command.

~

Roff waited up for us and he shouldn't have. He fretted over the wounds we'd gotten, although they were already closing. The healing sleep would finish them up for us. Gavin was feeling gun shy, I think; he insisted that Roff sleep downstairs. Roff hauled a pillow and blanket down and slept on the sofa in the underground living area.

"Tell us about these shapeshifters," René asked as we helped ourselves to a unit of blood in the safe house kitchen. Gavin finished mine after drinking a full unit himself.

"I don't know much; Kifirin told me that some of the Elemaiya have the gift of shapeshifting." I sat down at the small kitchen table with a sigh. "The other gifts include mindspeech, misting, foresight, that sort of thing," I said. "Saxom was able to tell who had what gift, maybe. He could sure sort out the Dark Elemaiya. I wonder if he wasn't of that race himself, at least in part."

"No way to tell unless your true sire is more forthcoming," Gavin grumbled. I'd been doing some thinking about my true sire. And about Merrill's statement that he couldn't lie and that everything he'd told me was the truth. The first part of his statement was bothering me more and more.

His words were, *I knew the vampire and werewolf races were dying on this world.* And that statement was followed by *You are the answer to so many things that were troubling me. I had to go Looking for your mother.*

He knew the vampire and werewolf races were in trouble. I was the answer. He'd had to search for my mother. I'd been created as the solution to a problem. Yeah, it bothered me.

I wasn't a love child conceived in some fling my mother had; it was calculated. And, if I were the answer to the problem he saw—the problem of the vampire and werewolf races that were dying, then I would have to belong to one race or the other.

My parents hadn't been werewolves, so that had been out of the question. Griffin had known I'd become vampire eventually. He'd known. If he hadn't planned it, he'd seen it. He admitted that one of his talents was foresight.

I didn't know at the moment how I truly felt about my mother's part in this. Griffin said that her ability to mindspeak with him encouraged her to come to him and have a child with him. Did she regret that after Howard Graham started beating her?

"Fuck," I muttered, rubbing my forehead with shaky fingers. "I want to go out for a while, Gavin." He frowned at me—was about to tell me no, but something in my expression must have stopped him. He shrugged and said nothing as I misted away.

There aren't many tall buildings in downtown Oklahoma City, and most of the lights are turned off during this portion of the night. I looked out over the downtown skyline anyway.

Dawn was close, but hadn't I gotten up during daylight before? It wouldn't kill me if I chose to sleep on the roof of the safe house. I hugged myself tightly, my knees drawn up to my chest. What did my father want from me? I wasn't naïve enough to think it was love.

∼

"My baby has already discovered the flaw in the tapestry," Griffin sighed. Amara sat at the kitchen island in the guesthouse, sipping a cup of tea in the early afternoon light shining across the English countryside.

"What do you think she'll do, Brenten?"

"What she should; think she was born as a matter of convenience for others. It won't stop her from doing what's right, love. She'll just hate me while she's doing it."

"Her life has been filled with pitfalls," Amara sighed. Griffin shrugged. "Tell me you don't love your daughter," Amara gazed at Griffin.

"I can't tell you that," he said and folded space. Amara didn't know where he went; she only knew he'd be back. Eventually.

∼

"Tony, you shouldn't be up here, dawn is coming." He'd used his newly acquired vampire strength to climb to the roof of the safe house and now settled lightly and noiselessly beside me. I looked at him for a moment, hoping the tear stains weren't showing on my face. That hope was short-lived.

"Lissy, why are you crying?" He put an arm around me. I wondered if René and Gavin knew he was here with me.

77

"Tony, if I tell you, then René will know. And then Gavin and Merrill and Wlodek and anybody else they choose to tell." I wiped my cheeks with fingers that trembled. Dawn was coming and we'd be forced to go inside soon so Tony's skin wouldn't blister.

"Baby, you have to tell somebody, don't you?" He tightened his arm around me.

"I don't think so," I said, betraying myself by sniffling.

"It has to do with dead relatives. And your father. I heard his words, too, baby. It didn't sound like you were a love child. He said he went looking for your mother because the vampires and werewolves were in trouble."

If Tony was putting two and two together, then the others probably were, too. Why didn't I just stand on a rooftop somewhere and blubber out my misery for the entire universe to hear? They were going to find out anyway.

"How did you manage to get away from Gavin and René?" I asked instead.

"They asked me to come," he said softly.

"Gavin's not afraid you'll jump me while we're alone together?"

"He was. That's why he asked René to place compulsion. I can hug and kiss you a little, Lissy. I can't go farther than that." The regret for that was thick in his voice.

"Compulsion," I muttered. "The most damning word in the vampire language."

"I'm happy to be vampire and I know you're not," Tony tucked my hair behind an ear. My strawberry blonde curls were long enough to do that, now.

"My husband's grave is that way," I pointed to my left, which was north of where we were. "Now I can't go there because the image of his brother's body lying on top of it will be in my mind. Dead because of me, Tony. Tell me how I'm supposed to live with that. Sara's dead too, whether they killed her or she died of a heart attack or whatever. Who else is going to die because of what I am? My father made me because of what I would become. He knew I'd be turned, Tony. That was the plan, don't you think?"

"I think he might have wanted to save the world, that's what I think." Tony nuzzled my cheek gently.

"And that's supposed to make me feel better?" I rose abruptly. "How was your childhood, Tony?" I looked down at him; he was still sitting. I reached for his arm and pulled him up easily, turning us both to mist. My mental sigh was passed to him as we sank through the roof and then through the upper floor and down to the basement, minutes before the sun rose. René was waiting patiently and Tony was ushered into his bedroom by his sire. I was jealous of that, even.

"Lissa," Gavin's breath was cool on my neck as he placed a kiss. "Come, cara. We will speak of this later." I put my arms around his neck and sobbed once as he lifted me and carried me into our bedroom.

~

Ken White was there to pick us up at ten the following evening. Gavin and I rode in Agent White's rental car; Gavin in the passenger seat while I sat in the back. I'd slept later than the others before waking sluggishly, and Gavin hadn't forced me out of bed.

Roff had been there waiting for me, patiently holding a bag of blood so I could feed. Gavin didn't interfere, either, when Roff crawled onto the bed and let me lean against him as I sipped my meal.

Now we were driving toward a hotel not far away; the person I was supposed to see was there with Agent Townsend. Ken parked the car and we climbed out to walk inside the hotel. Overhead, the sky was a dark, stormy blue and I worried we might get rain. Tall piles of cumulus clouds floated off to the west and I could see lightning. It didn't rain often during August in Oklahoma—usually it was dry and dusty. But if it did storm, it could be a good one.

The elevator dinged when we reached the third floor of the WaterMark Hotel; it was one of the nicest hotels in the city. Agent White led us to a room halfway down the hall, swiped a keycard and opened the door. Chris Townsend was inside, standing beside a man in his late sixties or early seventies, with graying hair that had once been black. Wrinkles lined his face and fading brown eyes studied me with a puzzled expression as I walked in. I went over to get his scent. This man wasn't connected to anyone that I knew.

"Charles is on the phone," Agent Townsend held a cell phone out to me. I blinked at him and Agent White.

"Charles?" I said, taking the phone.

"Lissa? Can you tell anything?"

"Charles, this man isn't connected to anyone I know," I said.

"You're sure?"

"Yeah. I'd know if he was connected to somebody I'd ever scented before. He's not." Charles sighed at my explanation.

"That's Everett Hancock," Charles informed me. "Anthony Hancock's father."

Oh, lord.

"Charles, I'm sorry. This man isn't related. He is also completely human, no other bloodline," I added. Charles knew what I was saying. Gavin wasn't surprised by my words either, but Agents White and Townsend sure were.

"Let me talk to Chris again," Charles said. I handed the phone back to Townsend. Charles told him to keep the information to himself about what I could do and instructed that he tell Ken White the same thing. Chris said all right and ended the call.

"We're still going to send him somewhere safe, just in case our friend gets wind of him," Chris said, meaning Everett Hancock. Were we going to tell Tony? I hoped not. I think he had enough on his plate right now. I just shrugged and nodded at Chris instead.

"Mom, the Head of the Council has given permission for you to visit with Tony," Deryn spoke with Corinne Alford on his cell. "It's not something they normally permit, but since we're wolves, they're allowing this and setting a precedent." Deryn was happy to be passing this news off to his mother; she worried that she wouldn't be allowed to see her oldest son again.

"How soon?" Corinne Alford wanted to go to Tony immediately. That wouldn't be possible.

"He's in Oklahoma City," Deryn replied. "The Honored One says you can visit as early as tomorrow. William Winkler is coming up from the Dallas Pack so you won't be alone in a sea of vampires. They'll set up a plane ticket for you as soon as you want to go."

"Can we do it tomorrow?"

"Sure. For Dad, too, if he wants to go along. Somebody will meet you at the airport." Corinne agreed and Charles, who was nearby, was already arranging for first class tickets from Denver to Oklahoma City the following evening. Deryn passed the flight information off to his mother and everything was set up before Deryn terminated the call.

"It's a relief actually, to know the old fart isn't Tony's dad after all," Deryn sighed, glancing at Charles. "I only met him twice and he was the biggest, grumpiest old gas bag you've ever seen. Tony only went to him when he had to."

"Was Anthony happy with your father?" Charles asked.

"Absolutely. Dad taught us how to fish and how to box. Dad's a black belt, too, so we learned Karate when we were young. Tony was the one who wanted to study Jiu Jitsu, Aikido, Wing Chun and several other disciplines. Dad drove him to all the classes until Tony was old enough to take himself. Tony won competitions, he was so good. He got his college degree in three years and then went right into the military—special ops, you know. It was no surprise that he kept getting promoted, and when they started looking for a replacement for the Director's job, he accepted but only on the condition that he could make the job hands-on. I hear Agent Jennings made the same arrangement." Deryn was proud of his older brother; Charles could hear it in his voice. "I'm just glad he's not dead right now."

"No, he's definitely not dead. He's been officially registered with the Council. All his papers were completed before he left for the states. He's no longer Anthony Hancock; that name with that face is too recognizable. All vampires change their names. Your brother's ID shows he's Anthony Rockland, now. A variation on his sire's last name, de la Roque."

"He didn't mention it," Deryn said. "It doesn't matter. Everett Hancock can be a memory, now." Charles nodded in agreement.

~

This was the second time I was awake in daylight. It was better this time—I was more lucid, even if the light did hurt my eyes at first. I'd jumped and gasped awake. Another dream had come, only this time I'd seen a young woman—a very young woman—possibly still in her mid-teens, who was begging someone not to send her away. She was quite pregnant and standing in a field of tall grass.

An older woman was shouting at her, telling the girl to take herself and her whelp out of her sight. If that was mom, she needed lessons in parenting, I think. That's when I woke inside the darkened basement, breathing hard and blinking away remnants of a disturbing dream.

"Raona, why are you awake?" Roff stopped chopping vegetables and came to me as soon as I made my way up the stairs and into the kitchen area. Concern clouded his face as he took my hand and led me to a seat at the tiny kitchen table.

"I had another dream," I said, wiping a hand over my face in an attempt to clear away my grogginess. Light was streaming through open blinds in the kitchen window. I squinted at it, attempting to see past the brightness to the day beyond.

Roff went to get a glass of water before I had the opportunity to ask. I gulped it; he'd added a few ice cubes and I thanked him for that. He merely nodded and sat down at the table with me. "Was this a troubling dream?" Roff asked.

"No, I didn't know the people in it," I said. "A mother was sending her pregnant daughter away—that's what the dream was. Jeez, talk about confusing," I set my water down on the table and rubbed my eyes.

"Raona, let me carry you back to bed."

"I can get myself down; you don't have to go lugging me around all the time."

"But I like this," Roff grumbled.

"You can't like hauling me around." Except that he did. And he insisted, so I was carried downstairs and placed carefully back in bed.

"Go back to sleep, my Queen." Roff gave me a careful kiss and pulled the blanket over me. I listened while he made his way up the stairs, hearing the faint thunk of the basement door closing. I snuggled against Gavin's wide back and closed my eyes, falling asleep quickly.

~

"Child, Dominic is likely in the U.S.," Wlodek informed Radomir over the phone. "Make arrangements for the jet to fly his brothers to Oklahoma City. I would prefer that you go with them, rather than allowing Russell to make the journey. I have another assignment for Russell, and I will feel easier if you are there with Lissa and the others. I will be assured of getting complete information this way."

"Of course, father," Radomir had stepped outside the hotel to take the call, in case his father had sensitive information to impart. "I will make arrangements to leave tomorrow evening."

"Get the address for the safe house from Charles; obviously you will have to move the others and find another place to stay. None of the safe houses in the area are large enough to hold all of you." Wlodek tapped a pen on his antique desk; Radomir recognized the sound and could picture his sire's hands as they toyed with the gold pen.

"I will, father," Radomir said, ending the call. He immediately called the vampire who scheduled the Council's jet as he walked through the hotel entry and took the stairs to his room.

"Russell, call the Honored One, he has another assignment for you," Radomir announced as he strode into the room. Lorenzo and Thaddeus watched Radomir closely; they didn't know what this meant.

"Do not fear, your brother has been spotted in the U.S.," Radomir informed them. "We are flying there tomorrow evening to join others who will help us in our search." Lorenzo breathed a sigh of relief at the news; he worried that the Council would abandon his brother's cause and Dominic would be lost to him and Thaddeus.

"Pack up, brother," Lorenzo slapped Thaddeus on the back. They walked through the connecting door to gather their things.

~

"Our Raona was up in daylight again," Roff informed Gavin, who'd finished a pint of blood and was tossing the used bag into the compacter.

"What did she do?" Gavin asked, concerned.

"She claimed she had another dream and wandered to the upper level, where she drank some water. I convinced her to go back to bed." Roff watched Gavin carefully for signs of anger; he knew to leave should a vampire became uncontrollable. Gavin sighed instead.

"I do not understand how or why this is happening. Please continue to watch her and make sure she returns to my bed. When the werewolf arrives, he can assist you in this."

"Of course," Roff nodded to Gavin, quite happy that the vampire hadn't gotten angry.

Winkler arrived two hours later and Lissa had only been awake for an hour, moving about sluggishly while she drank her usual amount of blood. "Lissa," Gavin lectured, "it would ease my fears if you will promise not to wander around should you rise during daylight hours."

~

I looked up at Gavin's face; he was standing on the other side of the refrigerator door as I was placing my unused third of a unit back in the fridge. "I'm not going shopping or jogging down the street, if that's what you're worried about," I said. "The light is too bright for my eyes;

I don't think I can just walk out in it without blinding myself. All I do is talk to Roff or whoever is awake."

"Ask the wolf to find a pair of dark sunglasses for you, cara," Gavin said. "This way, you may sit and talk with Roff and your eyes will be protected."

My mouth dropped open—I know it did. Gavin, making a good suggestion instead of cursing in multiple languages and chastising me for going upstairs during daylight? Unheard of. "Uh, okay. I'll see if Winkler will mind getting some for me."

The doorbell rang upstairs and Roff came down a few minutes later, followed by Winkler, Dalroy and Rhett. Where were we going to put everybody? I even said that out loud, I think.

"Lissa, we have already discussed this on the phone with Charles and Winkler while you slept late," Gavin smiled. "The home in Nichols Hills is still vacant and Winkler has secured it for us to use again. There is plenty of room there for everyone. Also, Anthony's mother and stepfather are coming for a brief visit; they will meet us here first. Radomir, Lorenzo and Thaddeus will be joining us as quickly as they can arrive; they are flying here on the Council's jet."

"Holy crap," I muttered. Our numbers were getting huge. "Does Tony know his mother is coming?"

"He has been informed—René has taken him shopping so he may buy a gift for her."

"Ah." That's why I hadn't seen either of them. Winkler came over, grinned at me and leaned down to give me a peck on the cheek.

"Babies are fine, we had a doctor's visit yesterday," he informed me before I could ask.

"Good," I patted his back before turning to say hello to Dalroy and Rhett.

"Do you think you could get me back to that restaurant that had the good chicken fry?" Winkler said, his nearly-black eyes twinkling.

"I can get you back there, but they stop serving at nine, dude," I poked Winkler in the ribs. It was past that already. "Maybe we can take you in the next few days and Tony's mother and step-dad can go with you."

"Sounds good. In the meantime, I need to eat something. We went straight to the airport after Rhett and Dalroy woke. I haven't had a chance to eat, yet."

"Jeez, Winkler, you could cave in," I teased. "Roff, do you have something suitable for tall, dark and furry, here?"

"I have a steak I can grill for him," Roff nodded. "I cooked chicken earlier; he may have the leftovers while I prepare his meal."

"I'll deal with that," Winkler nodded and followed Roff up the stairs. I trailed behind him with Rhett, Dalroy and Gavin right behind me. Winkler got reheated chicken while Roff slapped a steak under the broiler. "I like it rare," Winkler offered. Roff nodded and threw some vegetables together for Winkler. Winkler was perfectly happy with his steak; Roff left it bloody, just as Winkler prefers. We were talking and watching Winkler devour his meal when Tony and René came back.

"Mom and Dad should be here any time," Tony said, showing me a pair of earrings he'd gotten for his mother. His step-dad was getting a gift certificate from a popular sporting goods store.

"These are nice, Tony," I admired the earrings inside a small jeweler's box. They sparkled with rubies and diamonds—and not small ones, either. René had spent some money, looked like.

Tony had to give up his bank account and credit cards; everybody thought he was dead. René was providing for him, as a normal sire should. If he didn't have one already, René was probably arranging for Tony to have a credit card with his new name on it—Anthony Rockland. I hated that he had to give up Hancock; I liked that name.

The doorbell rang and Tony was up like a shot. René went with him to answer the door. Worriedly I searched Gavin's face; I hoped René knew to be circumspect; Tony's mother believed him dead until she'd learned differently, so this was a reunion. Gavin must have been on my wavelength; he nodded. I released the breath I was holding.

Corinne Alford was introduced to me, as was Tony's stepdad, Lucas Alford. Deryn resembled his dad, I noticed. Both had dark hair, brown eyes and a straight nose. Corinne had black hair like Tony's, and blue eyes, where Tony had gray.

Plus, she wasn't his mother. I knew that the minute she walked into the room. Everett Hancock didn't have a drop of Elemaiyan blood, and he wasn't Tony's biological father anyway, so Tony had to get it from someone else. At first, I figured that Corinne had an affair with someone who did have the blood. Now I knew better. At least one of Tony's parents had been of Elemaiyan descent; it just wasn't Everett Hancock or Corinne Alford.

I wasn't about to tell Tony that Corinne wasn't his mother. He loved her. Big time. And she loved him. I wasn't going to ruin that. I might tell Wlodek if he asked, or Merrill, but that's it. Tony didn't deserve the upset. Had Corinne wanted him to know, she would have told him.

"We're moving to another part of the city, so there will be room for all of us," Winkler informed Lucas Alford. Lucas was more than happy to meet the Dallas Packmaster; he was Second for the Denver Pack and he and Winkler were knee-deep in werewolf politics and intrigue in no time.

Gavin and I gathered our things together while the others talked; Winkler had rented an SUV, so it and the van would carry all our things to the house in Nichols Hills.

Rhett and Dalroy were set to provide security for us at night; Winkler was going to watch things during the day. Winkler would guard us with help from Lucas while he was here, and he'd arranged to bring in a wolf from the Oklahoma City pack when Lucas went home.

Oklahoma City had a werewolf Pack. I never knew, honestly. Winkler had to clear things with the local Packmaster—not just for this time, but the time before as well. It was courtesy to let the local Pack know you were in the area if you were a visiting werewolf.

We loaded up after an hour or so and Winkler and Gavin drove. Gavin remembers everything, and he clearly remembered the way to the mansion. I sat up front with him; René and Roff rode with us in the back seat of the van. "This is quite adequate," René remarked as we drove through the mansion's gates. He was right. The mansion covered the better part of half a block with a high brick wall surrounding it. Gavin and I had walked the perimeter of that wall many times.

"Gavin, what did you do with your paychecks from Winkler?" I asked. He'd been paid, just as I had.

Gavin laughed. "I never cashed them," he replied. "And once I took you with me, I'm sure Winkler canceled them."

"I ought to smack both of you," I grumped.

"I believe I'd like to see that," René observed.

"Stick around," I said. René laughed, this time.

"We would like our guesthouse," Gavin announced when Winkler tried to set us up in the main house. Winkler frowned but didn't argue. Gavin was revisiting the past; doing now what he hadn't been able before.

He placed our bags in the room he'd taken during our previous stay, which was slightly larger than the other bedroom over the garage. Roff took the other bedroom so he could be close to me. He unloaded all his groceries inside the small kitchen and seemed more than happy with his space. He also went to bed shortly after everything was put away. Gavin's cell rang—it was Radomir.

"Radomir is on his way with Lorenzo and Thaddeus," Gavin informed me after ending the call. I knew already; I'd overheard the conversation and Gavin had given out the new address. Radomir showed up twenty minutes later, so Gavin and I went to help them unload.

Winkler was still awake, thank goodness, and handed out bedrooms to the new arrivals. Radomir was placed on the third floor, next to Thaddeus and Lorenzo. Radomir would be watching them, I knew, in case there was any trouble. I wasn't getting any bad vibes off them and my skin didn't itch, so I was confident they were okay.

"Have you had dinner?" I asked as Thaddeus and Lorenzo explored the ground floor of the mansion. It was tastefully decorated and had abstract art on the walls. They'd eaten already; they'd brought a supply of blood in two good-sized coolers and those were promptly unloaded in a refrigerator inside the game room upstairs.

"Father wishes to speak to you privately," Radomir informed me quietly; he'd sought me out. I'd put a late-night snack together for Winkler in the main kitchen while Gavin helped René with another of Tony's lessons. I think it involved fighting more than one vampire at a time. I hadn't gotten that lesson, I recalled.

"All right," I nodded at Radomir and pulled out my cell phone. I'd never been to the roof of this house so I misted upward, going right through the roof and settling down to have my conversation with Wlodek.

"Hi, Charles," I said when he answered the phone.

"Lissa! We miss you," he said.

"Is that the royal we?" I teased.

"If it includes me, then the answer is yes," Wlodek had taken the phone away from Charles. I guess I was going to have to get used to the fact that they were both in Merrill's basement, with Charles's office right next to Wlodek. And, had that been a joke on Wlodek's part? Well, the sun was going to rise at midnight next time.

"Hello, Honored One," I said.

"You could call me Father. You are my youngest and prettiest, after all." Oh, lord.

"I may be your youngest, but Flavio has the prettiest title all locked up," I replied. That made Wlodek chuckle.

"I will be sure and tell him this; he has been a bit depressed lately."

"The most beautiful man on the face of the earth is feeling depressed? Whatever for?" I almost snorted. Almost.

"He feels responsible for nearly killing a certain little Queen," Wlodek replied. I wanted to refute that statement. I didn't. I couldn't say for sure how Flavio felt since I didn't know him that well. What I did remember is that he and Merrill both had been as tight-lipped as bivalves on the way back to London after the big brouhaha in New Mexico.

"Then tell him to stop," I said.

"Perhaps you should tell him yourself. He refuses to listen to me. Radomir has his number if you feel charitable sometime soon."

"Oh, right, I'm supposed to just call him out of the blue and tell him to stop being depressed because I say so and I mean it?" I asked in disbelief.

"I think he might appreciate that more than you know," Wlodek replied. "Now, on to other business. Have you been introduced to Anthony's mother, yet?"

"Yes," my voice was suddenly glum.

"Is she his mother?"

My silence for several seconds probably told Wlodek what he wanted to know, but I answered his question verbally anyway. "No, Father. She is not." It was Wlodek's turn not to speak for several seconds. More than likely it was because I'd called him Father, rather than the other information.

"Well," he sighed after a moment. "Well. It will not be a good idea to attempt to pry the truth loose at this point, and it may harm Anthony as well, should this information become public. I can trust you to keep this to yourself, my daughter?"

"Of course you can," I grumbled. I hadn't wanted to tell him, even. Unless he asked me point blank, that is. I think he knew that. We hung up shortly after that so I misted through the roof and into the house, where I went looking for Radomir.

"Radomir, the Honored One told me that you could give me Flavio's phone number," I said. I'd found him in the hall on the way to his bedroom.

"Here," I watched as the tall, dark-haired vampire took my phone and added the name and number into my phone book. I glanced at the number briefly when Radomir handed my phone back before hitting the call button. Flavio answered on the third ring. He hadn't recognized the number, I could tell.

"Bubba," I said tartly, "this is Sissy. You need to get out of that funk right now and I mean it."

Radomir had a hand over his mouth and he was snickering. "Lissa, is that you?" Flavio was shocked, I could tell. Anyone else might be too, if they were eighteen hundred years old and a member of the Vampire Council. Especially after getting a call like that.

"Yeah, it's me. Stop dragging around right this minute."

"Lissa, I was having a glass of wine with Oluwa." I was interrupting a meeting of some sort. I knew Flavio wasn't gay; he didn't have that vibe. Neither was Oluwa, so it wasn't a tryst. Oluwa had likely heard every word I'd just said, too.

"Then tell Oluwa I owe him a big kiss for the first time I saw him and a kick in the ass for the second time." Yeah, I don't know why I said it, either. It just came out. Radomir was now leaning against a wall and laughing out loud. I know Flavio heard that. Oluwa was laughing as well; it was a booming sound and coming through my phone loud and clear.

"You are no longer angry?" Flavio pointedly ignored the jocularity occurring all around him.

"I didn't say I wasn't still pissed. I'm pissed at lots of people, and Gavin's first on that list. You see how we're married now and all. I haven't kicked him out of bed over it." Radomir slid down the wall and was now laughing on the floor. "As far as the list goes," I continued, "I think you're probably tenth or eleventh, but I'll have to write the list down first and see where you fall. There's a separate list for bad guys —at least you're not on that one."

"Am I supposed to be pleased over that?"

"You should be, I'm determined to kill those guys," I said. "You're too gorgeous to even think about that."

"My appearance is keeping me on the good list of people you're angry with?"

"Nah, your sparkling wit kept you off the bad list," I retorted. "And you're a snappy dresser, too. What is it with you? Is there a vamp GQ somewhere and you're on the cover every month?" Radomir could barely breathe, now, he'd laughed so hard. Oluwa started laughing again over the vamp GQ comment.

"So, you wish for me to stop feeling depressed?" Flavio asked after a moment.

"That's why I called. If you were out flying kites or chasing butterflies with a net and wearing a big smile on your face while you did it, you probably wouldn't have heard from me."

"You suspect that I engage in these activities?"

"Bubba, I don't know what you like to do. I imagine you could get a kite in the air really fast, though, if you wanted to. And if you decide to fly a kite and have trouble, I'll mist your kite up for you."

"I think I would like to see that," Flavio said.

"All you have to do is ask."

"Perhaps we could have a glass of wine the next time you are in the country."

"Sure, Bubba."

"Is that slang for brother?"

"You know it, dude," I said and hung up.

∼

"She was trying to cheer you up," Oluwa wore a huge grin. He'd been cheered up in the most irreverent fashion imaginable. Flavio smiled.

∼

"Charles, this information is for the private records only," Wlodek offered a meaningful look to his assistant. Charles nodded. There was a special archive that he and Wlodek kept, containing sensitive information on some members of the race. "Anthony Hancock was adopted in some way. Neither of the people who claim to be his parents are his parents. At this time, we are unsure as to whom his natural parents are or if they still live." Charles tapped the information into his computer before removing the flash drive. It would be locked inside Wlodek's personal safe. Charles had compulsion placed long ago not to reveal any information stored within that safe. Charles's phone rang shortly after.

"Child, may I speak with my father?" It was Flavio, and to Charles's surprise, his sire sounded cheerful. Charles had a puzzled look on his face as he handed the cell phone to Wlodek.

"Child?" Wlodek said.

"Father, I received a call from Lissa." There was definitely a smile in Flavio's voice.

"Did you?"

"Yes. Radomir must have given her my number; he was there when she made the call."

"How is she?"

"Quite impish, father. I think I will call her that—Imp. It suits her and after her impertinent and disrespectful treatment of me, well, she deserves that name, I think."

"She was disrespectful?"

"Father, she accused me of dragging around, asked if I were on the cover of vamp GQ every month and wondered if I engaged in flying kites or chasing butterflies."

Charles was snickering now; his mouth covered so he wouldn't make so much noise. "Tell my own disrespectful child that I am not that stuffy," Flavio declared upon hearing Charles's muffled laughter. Charles removed the hand from his mouth and guffawed. Even the corners of Wlodek's mouth were lifting a little. Flavio started laughing. Wlodek's smile widened.

CHAPTER 6

The dream held me. I was standing in another place, one filled with trees fully leaved and a lightly wafting breeze caused shade and sunlight to dapple a small clearing. I found it quite lovely after remembering that I no longer had allergies or the fear that ticks might crawl up my leg and attach themselves somewhere.

The center of the clearing shimmered and glowed while the rest of the area remained in shade and shadow. I saw people appear in the midst of the shimmer and walk away from it, followed by more of their kind.

One of them, a boy of perhaps sixteen or so, drew my attention and I struggled for breath, sitting up in bed wide-awake, tearing myself away from the dream. I knew that boy—his face hadn't changed much. Xenides.

Waking during the day was becoming a regular occurrence, and I was thirsty again. I also remembered that I hadn't asked Winkler to get sunglasses for me. I walked out of the bedroom to search for Roff but he wasn't inside the guesthouse. The only way to the main house, if I walked, was through a big patch of sunlight. Deciding not to risk it, I misted through walls instead, flying from one place to another. The sunlight didn't bother me so much that way.

I was rummaging through Winkler's fridge when he came sliding in on the polished tile floor. He'd heard the noise and rushed in immediately to investigate. I shocked the hell out of him when I raised my head above the fridge door—I'd been leaning down to pull out a bottle of water. "Lissa!" he shouted. "What the hell are you doing out of bed? Baby, you'll fry!"

"Whoa, calm down, fuzzy britches," I said as Winkler hauled me over his shoulder, preparing to rush me into a darkened bedroom somewhere. "Put me down and I'll explain," I mumbled against his wide back. "By the way, do you have any extra sunglasses? My eyes water in sunlight."

Winkler let me slide off his shoulder. "You're not frying?" He still wore a stunned expression, his black eyes scanning me for sunburns.

"I have alien technology," I tapped the back of my neck. "They put some sort of shield disc under my skin. It keeps my body from being damaged by the sun," I explained. "It's supposed to last a hundred years."

"Are you kidding?" Winkler put his hands on the back of my neck and rubbed it gently.

"Nope."

"Alien technology?"

That made me laugh. "You should see the alien who put it there." Winkler would probably pee his pants if he saw the Larentii.

"If I hauled you into the yard you wouldn't die?"

"I'd be pissed, maybe uncomfortable and possibly asleep, but I've been assured I won't burn."

"Here," Winkler went to a drawer in one of the kitchen cabinets, pulled it open and drew out one of several pairs of sunglasses. "Lost and found," he informed me, handing the glasses over.

At least they were women's sunglasses, even if they weren't what I might have picked for myself. I put them on and breathed a sigh of relief. My eyes stopped watering immediately. "Now, sit down and tell me why you're awake," Winkler ordered.

"Hey, you're not the boss of me," I grumped.

"I used to be," he grinned.

"Yeah, yeah, kiss my ass," I muttered.

"Don't offer. You know I want to," he was still grinning.

"You and a bunch of other people," I retorted. Wait. A bunch of people had. Well, two, anyway. I wondered where Kifirin had gotten himself off to. "I've been dreaming, Winkler. That's why I'm awake," I said, trying to steer him away from the sex subject.

I took the top off my water bottle and sipped. The cold water felt really good; I was dry for some reason. Roff walked in with Corinne and Lucas Alford; they'd been out grocery shopping. Roff almost shrieked when he saw me.

"Raona, must I chastise you again?" He was doing his best version of righteous indignation.

"Roff, I'm awake. That's all there is to it," I said and drank more water.

"We were hoping we'd get chicken fried steak later," Winkler was back to grinning. "Roff and the Alfords picked up what you'll need to cook for us."

"Fine," I grumped.

"Come, we will put you in an empty room upstairs," Roff was trying to lead me away.

"If Gavin wakes and doesn't find me in his bed, you do not want to hear the cursing," I said. "Come on, I'll mist us back over." Corinne Alford gasped as I turned Roff and myself to mist and went through a wall.

"Now, must I tell you to go to sleep?" Roff was sliding me under the sheet. He ruined his gripe session by leaning down and giving me a kiss. I closed my eyes and was out in seconds.

"This is so good," Lucas Alford was helping himself to another plate of food. Roff was happy, too, I could tell. The werewolves, though? I've never seen anyone put food away like they can. Even the females don't have many qualms about eating (except Kellee, and she was just showing off for Winkler). I liked that about them. They had two apple pies waiting for dessert, too. Winkler asked Roff to buy the ingredients.

Thaddeus and Lorenzo had come in at one point while I was cooking, completely shocked that I could and would do this. For werewolves. We talked for a while, but they left before everything was done, going in search of something to amuse themselves.

Bill called Tony while I cooked, and I hadn't been privy to that conversation. Bill had a lead he wanted to follow, so we were going out as soon as the wolves finished eating.

The lead turned out to be in Stillwater, sixty miles north of Oklahoma City. Bill arrived at the house to lead the way, Winkler came along with us and Rhett and Dalroy stayed behind with the Alfords. I think Lucas wanted to go but Corinne didn't, so he stayed with her. Bill carried Winkler, Radomir, Tony and René in the car with him while the rest of us followed in the van.

After driving an hour, we parked outside a farmhouse west of Stillwater. A dirt road ran up to the house, with heat-browned grass growing in the space between tire tracks. The road wasn't used much; the grass stood tall in the center of that narrow track.

The farmhouse was neat, though, painted a pale yellow with green shutters. What caught my attention (and Gavin and René's as well), was the window glass was painted black, with thick curtains hung over that. Somebody didn't want light getting in. Not even a little.

"Let Lissa go in first," Tony ordered when we all piled out of vehicles. Bill wasn't arguing and Gavin only frowned, so I misted inside the house first. Ancient wood floors creaked beneath my feet when I materialized, though my steps were light across them. Cautiously I went to mist again, just to be sure; the entire house was deserted and darker than a tomb. I smelled vampire, just not one of those we hunted. At least not yet—the scent didn't smell evil.

Did Bill find this during the day? I sent to Tony.

Tony must have conferred with Bill; it took a few seconds before his reply came. *Yes, he said he got a tip on this place,* Tony responded.

There's nobody on the ground floor, but hold on for a moment, I want to check something, I returned, misting right through the floor. I don't know where the trap door was; I wasn't interested in that. What I found was a male vampire wedged in a tiny space with a human female, and they were terrified.

The woman looked to be in her early forties, so this was likely a love match. Visions of Vilmos and his companion flitted through my mind. Heaving a mental sigh, I shot back through the floor into the upper portion of the house and misted outside, materializing next to Gavin.

"Gavin, please come with me," I said. Turning to mist again, I hauled him a quarter of a mile away before he could protest and jerked my cell phone from a jeans pocket as I solidified. *Tony, keep everybody outside the house until we get back*, I told him in mindspeech.

What's going on, Lissy? Tony was very curious and a little worried— I could tell through his mental voice.

Tony, just hang on for a minute, okay? I tried to reassure him as much as possible while I dialed Charles's number.

"Lissa?" Charles was probably surprised to hear from me again so soon.

"Charles, I just found a vampire who's hiding out with a human female," I said, praying that they weren't going to be killed just because I'd found them. "The vampire is about three hundred years old with long blond hair braided down his back. The woman is in her early forties, I think. They're hiding under a house in north central Oklahoma and they're terrified someone will find them."

Charles was already tapping on his computer and Wlodek, who'd been listening in, took the phone. "Lissa Beth, what have you found?" he demanded.

"I don't know," I felt like sobbing. "Father, I don't think they're bad. Please tell me we don't have to kill them." Gavin's eyebrows rose when I called Wlodek Father but he didn't say anything. He was frowning, however, over the news that a vampire and his human companion were beneath the house.

"Probably Winston Byrnett," Charles's voice came over the phone. "The description and the age fit."

"He disappeared twenty years ago," Wlodek informed me. "He

requested the review for his companion and then disappeared with the woman before a decision was reached. His human companion was approved by the Council, but the news was never delivered. We were unable to locate him."

"So, other than the fact that he's feeding off the population, he's not rogue?" I asked.

"I would strongly suggest that he begin ordering his meals from the normal sources," Wlodek replied dryly. "If he will send his information to the Council, we will supply the paperwork that he didn't wish to wait for earlier."

"Okay," I heaved a relieved sigh. "Thanks." I terminated the call. "Come on, you may have to place compulsion while we do some explaining." I grabbed Gavin's arm and we misted back to the house.

"Just give us a few minutes," I told Bill, Tony and the others when Gavin and I landed beside them. "We'll be back in a bit." I misted Gavin and myself straight into the hidden basement. Gavin placed compulsion the moment we materialized; Winston was set to fight both of us. His companion huddled farther into the small cubbyhole that held a mattress and little else.

"You will answer all questions truthfully," Gavin added to his initial compulsion not to attack. The blond vampire nodded.

"Are you Winston Byrnett?" I asked.

"Yes," the vampire nodded. The woman whimpered and wept.

"Honey, we're not about to kill him—or you," I reassured her. She peeked out of a small space between her hands; they were covering her face.

"The Council approved your companion," Gavin took up the conversation. "The Head of the Council says that if you send your request, the approval papers will be forwarded to you. He also suggests that you order your meals from the recommended sources from now on."

"That's all?" Winston was shocked. "You tracked us all this time just to tell us that?"

"We weren't tracking you," I said. "We were after someone else, but we got a lead on you, instead. That's why we're here now. It might be a good idea to scrape the paint off the windows and move away. Somebody knows something," I added.

"We will," Winston nodded.

"Here," I pulled the cash I had with me from my jeans pocket. "Go spend the night in a hotel in Oklahoma City. Have your lady," I nodded toward the woman, "check on other property for you. I don't think coming back here is a good idea." I handed the money to the vampire.

"I haven't touched my bank accounts in nearly twenty years; I was afraid the Council would track me," Winston muttered, handing the folded cash to his human companion.

She accepted it, crumpling it in her hands in confusion. I probably had three hundred with me—I hadn't taken time to count it before we'd left Oklahoma City. It was enough for them to spend the night somewhere and buy the woman a meal.

"The Council isn't after you, Mr. Byrnett," I said. "But somebody tipped us off and my guess is they weren't vampire. I think you should gather your valuables and get out tonight." I'd seen an old truck under the carport beside the house. The woman nodded and Winston turned to help her off the mattress.

It didn't take long for them to gather what little they couldn't do without, and Tony and the others were shocked when Gavin and I walked out with the couple. Winston had a small safe he hefted into the back of the truck; the woman had clothes, photographs and a few other belongings. They were loaded up in no time.

"These people aren't connected to Xenides," I informed Bill and the others, who now stood by, watching as the truck was loaded up.

"Did you say Xenides?" The woman came over to us.

"Yes. What do you know?" Tony exercised compulsion. I swatted his arm; compulsion wasn't needed.

"Someone came to the door today and told me that an old friend of Winston's was coming to visit us tomorrow evening. When I asked who the old friend was, the girl called him Xenides. Winston says he doesn't know of anyone by that name."

Winston walked over to join the conversation. "I've never heard of Xenides," he said.

"She said that if we knew what was good for us, we'd wait until he arrived," the woman went on. "I didn't like her attitude, and Winston said since she was human, he wasn't really worried. Until you showed up tonight, that is." She raked a hand through dark brown curls, her blue eyes concerned. "We thought the Council was here to kill us," she muttered softly.

"What about Catulus?" Gavin asked. "Have you heard that name?" Wlodek had mentioned that name; Xenides had used it before.

"Fuck," Winston cursed. "You don't want to get anywhere near that one. He'll kill you and steal your women."

"How do you know this?" Gavin demanded.

"My sire knew him. Catulus killed him, along with my older brother. I was out; that's the only reason he didn't kill me as well. Catulus wanted my older brother's female and he wouldn't give her up. My sire and my brother tried to fight Catulus off but he was older and stronger."

"Then maybe you should keep on hiding until we can get rid of him," I said. "We'll let the Head of the Council know. Go on, get as far away from here as you can," I said.

"Here," Bill handed the keys to his car to Winston. "Let's transfer their things," he said. "Just let me know where you left the car," he added, "and we'll pick it up." He handed over a card, much like the one I'd gotten from Tony the first time I'd met him. Winston's eyebrows rose considerably. "We'll let Xenides think you're still here," Bill jerked his head toward the old truck beneath the carport.

"Will do," Winston nodded. "Sweetheart, have you ever lived in Texas?" he asked the woman, placing an arm around her shoulders.

"No, hon," she said. "Is that where we're going?" She looked up at him with a trembling smile.

"Maybe," Winston smiled at her.

"Here," Gavin pulled out his money clip and emptied it; there had to be at least a thousand dollars in it. He handed that to the woman. "For moving expenses," he said. The woman smiled at him and took the additional money. Bill got them inside the car; Tony and René moved their things. We watched as they drove away, turning east onto Highway 51.

"We'll all have to squeeze into the van," Bill sighed.

"We'll make it work," Winkler grinned. Roff, who'd been standing by watching everything, was completely fascinated.

"I will ride in the back, like luggage," he offered.

"Are you sure?" I asked. He grinned.

"Of course," he replied. "I have been in smaller spaces."

Gavin held me on his lap while Winkler drove. René, Tony and Lorenzo were in the seat behind us; Radomir, Thaddeus and Bill were in the seat behind them and Roff was folded up in the back.

I was glad we didn't have anyone else; they wouldn't have fit. We were packed so tightly inside the van, I felt as if we were riding in a vampire clown car.

"Are we going to stake out that place tomorrow?" René asked.

"Oh, yes," Gavin replied.

"Xenides is really old. We'll have to surprise him," I said.

"If he comes himself, he'll get a surprise," Gavin muttered.

Gav is worried about you, Tony sent. *He wants to strangle the bastard while he removes his head.*

Tony, I want to strangle the bastard while Gavin removes his head, I returned.

You may both have to wait; René wants Xenides' death so bad he can taste it, Tony replied.

"I was hoping to find evidence of my brother," Lorenzo offered timidly, breaking up the mindspeech with Tony.

"It was a long shot, but if he's with Xenides, we still may be able to get him back tomorrow. Providing Xenides sends him, or comes himself," Tony said.

"Why is Xenides interested in Winston Byrnett?" I asked. Nobody had an answer.

We ended up staying the night at a motel in Stillwater. Gavin plunked down an impressive credit card and paid for several rooms. He and Radomir wanted to be as close to Winston's home as possible, in order to get there as quickly after sundown as we could. Bill was on his cell, calling for other agents to watch the place during the day.

"Wait," I said to Bill before he hung up. "I have an idea."

~

Angelo muttered softly and angrily—he didn't want to go. Dominic (under Xenides' heavy compulsion) was going with him to pick up the vampire and kill his female companion. Winston Byrnett had been missing for years and Xenides had need of vampire reinforcements.

Only a few days earlier, many of Saxom and Xenides' turns had been killed in Great Britain on a single night. Xenides had rolled the dice and lost that round. Now, Xenides was actively searching for replacements to rebuild his army, and those vampires living below the Council's radar were ideal targets. Byrnett would do nicely. Angelo and Dominic could bring in the vampire; Xenides was going to stay with his newest female.

~

Dominic didn't want to be there. Never wanted to leave Europe. During more coherent moments, he cursed Xenides for forcing him to do unspeakable things. Dominic had been to the states before, but that had been with his sire and his brothers.

Now, following his abduction at the hands of Angelo and Xenides, he was trapped in compulsion and forced to stay in mental contact with Xenides when needed. Xenides felt oily and evil to him; he shuddered whenever the ancient vampire came close. Xenides laughed as Dominic recoiled at his nearness.

"Can't abide your Dark cousin, now can you?" he'd say. Dominic hadn't a clue what Xenides meant.

"Stop daydreaming and get in the car," Angelo ordered. Dominic was older than Angelo and wasn't susceptible to the younger vampire's compulsion. Xenides, however, would punish him if he didn't do as Angelo said, so Dominic slid into the passenger seat and shut the door. Angelo started the car and drove toward I-35.

∽

Gavin, Radomir and I were huddled inside one covered trench; Tony, Bill and René were inside another nearby. A handful of carefully selected agents were with Winkler, Dalroy and Rhett in a stand of trees behind us, far enough from the house that they wouldn't be seen, heard or scented.

Gavin had ordered Roff, Lorenzo and Thaddeus to stay at the hotel; they didn't have what he called "combat experience." Thaddeus and Lorenzo grumbled that I was getting to go, but René shut them up quickly. Tony lectured them as well, but I got him calmed down after a while. Now, here we were, waiting for Xenides or his minions to show up.

A black Mercedes rolled up the dirt road and stopped a few minutes later. Two vampires climbed out of the vehicle and approached the house cautiously. One I didn't recognize; the other was Dominic. He fit the description his brothers had given. *Time to go*, I sent mindspeech to everyone inside the bunkers. I misted Gavin and Radomir first, before going to collect Tony, Bill and René.

We were behind Dominic and the other vampire as mist; they were now searching through the house for Winston. We waited for them to walk out again, just to have more fighting room. One of the two—the one I didn't recognize—was cursing; he'd just realized Winston had fled. I dropped my passengers behind him and they went to work. Gavin had claws at the throat of one vampire while René collared the other, faster than the eye could follow.

"Tell him not to send mindspeech!" I shouted at René, who held Dominic with lengthy, razor-sharp claws at his throat.

"You will not send mindspeech," René hissed compulsion and Dominic sagged to the ground in relief. Radomir now held the other vampire tightly, as Gavin paced before him.

104

"Tell me your name," Gavin growled out a mind-bending compulsion.

"Angelo." I didn't interfere with Gavin's pacing or his growling; I learned what I wanted to know from Angelo's scent.

"You're one of the shapeshifters, aren't you?" I accused. Angelo jerked in Radomir's grip. Radomir cuffed him and he cursed.

"Answer her!" Gavin thundered.

"Yes," Angelo whined unwillingly.

"Yet you are not Dark Elemaiya," I went on. "You come from the other side. Why are you in league with Xenides?"

"He caught me and turned me," Angelo muttered as he twisted in Radomir's hands. I'd known that already—he had Xenides' taint about him.

"How many others has Xenides made?" I demanded.

"I don't know, he won't tell me. I've only been vampire for twelve years."

"Does Xenides have any misters with him right now?"

"Not now; someone killed most of what he had."

"Come, cara, we will take these two with us. The Council will deal with them. The jet is still in Oklahoma City after bringing Thaddeus and Lorenzo." At Gavin's curt nod, Radomir hauled Angelo toward the van Winkler was parking in the yard. René and Tony followed closely behind Radomir, Dominic held between them. Another van, driven by human agents, pulled up right behind Winkler.

"No," Angelo begged as Radomir shoved him inside Winkler's van. "Please kill me now. Do not send me to the Council."

"You will go to the Council," Gavin snapped and that was that.

Xenides was in the throes of a vampiric orgasm after feeding off Jordan, his newest human conquest, when Dominic's mindspeech came to him. *Xenides!* was shouted mentally before it was cut off.

Xenides grunted, concluding that he'd have to call in other reinforcements. He'd already collected as many rogues as he could from the surrounding area, and had sent them to a designated location. A handful of his vampire children were doing the same in other places. He didn't really need Byrnett, and Angelo and Dominic were no longer a necessity. Xenides dismissed them and went back to his lovemaking.

∼

"Brother, we will stand with you," Lorenzo was distraught; Dominic was chained and settled into a seat at the back of the Council's jet. Angelo was similarly manacled on the other side, and bound with Gavin's compulsion that he couldn't shapeshift. Who knew what he could become? I hadn't bothered to ask.

Dalroy and Rhett, acting as extra guards, were flying back to London with Radomir and the prisoners, with a brief stop in New York to spend the day. At least Thaddeus and Lorenzo had their brother back. I hoped Wlodek wouldn't be too hard on Dominic, since he'd been an unwilling victim in all this. Perhaps Wlodek could find a use for another vampire who could mindspeak.

We'd tried, numerous times, to get past Xenides' compulsion and get Dominic or Angelo to tell us where Xenides was. They couldn't give out that information. He couldn't be far away, and Bill had his people working diligently to check on recent home and hotel rentals. They just weren't getting very far. I figured Xenides placed compulsion on his new landlord to lie about it if asked. It wouldn't be hard to do.

Gavin sighed as the door was closed on the jet and the pilots prepared for takeoff. Winkler had come along as our driver; Bill had also come, fascinated by the entire process. Gavin allowed Bill to climb inside the jet for a few minutes. He'd watched, silently curious, while the prisoners were chained to their seats.

"They don't fool around, do they?" Bill asked when he'd come out of the jet.

"No, they don't." He had no idea I was speaking from personal experience. Bill left before we did; he'd come alone since he didn't

106

want his agents to know any more than necessary. I was more than happy to get back to the house in Nichols Hills afterward. I was still wearing the same clothes I'd worn the day before, though I'd showered at the motel.

Roff was fussing the minute we climbed out of the car, herding me toward the guesthouse. Gavin was smiling and following along behind. "Lissa," Gavin held his cell phone out to me as soon as I stepped out of the shower later. Gavin wrapped a big towel around me and settled me on the foot of the bed, drying my hair with a second towel while I put the phone to my ear.

"Hello?" I said.

"Lissa, tell me what you know of the prisoners," Wlodek ordered. Well, somebody sounded grumpy.

"Angelo is a shapeshifter and has Bright Elemaiyan blood. I don't know what he becomes when he shifts. Xenides is his sire. I think Merrill will have to ask some of the questions—Xenides has some pretty strong compulsion on him and Dominic."

"Merrill won't be able to get past much of the compulsion placed on Angelo, then, since Xenides is his sire. We'll have better luck with Dominic, I think. Do you think he went willingly with Xenides?"

"No. Not in the least. He finds Xenides repulsive. Only compulsion kept him with Xenides; Dominic was forced to do his bidding."

"I am still quite aggravated that Maxwell kept a mindspeaker from us," Wlodek growled. He was pacing; I could hear his footsteps. "If he had let us know, then Dominic would have been with us instead of available for Xenides to abduct." I was thinking that we couldn't know that for sure, but I also couldn't say otherwise.

"Well, Maxwell is dead, so we may never know what his purpose was, more than likely," I said.

"True," Wlodek agreed. We talked for only a few seconds more before hanging up.

"Would you like a bit of blood, Lissa?" Gavin pulled me against him, nipping my neck lightly.

"Sounds like you want some," I said.

"That is certainly true." He peeled the towel away and bent his head to my breasts.

❧

I was hearing voices before I came fully awake; someone was talking to Gavin. I moaned and attempted to shut out the drone by curling up in a ball on the bed and lifting the sheet over my head.

"Raona, you should wake now and bathe; the wolf and the others have important information," Roff pulled the sheet away from my face. I blinked up at him and then turned my head, seeing that Gavin was indeed talking with Winkler. I was naked under the sheet; there was no way I wanted to rise and parade in front of Winkler sans clothing.

"Roff, I'm naked under here," I muttered. Of course, Winkler and Gavin both heard. Winkler laughed; Gavin just frowned at me.

"Then I will bring your robe," Roff was off the bed and walking toward the bathroom. I could have misted out of the bed, but Roff had already gone to get my wrap. Sighing, I waited until he came back with it. Roff held it up so I could slip into it, though I was pretty sure Winkler was doing his best to stare.

I tied the robe around me and stalked into the bathroom with as much dignity as I could gather under the circumstances. Yeah, it wasn't a lot. "Raona, would you like help?" Roff followed me into the bathroom.

"That's all right. I can get this," I said. He looked disappointed. I shooed him out the door and closed it behind him.

After I was clean and dressed, I walked out to the small living area of the guesthouse, located next to the kitchen. Winkler was still there, having a snack that Roff put together for him. That man—well, werewolf—could eat better than anyone else I'd ever met.

"Lissa, come and sit, cara," Gavin patted the seat next to him on the sofa.

"What's wrong?" I asked. There had to be something wrong. Nobody asked you to sit unless there was.

"They found Sara Workman's body," Winkler said. "Bill called two hours ago. She was dumped out by Crescent; some kids found her body in a ditch. Looked like she'd been savaged by animals." Crescent was a small town forty miles north of Oklahoma City, surrounded by wheat fields and farmland.

"No surprise. Xenides' shapeshifters probably got into that sort of thing. She was already dead, though." I looked away from Winkler and Gavin. This was my own personal hell, I think. People were dying because they were related or connected to me. I was running out of relatives, too. The two cousins in Kansas were the last of the lot and they were Don's relatives, not mine.

"They're doing an autopsy to determine the cause of death," Winkler went on when I didn't turn back to him. I nodded wearily.

"Cara, you cannot accept the blame for this," Gavin said softly.

"Can't I?" I turned to stare at him. "If I hadn't walked into that stupid bar after Don died, Sergio and Edward would have picked somebody else to play their sick little game with. It wouldn't have been me."

"I'm alive because you walked into that bar," Winkler said softly. "Twice over, at least. From what I understand, Gavin's alive too, for the same reason."

"How many live because you are what you are, Lissa?" Gavin tucked me against his side. "How many will live in the future? You have no idea. You are upset and blaming yourself for this. That is understandable, but not the truth, love."

"Then why don't I feel any better?" I grumbled. "Stupid, fucking Xenides. Stupid, fucking Saxom. What did he want from all of this? What did he hope to gain?"

"The actions of a warped and twisted mind cannot be interpreted by logical means," Gavin said. "It is useless to attempt it. All we might do is prevent them from happening, if we can."

"Where are Tony and René?" I asked.

"They've taken Mr. and Mrs. Alford out to dinner," Winkler replied. "The Alfords are leaving tomorrow, so they're spending the evening together."

"Oh," I said and sighed. I hadn't talked much with Tony's mother. That hadn't kept me from wondering what she knew or where Tony had come from. I felt sure that Charles had already done research into medical records and that sort of thing. I wondered what he'd found. Poor Tony. I had a feeling his birth mother had given him up because she wasn't prepared to take care of him, somehow.

"Gavin, may I borrow your laptop?" I asked. I hadn't emailed or talked to Franklin and Greg in days. Merrill, either, for that matter.

"Of course, cara." Walking into our bedroom, he returned quickly with the case in his hands. Gavin emailed Charles or Wlodek often. He even had Wlodek's personal email account. I didn't have that. I'm sure it had to do with secret stuff that nobody else was supposed to know. Gavin opened up his Mac and settled it on my lap.

"I only want to email Franklin and Greg and Merrill," I said, entering Merrill's email address. I wrote that I was fine. I told Merrill what had happened in the last few days, but I was sure Wlodek already informed him since he was in the house, now.

In Franklin's email, I asked how Greg was doing. I was hoping Greg wouldn't read Frank's email; I didn't want him to think I was going behind his back. My email to Greg was as upbeat as I could make it. Shutting Gavin's laptop, I handed it back to him with a sigh.

Sara's body had been mauled after her death; Dominic was sitting in a cell at one of the Council's holding facilities. There wasn't anything I could do for Sara, but I should have told Dominic before he left that I'd been in his situation a couple of times myself.

Gavin took the laptop back to our bedroom after I was done, and while he was up, Roff came in and sat down next to me. "Two more days," he said and smiled.

"Two more days?" I didn't understand. Roff pointed to his neck. Now I knew. He wanted another climax. "You poor thing," I put my arms around him and leaned my forehead against his shoulder.

"I am extremely fortunate," Roff informed me. "I am the comesula to the Queen."

"You will not repeat that word outside this room," Gavin warned Winkler. He'd walked in just as Roff was letting the cat out of the bag.

"What word?" Winkler feigned innocence. "I didn't understand it anyway. Did you say comma sula?"

"It means companion," I said. "And it's one word—comesula. Roff's not local." I didn't point out that Gavin referred to the term Queen and nothing else.

My statement caused Winkler to frown at me. "What do you mean, not local?"

"I am from the High Demon's planet," Roff smiled. "Before that, my kind were native to Le-Ath Veronis."

"Come on," Winkler said, smiling.

"It's true," I grumbled. "Le-Ath Veronis means Heart of the Vampire, according to my sources."

"There was a werewolf planet, too," Roff said. "Although I do not know its name."

"It is empty now, just as Le-Ath Veronis is," Kifirin was there suddenly, examining an abstract sculpture on the small kitchen island.

He really did have an ear tuned to certain words. We'd said Le-Ath Veronis and Kifirin appeared from nowhere. He was prepared for Earth, too, dressed in jeans, a yellow polo and nice boots. Kifirin's dark hair was neatly styled and his lips curved slightly as he turned the small sculpture in his hands.

Winkler was out of his chair in a blink at Kifirin's sudden appearance. "Where the fuck did you come from?" he demanded.

"I cannot give information regarding where I came from originally, it has no name," Kifirin replied with a shrug. "Recently, I came from the planet named after me. The werewolf planet was named Harifa Edus. In the language spoken there, it meant Hunter's Eyes."

Kifirin set the sculpture down, his dark eyes focusing on Winkler instead. "There were six moons orbiting Harifa Edus; therefore there were six nights to hunt every month, which lasted twenty days."

"Geez, Winkler, that was werewolf heaven," I said. Winkler was still giving Kifirin the eye. He warily sat down again when he saw that neither Gavin nor I were upset at Kifirin's presence.

Kifirin came to sit beside me, so Gavin had to settle for a nearby chair. "Avilepha, you are correct—I am listening for certain things—

always. For now, you are upset because the ephu has taken the lives of your kin?" He placed an arm around me. Roff moved over a little to give Kifirin more room.

"Ephu?" Gavin asked.

"Evil one; devil perhaps," Kifirin offered. "One who brings harm intentionally? I came to see if Lissa wished to travel with me tonight, to steer her thoughts away from these things."

"Where?" I asked.

"I would like to take you to see the High Demons' planet," he smiled down at me. Honestly, that smile could induce orgasms. "We will not be gone long. In Earth time, that is."

"Good. I was feeling depressed and homesick, maybe this will take my mind off that," I said.

"That is as I'd hoped," Kifirin nodded and folded me away.

Twilight was falling on the High Demons' planet; Kifirin set me down in the middle of a street in the market district. "This is Veshtul, the capital city on Kifirin," Kifirin informed me.

"The planet really is named after you?" I asked. He smiled his angelic smile at me and nodded.

"I will make it so you will temporarily understand the language here," he said.

There were comesuli everywhere, locking up their shops for the evening, calling out to one another about evening plans or shouting for children who'd rather continue playing with friends.

I looked around me; it seemed such a peaceful place. The streets were paved with square bricks in many colors; the shop fronts were just as colorful, with none being more than three stories high. Even in the last light of day, it was something to see.

"If you wish to buy, you must do so now," a dark-haired comesula was ready to close his shop door.

"This is where they sell the best oxberry wine," Kifirin told me softly. "We wish to buy two bottles," he called out. The comesula came back with two bottles of wine and Kifirin handed over two gold coins. The comesula thanked him and trotted back inside his shop, closing the door for the evening.

"That is Roff's son, Toff," Kifirin said. I drew in a breath.

"Really? And you waited until now to tell me?" I hadn't gotten a scent off the comesula, but I hadn't questioned it—until now.

"He cannot know what you are," Kifirin said. "And I shielded his scent so you would not recognize him and give that knowledge away. I have brought you here while Roff and Giff are also here. I took them from a month in the future," Kifirin explained. "Things would become complicated if they saw you now."

"You are too weird for words," I said.

"It depends upon the language you use," Kifirin chuckled. "High Demons often use my name when they curse. Every bit of my anatomy has been described in erroneous detail when they are angry."

Kifirin carried the wine in the crook of his left elbow, while draping the other arm over my shoulder. "We will walk to the palace," he announced. We walked to the palace. I didn't see it until we came to the end of a street and made a right turn.

There it was, shining in the moonlight. The street we'd turned on was broad and led straight to the palace steps. The palace was huge and beautifully designed, with many pillars leading up wide steps, and there were domes and spires everywhere, all of it lit and shining in the twilight. It looked like something from a fairy tale or a science fiction story.

"The one who designed this palace was vampire," Kifirin explained. "He was brought from Le-Ath Veronis to draw up the plans and oversee its construction. Sadly, the High Demons forgot over the years that the vampires helped them many times in the past. They failed to provide assistance to any of the Dark Worlds when it was sorely needed."

"Yet here they are, enjoying a good life, while the rest of the dark worlds lie wasted," I sighed.

"True," Kifirin acknowledged. "I am taking you to meet someone inside the palace. I cannot introduce you to the Raona and Raoni; I cannot have them remembering you."

As information goes, that was certainly cryptic, but I didn't argue with Kifirin. I was feeling too calm and happy to be able to walk leisurely down a street in such a beautiful city, toward a palace designed by a vampire. "What was his name? The vampire that designed the palace?" I asked.

"Tybus," Kifirin said. "He was quite talented." I nodded in silent agreement.

The steps that led to the palace were many and wide, fashioned of pale marble with blue and gold veins running through it. The whole thing was beautiful beyond words. "You like this?" Kifirin asked.

"It's amazing," I said. Someone must have emptied the entire planet of that marble; it had taken so much of it to build the steps and the columns at the front of the palace.

"They nearly did use all of it," Kifirin agreed, reading my thoughts.

We walked into the palace through wide doors that led through a huge, oval entry. Guards were stationed outside those doors and I got their scent. It was something I'd never smelled before, but I would know it from now on. The guards paid no attention to us; it was as if they hadn't even seen us. Kifirin smiled.

We walked through the palace, past more guards and others dressed finely, going this way or that. None seemed to see us or note our passage. Kifirin eventually led me to the top floor of the palace; there were many more steps to climb to get there. Kifirin then pulled me toward an arboretum.

Nearly circular in shape, it was huge and had a high glass ceiling with glass walls surrounding it. Only the back wall where it connected to the palace was squared off and straight.

I went directly to the glass walls at the front of the arboretum; the view of the city from there was magnificent, with lights twinkling across an expanse of shops, homes and mansions in the distance. I thought about pressing my nose and hands against the glass so I could get the best view without any glare, but figured the caretakers wouldn't appreciate removing my nose and handprints later.

"I have wanted to meet you for a very long time." The voice was almost as beautiful as the man. Flavio was now the third most beautiful man I'd ever met in my life; I saw this when I whirled to see who'd spoken. Kifirin was now standing fifteen feet away, unwilling to interfere with this meeting for some reason.

"I am Erland Morphis," The man came forward, offering his hand. He had dark hair and darker eyes and his face was perfect if that were possible. He wasn't as tall as Kifirin, but that didn't matter.

What I thought as he held his hand out to me was that he'd likely cause males and females to sigh happily as he passed, just from the sight of him. The vibe I got from him was that he preferred males, but wouldn't turn down a female from time to time.

"How do you know of me that you'd want to meet me for a long time?" I asked as I took his hand.

"Nearly three hundred fifty years ago, I watched a vid-article from the Refizani planet," Erland Morphis replied. "I found it fascinating. A Queen Vampire, someone so rare as to be nearly nonexistent, was fighting Ra'Ak with abandon and blinding them, allowing them to be killed by others. Many races saw this—the ones that had space travel, that is. That is how the images came to them. And to me."

"It may have been three hundred fifty years ago for you," I said, feeling confused and disoriented. "It was a month ago for me." Erland Morphis' scent was different from the others we'd found inside the palace. It held a powerful spice that I couldn't name.

"I am a Karathian warlock," Erland informed me as if he were reading my thoughts. "I am eight thousand years old. My kind are nearly immortal, as many of the Wizards are."

"There are Wizards? Really? That is so cool," I said.

"Perhaps you should meet the Grey House Wizards, sometime," Erland smiled. Honestly, Helen had competition to launch ships now.

"Grey House Wizards?" I hadn't heard that before.

"They are the finest and most powerful of their kind," Erland said. "Different from the Karathians, as we dabble in some of the darker spells at times—we cannot help it, Karathia being on the boundary between the light and dark worlds, as it is."

"Do you dabble in the darker spells?" I wasn't sure how I felt about that.

"Never to cause an unwarranted death," he smiled again. "That would be against my principles and many who associate with me now would not continue to do so had I done things of that nature. Therefore, I stay within the neutral area when it becomes necessary to perform anything other than a spell of light."

"Well, that's a relief," I said.

Kifirin walked over and stood next to me. "We must go soon," he said, taking my hand and interrupting my conversation with Erland Morphis. Erland offered me a smile that held sadness.

Do not give any message or indication, Kifirin sent mindspeech to Erland Morphis. *She must not know so that things will proceed as they should.*

My heart weeps because there is no way to save her, Erland Morphis replied.

Do you think that pain has not been stirred thoroughly in my own heart? Kifirin leaned down and placed a gentle kiss on Lissa's temple. *We will go.*

CHAPTER 7

Ce left Erland Morphis standing in the arboretum, probably staring at the spot where we'd stood barely a blink before. Kifirin and I now perched on the edge of a volcano. Heat was rising from its depths but no lava was flowing.

"I have calmed it down somewhat; it erupted forty years ago," he said, his dark eyes gazing out over the caldera.

"Do a lot of damage?"

"Some," Kifirin admitted reluctantly. "I was angry at the time."

"What got your panties in a bunch?" I asked.

"It is not something I can discuss," he said.

"Big secret, huh?"

"Yes. Unfortunately."

"What do you call the volcano? Is it named after you too?" I smiled up at Kifirin.

"No, avilepha. It is called Baetrah, which means Fire Mountain."

"Roff said that the comesuli come here to ask you for favors."

"They still do. Sometimes I consider their requests." He'd said consider. He didn't say grant. I didn't push it—maybe it was one of those things you weren't supposed to know.

"The High Demons come here when they tire of their life," Kifirin went on. "If they throw themselves into the fire while in humanoid form, they give up their lives. While they are in full Thifilathi, the fire cannot harm them. It is the way they were made."

"You did that, if I recall correctly," my fists were on my hips.

"Yes," Kifirin sighed. "I did that. I made the High Demons. At times, I wish I had created them with better memories, or with more focus toward their responsibilities. Come, m'hala, it is time to go."

Kifirin dropped me off in the living area of the guesthouse, seconds after we'd left it. "That didn't take long," Winkler drawled. Sometimes, Texas comes out in his voice. Sometimes.

Kifirin left me there with both bottles of wine after a quick kiss. He just disappeared, as he always does. "How does he do that?" Winkler asked, rising and coming over to touch my cheek. Maybe he was checking to make sure I was real or something. Gavin rose, too, probably to make sure Winkler didn't get away with too much.

"He calls it folding space," I said.

"That's a theory that has been kicked around a bit, with variations on how it could actually be accomplished," Winkler observed. The genius Winkler was present, it seems. "Do you know how it works?"

"I have no idea, you're asking the wrong person," I said. "Maybe you should ask him yourself if you see him again."

"How did we miss this?" Griffin sat at a table inside a Falchani bar; Kifirin sat across from him. Two cups of untouched rice wine sat on the table between them. "All the *Possibilities* pointed in another direction. Now the *Absolute* shows up and it is disastrous." Griffin had fingers laced through his thick brown hair and he wanted to tug it out by the roots, he was so frustrated and upset.

"Only disastrous for the one," Kifirin blew a curl of smoke from his nostrils.

Tony sat next to René at the linen-covered table where they'd eaten their meal, sipping the last of their wine. The dinner was excellent, but Corinne Alford had the saddest expression on her face. Tony glanced briefly at his vampire sire before turning back to his mother.

"Mom, you'll always be my mother, no matter what," Tony reached across the table and took his mother's fingers. "I mean that. Nothing will ever come between us. You raised me, you and Dad," he nodded at Lucas. Lucas had done as much or more for him than most fathers Tony knew. He'd never been treated differently or slighted in favor of Deryn. They were brothers, too, even if they weren't blood kin.

"Mom, I know," Tony said. "I know I'm not Everett's. Or yours by blood. I'm yours because you wanted me."

Corinne Alford blinked across the table at her son before the tears fell. "How did you find out?" Corinne wept, her voice thick with emotion.

"I worked for National Security," Tony replied. "Don't cry. I've known for years, now. I went digging through the records. Somebody fixed the birth certificate, but there are no doctor or hospital records. I don't care who my birth parents are. They're not real to me. You are. You and Dad. Don't ever think I don't love you, because I do."

"I was pregnant by your father but that ended in a miscarriage," Corinne wiped tears away. "I went out running with the others three months afterward. Your mother had you in the woods, baby," Corinne sniffled. Lucas put his arm around her. "She left you. I scented the blood while on the run. I had to force the turn so I could pick you up and carry you out of there before the others found the scent."

"They would have torn me apart," Tony nodded his understanding.

"George Chapman helped me get the papers pushed through," Corinne named the Grand Master before Weldon Harper. "I wasn't about to give you up, Anthony. I think we had a bond the minute I picked you up."

"Old George did a good job; I almost didn't get past the records he paid for, they were so well done," Tony said. "Mom, that doesn't matter. René is a parent but you'll still be my parents. That's what I'm trying to say. René isn't going to stop me from calling or communicating with you, since we are what we are."

"I appreciate your intervention," Corinne smiled tearfully at René. "We'd have gone to Anthony's funeral instead if you hadn't done this for him."

"This is a first for me; before I had to hide my children away from their former family, it was the only way," René said softly. "Of course, none of their relatives were what you are. This makes things much easier."

"How many children do you have?" Lucas Alford was curious.

"I have had six, but only two are alive at the moment," René replied.

Xenides didn't care what the vampire's motives were; he was getting the information he'd desired; the date and the location for the Annual Meeting. He had others set up in Kansas in case the princess showed up. They'd been more than willing to help—for the right price and the opportunity to strike out at their Bright cousins, even if the blood percentage wasn't to their standards. It would still be a blow and an offer to further an ancient war. He turned his attention back to the one who stood before him.

"You are sure of this?" Xenides asked, looking over the copy of the invitation. The original had been carefully settled back inside the safe from whence it came.

"Yes," the vampire replied. "I desire payment in one way only, in exchange."

"And that would be?" Xenides' eyes narrowed. He preferred to settle payment on his own terms.

"I wish for a particular vampire to be killed," came the reply.

"And that vampire is?" Xenides demanded. The name was handed over. "Oh, do not fear," Xenides reassured his newly acquired spy, "We will certainly take that one down."

~

"Father, I think we should tell Lissa," Franklin was close to tears as he watched the IV drip slowly; it was attached to Greg's hand. He'd been hospitalized with pneumonia. Oxygen was flowing and Franklin and Merrill both wore surgical masks inside the room.

"I'm not sure it is a good idea," Merrill said. "Wlodek says this as well." Franklin disagreed with Merrill but didn't say it, settling for mentally cursing Wlodek instead. He knew that Wlodek was pulling the strings on this decision.

Wlodek had his own agenda; Lissa was tracking Xenides because he threatened the vampire race. Surely, there was enough time for Lissa to come and see Greg; he wasn't doing well at all.

The doctors were dismayed when Greg contracted pneumonia. It was a heavy blow to an already weakened system and now Greg was in and out of consciousness. It would mean much to Greg and Lissa both if she were allowed to come. Franklin sighed instead and bowed to his father's wishes.

~

Winkler drove Lucas and Corinne Alford to the airport during the day so they could catch their flight. He was just getting back to the house when he caught me filching another bottle of water from the fridge inside the main house kitchen.

"Lissa, this is getting to be a habit," Winkler said, leading me to a barstool at the island. I hadn't even had a dream this time; I just woke up anyway. I sipped my water and watched Winkler.

"You know, I haven't had to get rid of the water or the wine or anything else I've drank lately," I said. "And it hasn't made me sick, either. Usually I start feeling bad if I don't get rid of it within a couple of hours. Now, there's nothing." I drank more water.

"Have you told Gavin or any of the others about this?" Winkler raked a hand through thick, black hair. He was such a good-looking man, smiling easily when he was amused. At the moment, his nearly-black eyes betrayed concern—for me. I had no idea how Kellee could have plotted his death with her father. Well, there was greed, but still.

"No," I shook my head at Winkler's question. How could I explain to Gavin that I wasn't coughing up water or wine? He would have that vampire physician on the phone immediately, trying to find out what was wrong with me.

He was probably thinking about it already, and I might do the same if he were waking during the day and failing to eliminate everything ingested except blood. I had no idea what was going on with me—I didn't feel bad or anything. I felt fine. I was breathing, too, when I was awake during the day. I had no idea what effect that had on my rejuvenating sleep cycle. None at all.

"Come on, baby, let's get you back in bed." Winkler rose, but his cell phone rang. He pulled the phone out of his pocket. "It's Bill," he said and answered the call. I listened in.

"Mr. Winkler, we have a hit on Alif," Bill said. "Your software, actually. He was spotted in Chicago."

"What's happening in Chicago?" Winkler asked.

"The Vice President is attending a conference tomorrow evening," Bill said. "I'm in Chicago now. Is there any way we can get Lissa here for that?"

My eyes were widening in shock at Bill's words. "We'll have to wait until sundown," Winkler said, ignoring my frantic nodding. He was going to ask Gavin, Tony and René first. I never got to say, one way or the other, whether I wanted to go or not.

Frustrated, I bumped my forehead against the granite island. Winkler, still talking with Bill, came over and pulled my head up, settling it against his side and holding it there. He stroked my jaw and neck with one hand while he held the phone in the other. I listened to his heartbeat with one ear while I tuned in to the phone conversation with the other.

Bill was promising to send a jet for us tonight if we would come. He really didn't care who else showed up, as long as I came. Someday, I don't know when that might be; I wanted to decide for myself. I had no idea if that was ever going to be possible.

When Winkler hung up after a while, I glared at him as he looked down at my face. "Baby, we have to ask the others." He was defending his actions.

"You're just like the rest of them," I muttered and misted away.

I didn't want to get back in bed with Gavin; call it preemptive anger on my part. I imagined that a call to Wlodek would be made and a conference would be held among the testosterone-producing members of our group and then they'd decide whether Lissa would be sent in to take care of things. The schmucks.

I sat down angrily on the sofa in the living area, right in front of the window there. Granted the curtains were drawn, but there was still sunlight spilling around the edges. I curled up on the sofa and went to sleep there.

~

"What is she doing?" Winkler found Roff, and together they'd gone to the upper floor of the guesthouse to check on Lissa. They found her sleeping on the sofa, several wedges of sunlight hitting her body.

"I will take the Raona to bed," Roff was already gathering her up.

"I'll get the door for you," Winkler offered. Roff followed Winkler down the hall, and Winkler held the bedroom door open so Roff could carry the sleeping vampire in and place her on the bed beside Gavin.

"Too bad he doesn't wake when she gets up," Winkler said as he watched Roff arrange Lissa's limbs so she'd be comfortable when she woke.

"He would be angry if he did wake," Roff muttered.

~

"Cara, we are going to Chicago." Gavin was sitting on the side of the bed, waiting for me to wake. The conference was already over and I hadn't been consulted. Typical. Someone had also dragged me back to Gavin's bed, ruining my attempt at righteous anger.

123

Dammit.

"Did they convene the full Council to take a vote?" I muttered sarcastically.

"Lissa, is this any way to wake? Full of anger and sarcasm?"

"Gavin, if you want sweetness and light, I suggest you find another woman," I flung covers away and sat up in bed, refusing to look at him. "I was awake when Winkler got the call from Bill. I was trying to say yes when he asked if I could go, but of course the males get to make those decisions, don't they?" I misted off the bed before Gavin could put his hands on me.

"Lissa, you are not yet two years old as a vampire," Gavin reminded my retreating back—I was heading toward the bathroom as fast as I could after materializing on the floor.

"And yet Tony gets consulted on everything and he's not even two months old. Tell me how that works, Gavin?" I slammed the bathroom door. "Fuck!" I shouted. They probably heard me in the main house as I cursed.

"Lissy's upset," Tony glanced at René. René had been going over the laws concerning the companion vote. René sighed. "The law has changed recently," he went on with the lesson. "Before, the vampire was notified using correspondence. Now, if the vampire refuses to give up his human companion, he is brought before the Council and questioned. A decision is made after that. This change is a result of a recent event when an innocent vampire and his companion, along with his companion's infant daughter, were killed by a rogue assassin who had a taste for drinking from children. That, as you now know, is an automatic death sentence if it is discovered."

"He was the one Lissa was tracking while she worked for me. Isn't that right?"

"Yes," René admitted. "But you will not divulge that information to anyone," René laid compulsion. Tony nodded.

～

Gavin already had a bag packed for both of us when I stalked out of the bathroom. He wasn't speaking to me, either, which was fine. I wasn't speaking to anybody, including Roff. He looked hurt, but I wasn't about to thank him for putting me back in bed with Gavin. Sometimes, you had to make your point and you didn't need somebody going behind your back and undoing what you did in order to get that point across.

I climbed into the van, said nothing on the way to the airport and loaded onto the military jet that Bill sent for us. If the taxpayers knew they were paying to haul vampires and werewolves to Chicago at a moment's notice, I'm sure somebody was going to get upset over it. I hoped they'd be compensated, however, if I could take Rahim Alif down. Not that they'd ever know it was a vampire that took him down.

Bill was there when we landed, and had two vans ready to take us to a hotel downtown. The VP's speech was scheduled at the conference the following night. Roff reminded me that it was Thursday, September second, and was fingering his throat discreetly. Damn. I forgot all about that. "We'll get to that," I promised quietly.

The hotel overlooked Michigan Avenue and was huge. "The conference is held here and the speech tomorrow evening will be given in the largest ballroom. It's doubling as a fundraiser," Bill grumbled as we walked inside the hotel's foyer, which was richly decorated, with plenty of polished marble on the floors. Well, politicians will be politicians; even I knew that, and no opportunity to gather funding would ever be ignored.

"I'll go through the place tonight and see if I can find anything," I offered after we'd ridden an elevator to our floor. Gavin glared at me and Tony cleared his throat before stuffing his toes into it. "We'll go with you," he announced. Joy. I was going as mist. Now I was going to have passengers going with me as mist.

"Well, hell, let's take Bill, too," I drawled sarcastically. Some days, you should just keep your mouth shut. I hadn't learned that lesson, I guess. We shoved our bags into our sixth-floor room, made sure there wasn't any light that could get through and fry vampires and then every stinking one of them, including Roff, lined up so they could go with me as mist. It's a damn good thing they don't weigh anything when I haul them around like that. That's how Bill, Winkler, René, Tony, Gavin and Roff all ended up as passengers when we found the hole in the air duct.

The air duct was located over the hotel ballroom, with a large square cut out of it so somebody could crawl through and get to a nearby vent. It wouldn't be difficult to remove the vent cover and open fire on the ballroom below.

I also imagined that the hole had been cut with a vampire's claws. More compulsion had been used to accomplish that, I was sure. Security was too tight around the hotel for it to be anything else. I smelled the vampire that had been there, sure enough. It was somebody new—I hadn't scented this one before. The only other smell was that of a rat or something. I guess those things can get in anywhere.

Put us down, I want to examine this! Tony demanded. I sent blanket mindspeech back so anybody who could hear me would.

No! They'll come back and scent us! We'll be here tomorrow night, waiting as mist and see what they're about to do! Doofus! I misted right through floors and everything to get us out of there. The couple making love didn't even notice as I blazed right through their bed.

"They'd really scent us?" Bill asked just as soon as he'd become solid again inside our hotel room.

"Duh," I said. "I'd sure as hell smell it if somebody else was there. We don't need to muddy the scene; we just need to be back there tomorrow, waiting on them."

"In the meantime, I still want to check out the rest of the hotel," Tony had his arms crossed over his chest.

He was angry, Gavin was angry, René was angry on his vampire child's behalf and Roff was acting a bit sullen. Bill's only goal was to check the entire hotel for threats against the Vice President; Winkler had a smirk on his face—he was enjoying himself. The schmuck.

"Fine. Let's go through the whole damn thing, floor by floor," I snapped and gathered them all up as mist again. We did. We went through the entire hotel, floor-by-floor, room-by-room (the couple on the fourth floor was still at it) but didn't get the slightest scent of vampire. I didn't get a whiff of Rahim, either. He was staying away until he could pull off whatever he was planning, I'm sure.

"That was a bust," I snipped when we all dropped inside our hotel room again.

"I want to be there in the vent, waiting on them," Tony demanded.

"Tony," I held my head—I swear I felt a headache coming on, "You need to be downstairs in the ballroom. You can send mindspeech to me if you need to. I think Gavin or René should be with me; they can help slice up whoever is going to be inside the duct. This way, I can come quickly if there's a problem on the first floor."

"That would be my choice," Bill agreed. "I can hear Lissa's mindspeech when she sends it to me; I just can't send anything back."

Bill, I sent, *wake me up after the vampires go to sleep. I need to be up during the day, I think.* Bill nodded slightly to let me know he'd heard. Winkler and Roff might have a fit, but they were going to have to live with this.

I knew what Rahim smelled like—I'd matched the scent from a house in Georgia with that from a hotel room in Paris. His ass was grass if I ever caught up with him, and I sure as hell wanted to know if he were planning to come in during the day. The only person I wanted to get my claws into worse than Rahim Alif was his best buddy vampire, Xenides.

"I don't understand how you're doing this," Bill walked with me down the hall toward the elevator. I'd left Gavin sleeping the sleep of the dead in our hotel room. René and Tony were just as unconscious in the room next door.

I'd told Roff to stay with all of them and make sure they were safe.

He'd given me a wide-eyed stare and nodded. Yeah, he might be in trouble if Gavin woke up and found out I hadn't slept any.

"Can we get coffee, tea, or undiluted caffeine?" I rubbed my eyes as we loaded onto the elevator. Winkler was supposed to meet up with Bill downstairs. He was about to get a surprise.

"Winkler, don't even say it," I held up a hand before he could get the words out as Bill and I stepped off the elevator. "Our friend isn't—well—you know. He could be here at any time and we wouldn't know it. Therefore, I'm staying awake, just in case. Now, give me coffee and shut the hell up." Winkler shut the hell up and went to order a tall cappuccino for me at a coffee shop inside the hotel.

The caffeine had some sort of effect, I think. I was wide-awake after a while. Winkler and I hung around the front door of the hotel while Bill went to meet with some of his agents at the back. I knew he had agents scattered through the lobby, but I didn't try to pick them out. I knew the one I waited for.

Winkler was reading the Wall Street Journal while we waited; I'm glad he was making sense out of all that. My eyes crossed just thinking about it. Merrill read it, too—online, of course.

If I'd been depending on my eyesight to pick him out, I'd never have spotted him. He couldn't mask his scent, though, even with expensive cologne. Rahim Alif strolled into the hotel lobby dressed like a college student. He wore a T-shirt and cargo shorts—it was hot in Chicago the first part of September. Flip-flops, a baseball cap and a backpack slung over his shoulder rounded out his outfit. I elbowed Winkler as Rahim walked past us, on his way to the front desk. None of Bill's agents had a clue.

I listened carefully as the hotel desk clerk looked up his reservation. Rahim had booked a room under the name Raymond Andreadis. Rahim was passing for Greek. He was given a room on the eighth floor and was already walking toward the elevator when I sent mindspeech to both Winkler and Bill.

Bill, if you'll give me a couple minutes, I'll have him at the back door for you, I sent and ran to catch the elevator with Rahim. He nodded politely to me as I punched the button for the ninth floor.

He stepped off on the eighth floor as planned and the minute the door closed again to take me to the ninth floor, I was mist and trailing behind Rahim. I floated over his head while he slipped a key card in the slot, walked into his room and shut the door.

He wasn't tall; maybe five-eight or nine and I nabbed him, turning him to mist before he could set his backpack down. I didn't know what was in it and didn't want to wait around to find out. The Vice President was supposed to be in the building soon; he had the presidential suite booked on the top floor. I'm sure he smiled every time somebody gave him the presidential suite, too.

I'm coming with the package! I was doing my best to send to Bill and Winkler, I just didn't know if my mindspeech was going to penetrate a werewolf brain or not. I did my best, anyway.

I zipped Rahim through walls and down through floors, flying as straight as I could toward the loading dock at the back of the hotel. Bill was already there, talking on his cell phone when I misted to that huge block of concrete at the rear of the hotel. Winkler skidded to a stop nearby, a bare second or two later.

There were at least four more agents surrounding Bill, and they got the shock of their lives, I think, when I appeared out of nowhere, tossing Rahim at Bill's feet. "Don't move!" I shouted compulsion. Rahim shrank back on the concrete. *And don't send mindspeech*, I sent, just as a precaution. Rahim's eyes went wide. He'd heard me. Three agents were all over Rahim Alif like ducks on a June bug, as Don used to say.

"You're going to answer all their questions, aren't you?" I laid further compulsion, grinning at Rahim. He nodded and swallowed— hard. Once Rahim was in handcuffs, I had four agents looking at me as if I were from outer space or something.

"One of our special agents," Bill snapped at them. "Now, get this scum out of here." The agents hauled Rahim off. He wasn't resisting, I'd told him not to move. I might have to take that off later, I guess. I'd said it aloud, and didn't realize it.

"Don't worry about it," Bill waved a hand.

"I think we should stick around," I told Bill, who looked like he'd just accomplished the impossible and was overjoyed about it. "We still don't know who's gonna show up in the vent and Rahim might not spill that nugget in time if he's connected."

"You think he might not be?" Bill's eyebrows rose in alarm.

"I think he is, but there's something about it that bothers me," I said. "And have those guys check out his backpack, too. I sure don't know what's in that."

"We got it," one of the agents held up a hand after Bill yelled at him. They'd taken time to open Rahim's backpack. Good thing I'd told him not to move. The backpack was a bomb, with the detonator on Rahim's wristwatch. A quick movement of his hand and we'd all have gone up. Bill's agents were placing the backpack on the ground and backing away quickly; Bill pulled Winkler and me toward the hotel while calling for a bomb squad at the same time. Winkler and I stood at the hotel's back door while Bill barked orders into his phone from close by.

"Lissa Beth, have I told you lately how much I love you?" Winkler was hugging me now, his eyes still glued to the backpack lying on the concrete behind the hotel.

"William Wayne Winkler, I don't think I've ever heard those words come out of your mouth, and most likely you don't mean them anyhow. We're not inside a bar at the moment, you know." I pulled away and had my hands on my hips as I scowled at Winkler. I knew perfectly well how he preferred to pick up women.

"Lissa, you don't know that." Winkler turned dark eyes on me then. He looked hurt. I just shook my head. He was married, even if it had been a shotgun wedding, and his estranged wife was pregnant with twins. Not something to jump in the middle of, no matter how good he looked or how many times he said he loved me.

"Winkler, I do love you. I do. But there are too many things between us and you know it," I said softly, watching Bill talk to his agents, who were now holding a handcuffed and shackled Rahim Alif. Bill asked for transportation for the prisoner, along with the bomb squad, and he held Rahim's watch in his hand. Poor Bill. I sure hoped the government was paying him for the job he did.

"Lissa," Winkler sighed as we waited for Bill's backup to show. Winkler wasn't willing to let the conversation between us die.

"Winkler, we can't. That's that," I said. "And the fact that the Council married me off to Gavin while I was gone hasn't helped matters, either. They own me. They control my life, Winkler. As far as I can tell, that's all there ever will be for me." They couldn't place compulsion, but they didn't really need to, did they?

"That's all there ever has been for you," Winkler was stroking the back of my neck gently.

"Winkler, don't make me cry," I removed his hand from my skin and it took all my strength to do it.

The bomb squad arrived, followed by a van to take the prisoner. We watched as Rahim was loaded up and the bomb squad, all dressed in their special suits, went to examine the backpack.

Bill walked towards Winkler and me, a huge grin on his face as soon as the van hauled Rahim Alif away. Bill had just pulled off the coup of the decade, I think. "I'm thirsty," I said, and turned to go back inside the hotel. Somebody had a bottle of water with my name on it, I think.

Bill was fascinated as he watched me drink water. Winkler had a soda and Bill had coffee as we sat in the hotel coffee shop. I wanted to go lie down; I was exhausted but afraid to rest. Afraid that whoever had made that hole in the ductwork would be coming back.

I didn't know his purpose, or whether he was connected to Rahim or not. I did have his scent—there had definitely been a vampire there. The other thing I'd smelled, though, was a rat. Or a mouse, maybe. Definitely some sort of rodent. Maybe the hotel needed to call pest control. Or—maybe it was something else. I drew in a huge breath as I stood up.

"What time is it in England, right now?" I asked.

"About eleven or so," Bill said. "Why?'

"Winkler, let me borrow your cell phone." I held out my hand. Winkler frowned at me but handed his latest version smartphone over anyway. I dialed Charles's number as quickly as I could.

"This is Charles," Charles was giving a guarded answer to the strange caller ID.

"Charles, this is Lissa," I said.

"Lissa, I'd recognize your voice anywhere," he said brightly. He was shocked to be getting a call from me at the moment; I was supposed to be asleep. Like the calm assistant he was, however, he didn't even comment.

"Charles, I need to know how quickly one of those shapeshifter vampires can turn," I was fidgeting while I talked. "Is there any way we can ask that Angelo guy?"

"Hold on, I think Rad is at the holding facility now. Let me see if I can get him." Charles set the phone down and went off somewhere. I waited. And then waited a little more. It was probably only a few minutes, but it felt like hours to me. Charles came back. "Rad forced Angelo to tell him —it only takes a few seconds for him to turn, Lissa. Why?"

"I think I smell a rat," I said. "Thanks, Charles." I hung up and handed Winkler's phone back.

"We may be dealing with a shapeshifter vampire," I said softly as I sat down at the table again. "Which means he may already be inside the hotel, sleeping in a little rat hole somewhere. Or a mouse hole. Maybe even a squirrel hole." Holy crap. That's what I'd smelled. I knew it was a rodent of some kind. I got up again and took off for the front desk. Winkler and Bill were behind me in seconds.

"Hello, may I speak with the manager," I asked the girl behind the desk.

"I can help you," the girl said stiffly. I needed information and she was having delusions of grandeur.

"I want to see the manager," Bill hauled out his ID. Well, that was effective. The girl ran into the office behind the desk. The manager was out in no time, the girl right behind him, looking frightened. The manager had a slight paunch, thinning hair and washed out blue eyes behind expensive glasses.

"What can I do for you?" He asked Bill. Yeah, the woman was the least important member of this party.

"My agent here has a question for you," Bill nodded in my direction. Now I had everybody's attention.

"Have you had any problems lately with rodents of any kind?" I asked. "Has anybody reported seeing a squirrel, maybe, or a rat?"

"Now, how the hell would a squirrel get in here?" The manager snapped.

"Answer the question." Compulsion dropped into my voice.

"We've had three reports of guests sighting a squirrel but we can find no evidence of this," the manager was forced to answer and he sure didn't want to. He kept a clean hotel, thank you very much.

"Where has the squirrel been sighted?" I asked.

"Two of the sightings on the second floor," the manager replied. "The third time was in a guest's bathroom."

"Thanks for your help," I said and took off. Bill nodded at the manager and followed close behind me. Winkler just followed Bill—he didn't give the manager the time of day. "When is sunset?" I asked as we rode up the elevator to the second floor.

"Seven-thirty," Winkler said, checking his cell. Yeah, that's not handy or anything.

"Bill, do you or your agents have anything that might pass for a squirrel cage?" I asked, and wondered how strong it needed to be. Did the squirrel have vampire strength when it was a squirrel? That was a scary thought. How could you fight a squirrel? The thought made me snicker.

"What?" Winkler asked.

"Ever fought with a squirrel, Winkler? I snickered again, imagining a werewolf chasing a squirrel—straight to the nearest tree. Bill was on his cell, asking somebody to bring a pet carrier or cage of some kind. If we found the squirrel, we didn't need to be chasing the damn thing all over the hotel after sunset, and looking like a bunch of idiots while we did it.

I turned us to mist in the hallway, sending Bill a mental note to grab the security recordings if there were any, just so we wouldn't be seen disappearing on YouTube. We went through the second floor rooms, searching everywhere until I caught the scent inside a bathroom.

He was cute as a squirrel; I'll give him that, with his fluffy squirrel tail curled around him as he slept. Tucked away behind a stack of towels on the lower shelf of the vanity, he slept the sleep of the vampire shapeshifter dead. Snatching him up, I turned all of us to mist again and flew toward our floor.

Bill's agents were there already, waiting for us. I dropped Winkler and Bill on the floor outside the bank of elevators and then turned back myself, still holding onto my little squirrel buddy. We ran for Bill's room, Winkler grabbed the carrier from an agent and I stuffed the squirrel inside it just as the sun went down.

CHAPTER 8

I'd never seen a rabid squirrel before, but this one came close. He was frantically scratching, clawing and biting at the door to his cage as soon as he woke. Bill and Winkler followed me to my room; I opened the door to find an angry Gavin waiting on me.

He couldn't say anything right then; there were too many others around. And the fact that I had a cage with a squirrel in it didn't help his temper any, I could tell. The squirrel was still banging around inside the carrier, chewing on the wire door of his cage, but so far, he hadn't broken through it. Thank goodness.

It's a vampire shapeshifter, I sent to Gavin, Tony and René. Tony and René had come through the connecting door the moment they'd heard our door open—I don't think they wanted to be anywhere near Gavin's temper, either. Poor Roff was cringing in a corner.

Bill sent his agents off—the speech/fundraiser was supposed to start at eight and we still needed to get down there in case there was anything else going on. René volunteered to stay in the room and watch the squirrel while the rest of us went toward the first floor.

Gavin growled when I said I still wanted to go to the hole in the ductwork, just to see whether anyone else showed up. Tony was dressed for the do already, and Bill and Winkler jumped into suits really quick. I hadn't had a bath or a change of clothes and I didn't have time to do anything about it now. Tony and Winkler went with Bill; I turned Gavin to mist and we were off.

We listened to half of a boring speech, hovering as mist inside the duct before somebody showed up, and that somebody was female and human. Her black hair was pulled back tightly in a knot; she wore little makeup and was dressed in leather pants and a tight-fitting tank top.

She was all business, though, no doubt about that, and I figured she'd done this many times before. A small black case was settled at her feet and when she knelt down to open it, I saw it held a gun that had been taken apart. She was prepared to reassemble the thing when Gavin and I materialized next to her.

Gavin had her throat in his hand so fast she didn't have time to squeak and her eyes were huge as she stared at his face. He was pissed, all right—his eyes were red and his fangs were out.

"What are you doing here?" Gavin growled. "Answer me!" Compulsion was thick and mind-bending in his voice.

"Kill th-the m-mayor and the v-vice president," she stuttered. Yeah, I'd have been terrified, too, if I were in her place. Actually, I had been on the receiving end of Gavin's compulsion. I knew exactly what that felt like.

"Who sent you? Who do you work for?" Gavin demanded.

"Richter," the girl whispered. Gavin was squeezing her neck. He let up, now. "H-he was supposed to b-be here," the girl went on. I was calling her a girl, but she was in her thirties. That's what her scent told me, anyway.

"Bjorn Richter?" Gavin pulled the girl's face closer to his. She closed her eyes as he snarled in her face.

"Y-yeah," she could barely speak; Gavin's hand had squeezed again.

"Anyone else coming?" Gavin's voice was a dangerous purr, now. I was seeing the Gavin that went out and killed. He was in Assassin mode, no doubt about that.

"No," she struggled to shake her head.

"Good. Lissa, get us back to the room quickly," Gavin ordered. I got the three of us back to our hotel room as fast as I could haul mist in that direction.

Gavin threw the woman forcefully to the floor when we arrived and then stalked toward the squirrel's cage. "Richter!" Gavin thundered. "Turn to vampire and face me now!" I sure as hell hoped nobody was out in the hallway listening.

The squirrel cage blew apart when the vampire materialized and René crouched, claws extended, ready to help Gavin fight the rogue if needed. I had no idea who Richter was, but René and Gavin did. Honestly, he was cuter as a squirrel. As a vampire, he wouldn't trigger anybody's radar, with light brown hair and dark blue eyes.

The girl was now crawling across the floor, trying to get away from everybody. I watched her. She shouldn't have pulled the knife. I was beside her and had that thing jerked out of her hand and her body flung into a wall so fast she didn't know what hit her.

"Do not move," I snarled at the girl, placing the same compulsion for the second time that day.

Richter, his eyes going red and fangs and claws popping out, was facing off against Gavin and René. *Tell him not to shapeshift*, I sent to Gavin. At least Gavin had enough sense left to do that instead of ignoring me.

"You will not shapeshift," Gavin laid compulsion. Richter was about a thousand years old, as near as I could gauge it. More than young enough for Gavin to destroy his brain with the compulsion he had.

Richter was also not one of Saxom's—or Xenides' get, for that matter. Not in the family, so to speak. I figured he was a mercenary or something, and in it for the money. I also figured Rahim had plenty of that backing him up.

"I wish to be taken to the Council," Richter hissed. Gavin hadn't told him he couldn't speak and Richter was doing what he could to prolong his life. Roff, still huddled in a corner as far away as he could get, watched the whole thing, his eyes wide with shock.

"Sorry," Gavin hissed right back. "The Assassins and Enforcers have orders to terminate you on sight." Richter didn't have time to blink—Gavin blurred as he flung out a hand and Richter's head smacked against the wall and then bounced across the floor, leaving a trail of ash behind it. The girl shrieked.

Lissa! I was getting mindspeech from Tony. *We have problems!*

Oh, lord.

"Tony's calling for help," I yelled.

"Stay with that one," Gavin ordered René, pointing toward the girl. René barely had time to nod before Gavin and I were mist.

There was chaos in the ballroom and three snipers were shooting into the crowd. People were running toward the exits and getting knocked down and trampled by those faster and more frightened. How the hell had the snipers gotten in to begin with? I didn't have much time to ponder that question. I went after the shooters, scaring the daylights out of all three as I picked them up, turning them to mist with me.

Bill, get your guys to the back, I'll drop them there, I sent. Tony was included in that sending as I headed toward the loading dock for the second time that day. Bill somehow commandeered six agents amid all the turmoil inside the ballroom and they showed up in the alley behind the hotel in minutes.

Dropping now, I sent and Bill shouted at his agents. Three snipers were tossed onto the loading dock, guns and all. The bullets aimed at the snipers flew right through Gavin and me as harmless mist before becoming solid again, once their momentum carried them past us.

The snipers, however, weren't so lucky. Two died right then and the third was hauled off in an ambulance. I set Gavin down in a shadowy corner and Bill had to call his agents off us; their rifles were trained on us as we walked into the artificial brightness covering the loading dock.

"Is that everything?" I asked hopefully. I was tired and hungry, too. I hadn't eaten, yet—there hadn't been any time.

"For now," Bill sighed.

"We, uh, have another shooter upstairs," I said quietly. Bill's agents were talking with the medical examiner's employees; they were there to pick up the bodies.

"Let's go," Bill muttered. "Secure the scene," he yelled at the agents over his shoulder.

"Yes, sir," came the reply.

Tony was there to meet us as we walked through the hotel's back door; he'd been keeping the VP safe during the shooting, it appeared. Yeah, the second most powerful man in the U.S. had recognized Tony, all right; he stood right beside the former Director of the Joint NSA/Homeland Security Department with absolutely no qualms. I sure as hell hoped he knew how to keep a secret, or compulsion would surely follow.

Bill assigned two agents to the VP, who led him away. Tony fell in step with us and we all rode up the elevator together. Bill pulled his gun out as we walked inside our hotel room, stepping around two piles of ash that used to be Richter and Richter's head. Bill stopped and stared at the girl, who was still plastered against the wall.

"Seraphim," Bill muttered. Tony nodded. That name didn't mean anything to me, but then Richter's hadn't, either. Bill pulled his cell out and dialed a number. "Send three agents up to the sixth floor," he barked.

René, who'd stayed behind to watch the girl, moved aside to give Bill room. Roff walked out of the bathroom, looking pale.

"Are you all right?" I asked him.

"Yes. I felt ill for a bit but I am fine, now," Roff nodded, coming to stand beside me. I put an arm around his waist and hugged him—he looked like he needed it. Bill's agents came and hauled Seraphim away in handcuffs. Gavin snorted at her name.

"People think it means a beautiful angel," he remarked. "References say it means burning ones, or fiery serpents."

"Either way, she can cool her heels in the pokey," I muttered. "Is there anything to eat? I'm starved." Roff stared at me for a moment before dragging me into the bathroom and closing the door. Roff and I were both happy when we came out again.

"Lissa, I wish to speak with you. Alone." Gavin put emphasis on alone. The lecture was coming. Gavin was pissed and he was going to let me have it. And I was exhausted, too. At least he'd slept.

Winkler made his way into the room; he'd been downstairs sorting everything out in the ballroom. He was in one piece and unhurt, looked like. Gavin grabbed my arm and hauled me out of the room. "Turn to mist and get us to the roof," he growled in my ear.

I sure hoped he wasn't in a yelling mood; I didn't think downtown Chicago was ready for loud cursing in multiple languages. Poor Bill might have a real job on his hands keeping that out of the media.

News trucks and reporters with camera crews were crawling all over the street below us and sirens were wailing up and down Michigan Avenue when Gavin and I landed on the roof. The hotel had yellow tape pulled across the front and ambulances waited outside. Gavin ignored the entire scene as we sat down on the roof of our hotel.

"Lissa, do not ever leave me like that again," he grumbled before his mouth was on mine and his arms were crushing me against him just as tightly as he dared. After a while, he was satisfied just to hold me in his lap while we watched ambulances and police cars come and go below us. It wasn't long before my vision blurred and I fell asleep, though the night was still young.

"Is she all right?" Winkler asked. He'd waited inside Gavin and Lissa's room, as had Tony, René and Roff, and watched in concern as Gavin carried Lissa in.

Bill had already asked someone to come and clear away the mess on the carpet. The housekeeping staff had come and vacuumed up Richter's ash, thinking it was dirt. Bill was Director of the Joint NSA/Homeland Security office; they weren't about to argue with him about piles of dirt on the carpet. Bill had then gone downstairs to see to things there.

"She's asleep," Gavin whispered.

"She's been up all day," Winkler said. "Did she tell you she caught Rahim?" Gavin placed Lissa on the bed and covered her with a blanket after removing her shoes.

"No, she neglected to mention it," Gavin said. "Let us go next door where we can discuss this without disturbing her."

Gavin and the others walked through the connecting door. Roff stayed behind and crawled into bed with Lissa the moment the others were gone, pulling her against him.

"Rahim Alif, the mastermind behind the recent Paris hotel bombing, as well as several other terrorist attacks, was apprehended yesterday, hours before the Royal Hotel in downtown Chicago was attacked by snipers. The attack came during a speech given by the Vice President in a hotel ballroom." The reporter stood outside the hotel, using it as a backdrop for the newscast, and an inset photo of Rahim was displayed on the television screen.

I was sitting up in bed and sipping on a unit of blood that Gavin handed to me. I'd slept the rest of the night and then through the following day before waking again at sunset. Gavin sat beside me and nuzzled my neck and shoulder while I drank my dinner. Roff was in the shower and I was going in as soon as he got out. Gavin's cell phone rang. He answered.

"Honored One?" Gavin said, after reading the caller ID.

"Is Lissa there?" Wlodek asked.

"Yes, Honored One," Gavin answered.

"Excellent work, taking Richter down," Wlodek praised Gavin.

"Thank you, Honored One," Gavin replied.

"Let me speak with Lissa," Wlodek said. Gavin handed the phone to me.

"Father?" I said. I didn't know what he wanted.

"I understand you captured Rahim Alif."

"I did," I said. "He was dressed as a tourist and using a Greek name. He smelled just like he always does, though. Evil."

"Is that how you recognized him—because he smelled evil?"

"Not completely. I had his scent from a house in Georgia and the hotel room in Paris. It wasn't hard to detect him. I knew who he was the minute he walked through the door."

"And you were instrumental in capturing Richter?"

"Yeah. He was a squirrel." I heard Charles snicker in the background.

"Lissa, this is no time for humor."

"But he was. A squirrel, I mean. Richter was a vampire shapeshifter. He turned into a squirrel. He was hiding inside the hotel as a rodent for several days and probably feeding off the hotel guests while he was here. That's how we found him; he was sleeping behind some towels in a hotel bathroom."

"That may explain how he managed to hide from us for so long," Wlodek muttered after a few seconds.

"Nobody would be looking for a squirrel if they were after a full-grown vampire," I agreed. "He's dead, now. Gavin's pretty quick with those claws of his."

"I have seen that for myself." Wlodek sounded as if he were smiling. He must have wanted Richter bad. "Let me speak with Gavin again." I handed the phone back to Gavin.

"The compensation will be deposited in your account," Wlodek said. My eyebrows rose over that. Gavin was getting a bonus? Damn. I worked for free. I sighed and slid off the bed. Gavin reached out for me but I was already too far away. Roff came out of the bathroom so I went inside to clean up.

"Fledgling vampires are not allowed to earn money," Gavin said later as I was trying to convince my hair to cooperate after a shower. "They are dependent upon their sire for their needs while they learn."

"Uh-huh," I sighed and gave up on my hair. "Is Merrill still carrying the load, even though I'm married off to you?" I was now stuffing my toiletries into the little bag I had.

"He is insisting," Gavin said, stepping back—my elbows were flying a bit as I packed up. "If you want anything, cara, you only have to ask."

"I see," I said, shoving my comb into the bag and zipping it up.

"Lissa, I do not make the rules."

"Really? I thought you were a member of the Aristocracy—you

know—those vampires who got together to make the rules." I stalked past him and through the bathroom door.

"Who told you about the Aristocracy?" Gavin was right behind me, demanding an answer.

"I'm not going to tell you. How long were you going to keep that to yourself?" I snapped, flinging my toiletries bag into a suitcase lying open on our bed.

"You are a member as well, as my vampire spouse," Gavin pointed out. He wasn't helping his case any—he was merely digging a deeper hole.

"Yeah? How about that?" I zipped the suitcase. "I pity the next female who gets turned, you know." I lifted the suitcase off the bed as if it weighed nothing. "She'll be paraded in front of all those vampires and sold off to the highest bidder, if she isn't already under some vampire's thumb. You people need to come out of the dark ages." I headed toward the door and then turned back as the thought hit me. "You know what? Scratch that," I pointed an accusing finger at Gavin. "You need to come out of the cave." I flung the door open and stalked into the hallway.

"What precipitated this argument, cousin?" René walked into Gavin's hotel room after Lissa stormed angrily out the door. He'd heard the entire argument from his and Tony's adjoining suite.

"Wlodek," Gavin sighed. "She didn't know that young vampires are not allowed to earn money. Wlodek informed me that the reward money for Richter would be deposited in my account. Lissa overheard and now she is upset."

"She captured him, cousin. You just relieved him of his head." René slapped Gavin on the back. Gavin growled low. "How much was it, anyway?"

"Fifteen million pounds," Gavin grumbled.

"I think you owe Lissa," René laughed and went to find Tony. Roff was staring at Gavin when René left. He didn't understand. The Raona had no money? She was the Queen. He shook his head and trotted out the door after Lissa.

"I didn't make that rule," Gavin announced to an empty room.

As plane rides went, that one sucked. The weather was bad—there was a storm over Missouri and I thought I was going to have to mist everybody out of the plane, including the pilot and copilot. Gavin had me out of my seat and crushed in his arms after we dropped several hundred feet at one point. Roff was terrified and holding onto whatever part of me Gavin didn't have locked up. I was never so glad to see the Oklahoma City airport in my life when we finally landed on solid ground.

Winkler even looked gray when we stepped off the plane. The bags were taken off and we rode a shuttle to our van. I heaved a huge sigh and buried my head against Gavin's shoulder as we drove toward Nichols Hills.

"Cara, we'll take a drive as soon as we get to the house," Gavin murmured against my ear. We did take a drive—a long one.

"This was my house," I said as we drove past the property. It had a *for sale* sign in the front yard. I wondered who'd get the money now. Of course, none of my belongings would be inside it anymore; Sara had probably sold all of it in a garage sale and I told Gavin that.

"Do you want the house, Cara?" Gavin asked me gently.

"It doesn't have anything that I want now, Gavin. What would I do with it, anyway?" All I had left were memories and those I carried with me—both good and bad.

"Sometimes I am jealous of your first husband," Gavin said.

"Why?" Gavin was driving and he turned to look at me briefly, his dark eyes raking my face when I asked the question.

"Because you said yes when he asked," Gavin turned away from me again, easing the van down the cul-de-sac I used to live on. "Lissa, I know I got you by trickery and default. I think I would have tried to kill anyone else that might have taken you away." His mouth was set in a grim line as he steered the van away from my old street.

"You always get what you want?" I asked, studying his face. A bit of sadness touched his features. I could tell he regretted many of the things that lay between us.

"You were the first thing in a very long time that I truly wanted," Gavin admitted quietly.

"I thought you were going to kill me for a long time," I mumbled and turned to look out my window.

"I would have paid for that in ways you cannot imagine," Gavin informed me, pulling onto Reno Avenue. "Bill gave me the results of Sara Workman's autopsy before we left Chicago." He was changing the subject.

"What did they find?" I almost didn't want to know.

"Heart failure, just as you said, cara."

"I wonder if he still wants to capture me," I said, meaning Xenides.

"I'm sure he wants you more than ever, love. He sees the potential in you. He could destroy countries with you, cara mia. That's what he thinks to do when he has you in his grip. He would have a good start, even without your help, if he and Alif had managed to kill the Vice President in Chicago." Gavin's words worried me, and I wondered who those two planned to target next.

"What a comforting thought," I slapped a hand over my face. Gavin drove us to a nearby motel that didn't look too bad, secured a room, called René to let him know we wouldn't be back for a while and proceeded to love me senseless.

Sunday, September fifth, Gavin and I rose at sunset, showered and checked out of our motel room. The young woman behind the desk was eyeing my ring as Gavin and I turned in our keys before we left.

"That looks expensive," she said.

"I'm sure it was," I smiled at her. Gavin gave me a dark look and shooed me out the door.

"I suppose you're wondering why I never bought you a ring," I grumped when we climbed into the van. Gavin turned sharply to look at me as he put the van in gear and backed out. "I'm not about to ask Merrill to pay for it," I said. "When I can get to my own money, you'll have one."

"Are we back to the money thing?" he asked quietly as we headed toward I-35.

"No, we're at the ring thing," I said. "There's nothing I can do about the money thing."

When we arrived at the house in Nichols Hills, we found a werewolf from the Oklahoma City pack there. Winkler had asked him to move in for the present. The Packmaster for the Oklahoma City pack was there, too, and I was shocked to find that I knew him.

"Jerry?" I walked up to him while he shared a drink with Winkler and the other werewolf, whose name was Michael.

"Do I know you?" Jerry asked, frowning at me. He was getting the vampire scent, just as Michael was. They were supposed to know why they were here, weren't they? At least their hackles weren't up and they weren't growling.

"Yeah, or you used to," I said. Jerry was the assistant Chief of Police for the city. Gavin came up behind me, just in case I needed protection, I think.

"Jerry, this is Lissa," Winkler introduced us. The light went on for Jerry right then.

"Holy shit," he said, and held out his hand. "That's what happened to you."

"Yeah, that's what happened to me, all right," I said and shook his hand.

"We miss you down at the courthouse," Jerry said, his eyes crinkling at the corners as he smiled at me. Jerry was in his eighties—as a werewolf. Everybody at the courthouse thought he was thirty-seven.

"I miss lunch," I countered. Jerry laughed.

"Jerry, this is Gavin, my husband," I introduced Gavin to Jerry. Jerry nodded and took Gavin's hand when it was offered.

"I'm sorry about Don," Jerry told me.

"Yeah, me too," I said. "If he were still alive, I wouldn't be here right now."

"Does what you are now have anything to do with David and Sara Workman's disappearance?" Jerry asked.

"Sort of," I said.

"Lissa's special, and now everyone is trying to get their hands on her," Winkler said. "Threats have been made and we're trying to get to the bottom of all of it. We're working with the Director of the Joint NSA and Homeland Security Department on it."

"Are you kidding me?" Jerry couldn't believe that.

"There's a special division of the FBI that has vampires and werewolves," Winkler grinned. "Obviously not many know about that."

Michael had been listening to our conversation and couldn't hold back any longer. "Is the Director looking for recruits? Man, I'd love to work for the FBI and not have to hide what I am from my coworkers."

"Bill will come by tomorrow afternoon," Winkler said. "He's tying up loose ends in Chicago right now."

"In on that terrorist thing?" Jerry asked.

"We were all in on that terrorist thing," Winkler chuckled. "We just got back yesterday. Bill's department is taking all the credit for capturing Rahim Alif—we just can't announce on the nightly news that four vampires and a werewolf handled the whole thing, now can we?"

"That's all the news is about right now—the capture of a terrorist on U.S. soil," Michael snorted. "They're saying the Vice President may have been the target."

Xenides considered tossing the television across the room, but the hotel staff would receive complaints if he made too much noise so late at night. Rahim had allowed himself to be captured by U.S.

authorities. Rahim had slipped up one time too many and Xenides hadn't been close enough to pick up the pieces. The fool.

Xenides' human snipers were dead—two had been killed on-site and the third died on the way to the hospital. Nobody would get information from them. Director Bill Jennings had accomplished what Anthony Hancock had failed to do, however, capturing Rahim.

Jennings was becoming a bigger problem than Hancock. Xenides growled—Jennings had the little princess, still, and that angered the ancient vampire greatly.

The news was now reporting that Seraphim had been captured, but she knew next to nothing—Richter made sure of that. Xenides hadn't been able to reach Richter, so he was likely dead or captured.

Xenides had placed compulsion, however, for Rahim and Richter not to reveal anything about him or his plans. He was safe. He'd just have to go looking for other human scum to do his bidding; Xenides had already gathered as many rogue vampires as he could. An idea occurred to him, however, and he smiled before lifting his cell and dialing a number.

"He's not responding to the medication as well as we'd hoped."

The physician's words dealt a blow to Franklin, who'd spent yet another night at the hospital. He was exhausted and Merrill had gone off to check on the reported sighting of a vampire the Council was tracking. Greg hadn't wakened and Franklin was worried that he'd slipped into a coma. He didn't ask the question however; he was too afraid to learn the answer.

"Is there anything else to try?" Franklin rubbed his eyes.

"I'm ordering new antibiotics; we'll see how that goes," the doctor replied.

Franklin watched as the physician walked down the hospital corridor, away from Greg's room. He considered calling Merrill and then thought better of it. His fingers itched to call Lissa too, only Merrill had forbidden it. Franklin walked inside Greg's room instead, prepared to sit at his bedside again. Sliding onto a chair, Franklin leaned his head against the edge of the hospital bed, near Greg's hand and closed his eyes.

~

Monday, September sixth came along, as did Director Bill Jennings. Michael Robinson, our new werewolf guard, was doing his best to work up the courage to ask Bill for a job. I intervened and sent Bill mindspeech. Bill's eyebrows lifted slightly and he nodded.

I realized background checks and things would have to be done, but Bill would consider it now. Some people were just too shy to ask for something they wanted for themselves. I had no doubts that Michael would be a good hire—I got good vibes off him all around.

"I spoke with the President," Bill said aloud. Everybody turned to listen. I was sitting at the kitchen island having a glass of water; Roff was sitting next to me having a sandwich after fixing one for Winkler and Michael. Tony, René and Gavin were off doing training again, from which I had been excluded.

Roff's sandwich actually smelled good; it was roast beef, thin-sliced with tomato, cheese and lettuce. I got up and made one for myself, asking Bill if he wanted something while I worked. He smiled and nodded, so I put two sandwiches together and then settled on my barstool to eat while we listened to Bill.

"The president wants to give you another commendation," Bill took a bite of his sandwich.

"Ummm," I was busy chewing a mouthful of roast-beef sandwich and it tasted like heaven. I closed my eyes and sighed in pleasure. I could taste it! That was amazing. Winkler was watching me, a look of fascination crossing his features.

When I swallowed, I said, "Bill, I haven't looked at the last one. Or the Medal of Freedom." I felt embarrassed over that, but so many things had happened at that time, including Tony's betrayal, that I'd handed it back to Merrill and refused to read the letter or open the medal case.

149

"How are you eating that?" Winkler interrupted. He was shaking his head in confusion. I was enjoying my food.

"Honey," I turned to study his handsome face, "I feel a lot more like I do now than I did a while ago." That wasn't mine—I was quoting an old friend, Bill Scholes, who'd lived close to Don and me. He'd moved away when he retired and we didn't get to see him after that. I missed his philosophical musings. I smiled at Winkler and took another bite of my sandwich.

"Raona, I hope you do not have to be sick later," Roff was concerned, too; I could tell.

"We'll see. I haven't coughed up any wine or water lately, and I always had to before."

"Lissa, I have a confession to make." Griffin was suddenly in the kitchen, scaring Bill, Winkler and Michael half to death. Well, Kifirin and the Larentii weren't the only ones with Nexus Echo. Winkler looked as if he were about to pull me to safety and start fighting with Griffin. I patted his arm.

"Winkler, this is my father," I said, nodding in Griffin's direction.

"You're the werewolf?" Griffin held his hand out to Winkler. Winkler took it, still eyeing my natural father with distrust. I knew what that look on his face meant; he couldn't scent Griffin any better than I could and the news that I had a father was shocking.

I'm sure Winkler had all the old records on me, just as the vampires did. More than likely, he knew all about Howard Graham. Griffin was reading Winkler's mind, too.

"That man was never Lissa's father," Griffin huffed. He turned back to me, then. "Lissa, sweetheart, I gave my blood to you after you were wounded on Refizan. It was during the day and you were nearly asleep. That's why you don't remember, baby. My blood will allow you to walk in daylight and eat normal food if you want. You can still live on blood, but you don't have to. I also removed the shield disc on the back of your neck. You don't need it, now."

I was gaping at him, my mouth likely hanging open in shock. Griffin offered a crooked smile. "The blood of my kind can do wondrous things, little girl. Did you think I would hold back from that as soon as I had permission?"

"I don't know what you might do," I mumbled, staring at my half-eaten sandwich. "Do you want something to eat or drink?"

"Something to drink would be nice," he agreed. Roff slipped off his barstool before I could and brought Griffin a glass of wine. Griffin sat down with us to drink it.

"You don't look old enough to be Lissa's father," Bill said. He was getting information he never thought existed.

"I am more than one hundred thousand years old," Griffin smiled at the Director of the Joint NSA/Homeland Security Department. Michael was the one who gasped. I did my best not to look shocked, even though I was.

"Can you tell us where Jimmy Hoffa is?" Winkler grinned and stuffed a corner of his sandwich in his mouth.

"I could, but that is considered interfering. I can't do that," Griffin was also grinning now.

"Now we know why Lissa's special," Winkler responded.

"Lissa's special for many reasons and not just because I'm her father," Griffin replied.

Tony seemed a little worse for wear when he, Gavin and René wandered into the kitchen. He looked like he'd been in a fight and I wondered what Gavin was teaching him. Whatever it was, I wasn't getting those lessons. "Dude, you look like you need a good laundering," I lifted the tail of Tony's shirt; it was hanging out and appeared to have slid through the grass more than once.

"Are you calling me dude?" One of Tony's dark eyebrows lifted.

"I called you dude, dude. Want to step outside now?"

"I don't need another ass-kicking," Tony grinned, a dimple appearing in his cheek.

"Uh-huh," I said, handing Gavin an accusing stare.

"Cara, he needs to know these things," Gavin huffed. Griffin laughed.

"Where's that superhero costume now?" I poked Tony in the ribs.

"I landed on a planet with bigger, badder superheroes," Tony said. "Have to work my way up again."

"Poor thing." I patted Tony's back. Gavin frowned and cleared his throat. I slid off my stool and went to him. "Poor thing," I patted him on the back. René burst out laughing.

"Cara, if your father were not here," Gavin threatened.

"He means that in the nicest way possible," I patted his flat stomach. I was thinking that most men would kill to get abs like that.

"She just paid you a compliment," Griffin said, sipping his wine.

"I failed to hear it," Gavin grumbled.

"She thinks that most men would kill to have a body such as yours," Griffin smiled mischievously. Tony snickered.

"And that's why I didn't say it out loud," I said, smacking Tony on the arm.

"I should go, Amara is telling me dinner is ready," Griffin stood and gave me a lop-sided grin. "Lissa, will you give me a hug before I go?"

I wasn't sure how I felt about that, but I gave him one anyway and asked him to tell Amara hello for me. He hugged me tightly before he left and kissed the top of my head. Then he was gone as quickly as he'd arrived.

Gavin was waiting to pounce, and as soon as Griffin was away, he snatched me up and hauled me out of the house.

I got a lecture inside our bedroom on being more circumspect, and it didn't do anything to improve my mood. I heard Roff at one point; he'd sneaked inside the guesthouse to make sure things were all right and when he heard Gavin handing out the lecture, he left again.

How was I to know that teasing with my friends wasn't acting in a dignified enough manner? I was born in the wrong century for Gavin. I was sitting on the bed, my back against the headboard with my arms crossed angrily over my chest. I wasn't even looking at Gavin as he had his little fit.

I had no idea why he was so out of sorts at the moment. He finally let me go after an hour because I hadn't responded to any of his complaints. I wasn't speaking to him right then. He probably didn't care.

"Raona, the wolf was watching you closely and you put your hands on Anthony. Gavin did not like that," Roff whispered to me later, after I'd gone out to the grounds for a walk in the dark. Roff caught up with me while I made my third swift and angry lap around the fence.

"He should know by now that I'm not about to jump in bed with either of them," I grumbled. I'd had plenty of opportunity with both while Gavin had been absent. Why would I consider it now, while he was here?

"I think he wants your attention," Roff was doing his best to keep up with my swift, angry strides. He wasn't a vampire and I realized that after a bit. I slowed down so he wouldn't have to trot.

"What's your suggestion, then?" I asked. "I can't bake him a pie or anything."

"What would you do for your first husband, Raona, if he were still alive?"

That question made me stop in my tracks and Roff almost collided with me. I sighed, rubbing the space between my eyebrows.

"What is it, Raona?"

I looked up at Roff's face. How had I forgotten that he was more than three hundred years old? How? "Don got depressed every now and then because he couldn't do what he wanted to do or treat me the way he wanted to treat me. He wasn't in good health for a long time and well," I didn't finish.

"Perhaps Gavin would like to take you home, Raona, so he could protect you. He did not like it at all that you were up in daylight, capturing criminals while he slept. I believe he feels inadequate in some way."

"But he shouldn't—I wouldn't want to take him on, I've seen him fight," I said. "Come on, Roff, let's go back inside." It was nearly four in the morning, which meant two good hours of night left. I found Gavin reading in the bedroom when I went looking for him.

"Gavin, come with me for a minute," I put my hand on his cheek. He looked up at me, his dark eyes puzzled.

"Where are we going?" he asked, setting the book aside after marking his place.

"It'll be a surprise—I have to turn you to mist," I said. He allowed it without arguing, which surprised me. It only took a few minutes to reach Centennial Freeway, the highway that passes by the state capitol. There was a deep blue, cloudless sky all around us, with a few stars winking far off in the distance.

The statue of The Guardian atop the capitol dome was lit up and beautiful as we circled it. When you're in an airplane or a jet, that noise is all around you when you fly. All Gavin and I had was peace surrounding us as we flew.

I had never imagined stepping onto the top of the capitol dome and leaning against The Guardian so I could kiss Gavin, but I did. The winds whipped our hair and clothing but neither of us minded.

I love you, Gavin, I sent. He kissed me harder and deeper. When his fangs nipped my lower lip and then moved to my throat, I didn't object.

CHAPTER 9

*J*didn't wake in the day after Gavin and I continued our lovemaking in the bedroom, but I did dream. Why are my dreams so disturbing, now? If I'd felt comfortable asking Griffin, perhaps he could have told me. I didn't feel comfortable with that so I was left with a conundrum of sorts.

I saw the High Demons' palace in my dream, but somehow I knew that the time in which I saw it was far in the past. The High Demon King presided over what I imagined was his Council.

"The Ra'Ak have taken Harifa Edus, Raoni," a High Demon informed the King. "Only Le-Ath Veronis now stands out of all the worlds in the Dark Realm."

"Are you willing to go and help the vampires?" The King snorted, blowing a bit of smoke from his nostrils. "We are safe here, are we not?" He looked like a king, his face handsome and stern, his eyes a deep blue as he gazed out at his Council.

"I would go, if you asked it of me," The High Demon backed down, muttering.

"Nedevik, I think you would be alone in that venture," the King replied. "My troops do not wish to go. What care have we if the others die? The balance will be maintained as long as Kifirin stands."

"The Veronis Imperea is asking us to accept the comesuli—they are the most vulnerable to the Ra'Ak. She says they will work for us if we offer them shelter." Nedevik's words drew the King's interest.

"Are they willing to work our fields and tend our herds?" the King asked. He was intrigued by the idea, I could tell.

"As well as cook, clean, and manufacture clothing, wine and other necessities; they eat just as we do," Nedevik replied.

"How will they come here?" The King thought of a major obstacle.

"The Queen of Le-Ath Veronis has offered payment to several Karathian warlocks to accomplish this. They are standing by if you give consent, Raoni."

"What say you all?" The King set the question before his Council. He had a nearly unanimous decision in a very short amount of time. The High Demons saw profit in bringing the comesuli, although they refused the subsequent request to harbor some of the vampires as well.

"We do not need those creatures," the King waved a hand in dismissal and the fate of Le-Ath Veronis was decided on a beautiful afternoon, upon the planet named after a god. I was weeping when I woke at dusk. Thankfully, Gavin was already awake and out of the bedroom. How could I tell him what I'd seen? I was still wiping tears as I had my blood and took a shower.

"Raona, Gavin said to bring you to the main dwelling as soon as you were up and dressed," Roff was in the bedroom, waiting for me to come out of the bathroom. I nodded at him. He would probably know the answers to the questions I had, but they would have to wait until I could ask them without crying.

I followed Roff down the stairs to the ground and then over the green and well-kept yard to the main house. Bill was there with Tony, René, Gavin, Michael, Winkler and a pile of luggage. Gavin or Roff had packed for me while I slept. Bill seemed grim and Tony looked angry. René and Gavin had no expression, which was normal. Winkler didn't really care, I could tell.

"What happened?" I asked.

"Lissy, we need your cooperation on this, even though we know how you feel about him," Tony said, working to get his anger under control.

"Feel about whom?" I was getting a bad vibe about this, whatever it was.

"Lissa, Lawrence Frazier has been taken," Bill supplied the information. The news caused me to draw in a painful breath. Larry—Tony's friend who'd taken blood from me while I'd slept (and that after I'd pulled him away from a boatload of pirates in the Arabian Sea) had been kidnapped.

"Taken by whom?" I was now attempting to stop the quivering of my skin; I had no love for Dr. Lawrence Frazier.

"We think either Rahim Alif's colleagues or those associated with Xenides. Agents White and Townsend said they had both vampire and human scents from his home in Maryland. Lissa, we can't allow his knowledge and expertise to fall into the hands of the enemy," Bill was pleading with me to understand the urgency of the situation.

"You know what he did to me?" I was hugging myself.

"I know, Lissa. I was briefed by Director Hancock," Bill nodded in Tony's direction.

"Cara, think," Gavin said. "If Xenides controls Frazier, he could cause a great deal of damage to all. With Frazier's knowledge backing these rogues, the influenza vaccine could only be the beginning of more terrible things."

"Dear God." I shuddered at Gavin's words.

"Little rose, we will be with you," René offered, his brown eyes smiling kindly and his fingers brushing my neck briefly.

"Lissy, this is important," Tony said. "Larry could be forced to supply a vampire DNA solution to kill presidents, heads of state, diplomats, world leaders—anyone that Xenides or Rahim Alif's contacts and associates desire. It would be easy if vampires were involved. Only a small amount of compulsion and they can get in anywhere. You and I have seen this already." Tony was begging me to get on board with this.

"Fine," I muttered. "Where are we going? I see I'm packed already."

"Maryland first, and then wherever the leads take us," Bill replied. "Our jet is waiting; we just have to get to the airport."

At least the flight was uneventful and we landed at Dulles in four hours, leaving enough time to drive to Larry's home in Chevy Chase to sniff around.

"Two vampires," I said, as we walked inside the house. It was a nice house—a two-story brick that had been renovated. Both vampires had Xenides' scent about them, not Saxom's. Therefore, these would be younger. Three humans were with the vampires; their scent hung heavy in the house. I didn't smell blood or death, so Larry was alive when they'd taken him away.

I let Bill know that. He and Tony both breathed a sigh of relief. I wasn't sure how I felt about Tony's reaction. The guy must have been a friend, but after what he'd done to me, I wasn't feeling charitable toward Tony or Larry at the moment.

"He was taken yesterday," Bill explained as we concluded our search. It was now Wednesday, September eighth; Roff (and his watch) made sure I was updated as we boarded the plane in Oklahoma City.

"As near as we can figure, between two and six in the morning," Bill gave the particulars on Frazier's kidnapping. "He didn't leave the hospital until after his rounds were finished at midnight, and we have records of an email sent after one a.m. from here at the house."

"Bill and I have checked all the flights out—there weren't any commercial or private flights scheduled during the time he was taken," Tony said. Now I knew why he and Bill had been huddled around Bill's laptop during our flight. Even I knew the vampires would have to hole up somewhere for the day unless they were willing to be hauled around in body bags. Somehow, I couldn't see that happening with Xenides' bunch.

"Larry the lizard still has patients?" I stared incredulously at Bill and Tony. That bothered me—a lot.

"He has some of the cases that come back to us; potential germ warfare and that sort of thing," Tony frowned and coughed into his hand. He hadn't appreciated the lizard comment. Gavin was now frowning at me as well—I wasn't being circumspect. Again.

"And how much of that sort of thing is Frazier responsible for?" I snapped at Tony. Germ warfare? That sounded right up Frazier's alley.

"Lissa, we understand that you dislike this man," Gavin placed an arm around me, pulling me against him in a tight grip. He was silently telling me to shut up. I shut up. For the moment.

"Where do you think we might start looking?" René asked.

"Any dead bodies?" The words just came right out of my mouth as I pulled away from Gavin.

"We will be looking for slashed throats or for those who are listed as missing," Gavin added, pulling me against him again. "Or reports of weakened conditions with no medical explanation."

Bill made calls, asking for updates. "Does a burglarized blood bank interest anyone?" he asked, terminating a call. I slapped a hand over my mouth before Gavin could.

The blood bank was near the National Naval Medical Center, where Dr. Lawrence Frazier's patients were hospitalized. No doubt, the vampires were using his knowledge to their advantage. Bill got us into the building after hours by flashing his ID.

The Deputy Director of Operations met us there, although he had no idea why the newly appointed Director of the Joint NSA/Homeland Security Department was interested in his break-in. Bill wasn't about to tell him, either.

"The door was forced," the Deputy Director informed us after we were led to the break-in site. It was a metal door at the back of the facility, where employees came and went.

"Was anything taken?" Bill asked as we examined the replacement door.

"Some medical equipment—needles, bags, IV poles, tubing, just about anything necessary to take blood or give a transfusion, plus frozen blood from the freezer. Those vandalized rooms are still taped off, but the military police have already processed everything. We were going to clean it up tomorrow." The Deputy Director was military, with a buzzed haircut and neatly creased clothing. He didn't appreciate the mess left behind and wanted it gone as quickly as possible.

I learned the blood bank was one operated for the armed services and that was why military police had investigated the crime scene. All of us examined the vandalized rooms. Equipment and supplies had been flung recklessly about, but the scents inside both rooms told me that the vampires, one of the humans and Lawrence Frazier had been there. Winkler moved behind me—his nose was good, but he couldn't separate the scents as well as I could while he was human.

"I'll see about making contacts and running any fingerprints and other evidence in the morning," Bill said, thanking the Deputy Director and shooing the rest of us away from the building.

"It was them," I told Bill as soon as we were inside the van he'd commandeered for us. "Both vampires, Larry Frazier and one of the humans."

Bill grumped about that—if he released the information we had, NCIS would come in to investigate further on the blood bank break-in. I figured Bill was going to call the President as soon as the man was up and coherent in the morning.

We had a hotel set up for us, and Roff and Michael's room connected to ours while Tony and René's room was across the hall. Winkler's was down the hall a bit. Bill called in day guards, so nobody would disturb or attack us. Winkler, Michael and Roff were going to sleep part of the day, too—they'd been up most of the night, just as we were.

~

"Lissa, wake up," Winkler shook my shoulder. Bill, Michael and Roff were standing right behind him. I figured Winkler was the brave one of the bunch; the one willing to wake a vampire during daylight, anyway. Thank goodness, I'd gotten my PJs on again after Gavin's amorous advances before daybreak.

"Winkler, I hope there's a good reason for this," I slapped a hand over my face, trying to convince my eyes to open. Yeah, I knew he and the others were there by scent only.

"Bill needs you," Winkler said as I removed the hand from my face.

"What's up?" I asked, blinking at the four faces staring down at me.

"Admiral Hafer has been abducted," Bill answered my question.

"My other favorite person," I grumped. "If you tell me a senator from Oklahoma has been abducted next, my life will be complete." I sat up with help from Winkler and pushed hair away from my face. I couldn't begin to imagine what I looked like right then.

I allowed Winkler to help as I slid out of bed as quickly as my sluggish brain and body would allow, before running into the bathroom and almost slamming the door. There's nothing like a male committee watching you wake when you have bedhead and are wearing rumpled pajamas.

I cleaned up and dressed as quickly as I could, scribbled out a note for Gavin and left it with Roff (he and Michael were staying to watch over Gavin, Tony and René) and off we went. It was three in the afternoon and hot in the D.C. area as Bill drove us to the site. Admiral Hafer had been abducted from his home, just as Larry Frazier had. The same scents from the blood bank were inside Admiral Hafer's house.

"Did Frazier and Hafer know each other?" I asked, after telling Bill what I'd scented.

"It's possible—Larry Frazier worked with most branches of the military," Bill acknowledged. "NCIS is definitely involved now, and I have to share information as much as I can, although the President is keeping all of you out of it for the moment. I had to agree to this in order to get the information exchange from them."

Bill didn't sound terrible happy over that revelation and I wondered what Tony was going to say about it. He knew Larry Frazier better than any of us. Maybe he would know if Hafer and Frazier knew one another.

"Lissa, do you want a drink?" Winkler herded me into a bar after Bill dropped us off at our hotel.

"I'd rather have a cinnamon roll," I said. We found one at the hotel coffee shop on the main floor. My cell phone rang while I was wiping gooey frosting off my face. It was Merrill.

"Lissa, sweetheart, I didn't expect you to answer. I was going to leave a voice message," Merrill scolded lightly.

"Didn't you have the talk with Griffin?" I asked, licking more frosting off my fingers.

"Lissa, what are you doing right now?" Merrill asked.

"Eating a cinnamon roll," I answered honestly.

"Perhaps Griffin needs to provide more information than he has," Merrill muttered. "He can be cryptic at times and this was certainly one of those times. He can't interfere, but from the conversation we had, I got the idea that Director Jennings needs to contact a friend of mine—a werewolf named Daniel Carey. He was working with Admiral Hafer not long ago. He may be back in Corpus Christi; he's the Second for the Pack, there."

"I've met him," I nodded. "He's Shirley Walker's Second."

Winkler's ears perked up at Merrill's message; he was hearing it almost as well as I was. He knew Daniel Carey, too, I realized. Daniel and Shirley had come to the beach house when I was working for Winkler.

Winkler pulled his phone out and dialed a number before Merrill could hang up the phone, and he did hang up—somewhat abruptly, I thought. I wanted to ask about Greg, but didn't get the chance. I hadn't asked Gavin to borrow his computer lately, either, and I wanted to see if there were any emails from Franklin and Greg.

Winkler was talking with Daniel Carey while my mind wandered a little, and I realized I was more tired than I thought. "Admiral Hafer's been kidnapped," Winkler told Daniel, bringing me back to a normal orbit.

"I heard," Daniel said on the other end.

"Someone named Lawrence Frazier was kidnapped as well," Winkler said. "Do you happen to know if they knew each other?" There was a lengthy silence on the other end. I was watching Winkler's face carefully, now. Daniel decided to talk.

"This involves state secrets," Daniel said. "A vampire helped me out with this, otherwise Anthony Hancock's name would have been splashed all over the media and the President might have gone down with him."

"Which vampire?" I got in on the conversation now.

"Is Lissa there with you?" Daniel asked.

"She's here and we're working with Director Jennings on this," Winkler said.

"Merrill helped me with this," Daniel sighed. "Hafer had dirt on Hancock—said he approved a risky experiment on six top agents. The agents were dying, the last I heard. Hafer wanted you, Lissa, and if he didn't get you, he was going to cause a lot of trouble. I think Dr. Frazier was his informant on the experiments."

"I guess Dr. Frazier was trying to cover his own ass," I grumbled. "Since it was his experiment. He was the one to go ahead and try his little concoction on humans without going through the proper procedures."

"You know about this?" Daniel asked. Winkler still held the phone but Daniel was talking to me, now. Winkler handed the phone over. He could still hear the conversation, after all.

"Yeah, I know about it," I muttered into the phone. I was hip deep in the middle of it at the time, since Frazier was taking my blood to do his little experiments. "Those six agents are still alive as far as I know, because I got outside help to cure them," I added. Winkler's eyebrows lifted at that information. "Do you know how well Hafer knew Frazier?"

"Frazier was Hafer's physician a few years back. Hafer had a hip replacement, plus one or two serious repairs done on his heart. The whole thing was hushed up and never made public. Frazier was the perfect person for that, obviously."

"I don't know why Bill doesn't have that information," I told Daniel.

"You have no idea what can be erased from the records if you're high enough up," Daniel replied. "Poor health could have forced Hafer into retirement, and that would have kicked him off a lot of defense committees. He didn't want that. I don't know why, he never told me. That's all I know, Lissa. And remember, you never talked to me about this."

"Of course not," I said and hung up when Daniel terminated the call.

"Let's go find Bill," Winkler said, tossing his coffee cup into a nearby wastebasket. I dropped the rest of my cinnamon roll in the trash, too. It had gone cold and my appetite disappeared while I spoke with Daniel.

❧

"Hafer was planning on exposing the experiments?" Bill paced in front of us. Gavin, René and Tony had wakened and Roff and Michael, who were sharing a room, sighed happily and went to dinner. They were planning an early night.

Tony was growling until René got him calmed down—he hadn't known about Larry's duplicity, either. His friend had been willing to let Tony take the fall, even though he was more responsible, in my opinion.

Larry was the physician and the research biologist; he should have known not to take shortcuts. Vampire DNA would kill humans if introduced into their body in small amounts. I gasped, I think, when the thought hit me.

"Lissa, what is wrong?" Gavin came to my side quickly and began rubbing my shoulders.

"Who came up with the idea to introduce vampire DNA into the flu vaccine? Who told Rahim and Xenides how to do it? Do you think that Larry Frazier was under Xenides' thumb all that time?"

"Lissa, I think you're jumping to conclusions," Bill said.

"Larry was in Oman, tending to a few patients who'd been brought in from Afghanistan. That's why he was on the Navy ship afterward when the pirates hit," Tony said. He was trying to piece this together, just as I was.

"They knew he was on that boat," I muttered. "Those pirates were out there, waiting, I think, for somebody to come and get them. They didn't seem interested in going anywhere with their hostage."

"Rahim may have paid them to take Larry—he was the only one they kidnapped, but they shot several others getting him off the ship," Tony nodded.

"So, Xenides, or one of his brothers or children placed compulsion on Larry while he was in Oman? Is that what you think?" Bill asked. "That Rahim may have gotten a vampire into the country and close enough to Frazier to do this?"

"That's what I think, but since I don't have proof, right now it's just a theory," I said. "Regardless, somebody figured out how to put vampire DNA into the flu vaccine and now at least two vampires have Larry Frazier and Admiral Hafer. Frazier probably pointed those vampires in Hafer's direction, so he'd be taken. How does that fit into the equation?"

My breath was shaky, now. How much damage could Xenides do with Dr. Larry Frazier in his clutches? What did he want with Hafer? I couldn't figure that out unless it was for information of some kind. That made me even shakier. Tony, I learned, was thinking the same thing. Only he was in a better position to know what Hafer might be able to hand out as far as information and state secrets went.

"It's not looking good," Tony rubbed his forehead as if he had a headache. René was watching over his newest vampire child with concern. Gavin pulled me tightly against his chest. He knew I was upset. I was shaking after all.

"Sounds like we need to find these guys fast," Winkler said. He'd been standing nearby, listening to everything.

"Let me make some calls." Bill was frustrated, I could tell. He was beginning to show signs of wear, just as Tony used to. Bill left us, walking out our hotel room door. A guard was posted outside and he fell in behind Bill.

"Lissa, have you eaten?" Gavin pulled my chin up so he could see my face.

"She had half a cinnamon roll earlier," Winkler said. "That isn't any kind of meal." René went to the locked cooler, pulled out a bag of blood and tossed it to Gavin, who wasn't satisfied until I'd drank as much of it as I could. He gave the rest to René, who locked it inside the cooler.

"Gavin, do you think Xenides may have made Larry Frazier forget what vampire DNA would do to humans as soon as he gave Rahim information on how to get it into the flu vaccine?" I asked while we waited for Bill to return. "I mean, he went ahead and just shot that stuff into six guys without a second thought."

Gavin was now sitting beside me on the bed. I had my back to the headboard and my knees drawn up to my chest. I'd pulled my shoes off, of course. Gavin was also lounging on the bed, but he had his long legs stretched out in front of him and had kept his shoes on. Oh, well. It was a hotel.

"Lissa, Xenides could have placed compulsion for Frazier to believe the vampire DNA was harmless, or any number of other things to get him to willingly cooperate." Gavin lifted a stray strand of hair off my forehead and smoothed it behind an ear.

"Gavin, I can't tell you how fucked up and scary that is," I leaned my forehead on his shoulder.

"Little rose, do not fret," René said. "There are enough of us here, I think, that we can take care of this quickly. Anthony has experience in this area, as does Director Jennings. We will find these perpetrators."

"Was that out of character for him, Tony?" I was looking at Tony now. "Did Frazier cut corners before or was he rushing things when he took my blood?" It still irked me, and I didn't understand how Tony had agreed to it.

"Larry was a bit on the adventurous side at times," Tony admitted, crossing his arms over his chest and refusing to look at me. "It could go either way." His gray eyes held worry and more than a little guilt before he'd turned away.

"I think we should not go down that road," Gavin murmured, pulling my head against his shoulder again.

Bill was back in a few minutes, phone in hand. "We've got two receptions at the White House, plus a speech tomorrow." He didn't look happy. "Hafer knew the schedule, according to my contacts." Well, if Hafer knew, then Xenides probably knew, too.

"Lissa and I can handle anything during daylight," Winkler offered. "Michael and Roff can stay here with the other three."

"I want Lissa there at the night event, too," Bill said.

"Lissa has to sleep sometime," Gavin announced. Yeah, I was thinking the same thing. I was tired right then, but I wasn't saying that.

"She can sleep in until ten—the first one doesn't start until one in the afternoon," Bill said. "I think we can get her there by the right time. I just want her nose and her other abilities on these things. The President has been notified and the First Lady is going to be at all three events. I'm sure you all know what happened the last time we had a problem."

"What can we do tonight?" Tony asked. He was restless from inactivity.

"NCIS passed over a couple of leads," Bill said. "We can check those out." Tony nodded eagerly and René was prepared to indulge his child. We walked out of the hotel with Bill after he called for a van.

Our first stop was a convenience store that looked as if a bomb had hit it, only there hadn't been any bomb. The night clerk had been killed the evening before and the security DVR had been destroyed after the disc was stolen. Bill explained all of this to us before we climbed out of the van.

Yellow police tape was still strung up everywhere and the business was obviously closed. The convenience store was part of a chain, so a security guard had been hired to keep vandals away. There were also two D.C. cops there to help.

Bill showed his ID when we walked up, so barricades were moved and we were allowed inside. Broken glass and bits of twisted metal and shelving were everywhere. If Gavin hadn't held me up, I would have fallen, I think. I smelled Larry Frazier and one of the vampires. Except the vampire had a little extra. "What's wrong?" Bill and Tony were asking at the same time.

"Tony, I thought you'd have the sense to destroy whatever blood was left." I was angry and gasping out an explanation as best I could. The vampire had received some of my blood—I could smell it. "Gavin, what does this mean?" He'd gotten my blood plenty of times, most recently the night before.

"Lissa, I do not know," Gavin whispered, his expression troubled.

"Take blood now, and then see if you have any of my talents." I was praying that he wouldn't, but I had to be sure.

"Lissa, first tell me what you wish for me to try." Gavin was worried; I could see it in his face.

"Try misting. The humans could turn almost instantly," Tony said. I was now surrounded by all of them.

"Cara, do you want the climax?" Gavin moved against me and murmured in my ear.

"Gavin, no." I didn't want that embarrassment, though I knew the bite would be more painful.

"I will be gentle," Gavin said softly, breathing on my neck. I stiffened when his fangs pierced my skin but he held me tightly, and René was at my back, helping Gavin hold me still. He took perhaps a mouthful before pulling away.

"Just concentrate on turning to mist," I said, rubbing my neck. I could have saved my breath; Gavin was way ahead of me and already turned to mist. "Oh, dear God," I moaned.

"It should only last for half an hour at the most," Tony said, so Bill set about timing it.

Can you hear me? I sent to Gavin.

Cara, I hear you always, he replied.

But I've not heard more than a single word from you before, I returned. I went to mist just so I could see Gavin's mist—it was a bright gold.

Cara, I see your mist—it is a blinding white, Gavin was excited, now. I turned back to myself and we waited. Gavin's effects wore off closer to the hour mark. He was smiling when he returned to us.

"It must be because you took the amount you did and got it directly from her," Tony sighed. Bill was nodding and agreeing.

"I know how this happened," I looked around at the devastation. It wasn't as good as what I could do, but it was impressive anyway.

"Lissa, what else can you do?" Gavin gave me his best, longest suffering tone.

"Uh, blow things up with my mist," I hung my head. "I told Franklin and Greg, but Merrill had other things on his mind right after I got back from Refizan. He wasn't paying attention when I mentioned it."

"What did you blow up?" Gavin frowned deeply, his brows drawn together with worry. He never showed this much emotion. Never.

"A temple."

"How big was this temple?" Bill asked.

"Pretty big," I stared guiltily at my feet. "If I'd used everything I had, this store would have been scattered for a mile, I think." I looked up into Gavin's concerned face.

"Lissa, you frighten me at times," Gavin said.

"So, now we have the how, we just don't have the why," Bill said.

"What is the other lead?" Tony asked. I ignored him—didn't feel up to talking to him at the moment. His and Frazier's faux pas was getting us deeper into trouble as time went on. We climbed into the van and drove to the second crime scene.

"Hafer was here, with the other vampire," I said, sniffing around the second convenience store. At least it was still intact. This clerk was also dead; his blood still permeated the front of the store. The DVR disc was missing here, just as it was in the last place.

"Why are they hitting convenience stores?" I couldn't figure this out at all. If the humans were hungry, there were vending stands up and down the street. "Was this one robbed?" I walked over to Bill.

"It was," Bill nodded. "But we think that's just a cover."

"What if it isn't?" I asked. "What if they can't get cash or money some other way without robbing someone?"

Gavin had his phone in his hand so fast I never saw him reach for it. Charles was on the other end in seconds.

"Have any accounts been frozen recently?" Gavin asked curtly.

"We got a few names from the shapeshifter," Charles replied. "The Honored One had me freeze their assets."

"I think we are tracking them now; they have killed in the course of a robbery," Gavin informed Charles. Wlodek must have been standing at Charles's elbow listening in, because he was on the phone immediately.

"What is happening?" Wlodek demanded. Gavin gave a report, including information on the kidnappings of Larry Frazier and Admiral Hafer, plus the unwelcome news that Larry still had some of my blood and that he'd given it to at least one of the vampires to duplicate my talents. Wlodek cursed when Gavin informed him that I could make things explode with my mist.

"Remind me to have a talk with my child when you bring her home," Wlodek muttered angrily. Great. Something to look forward to. My life wouldn't be complete unless I was in trouble with somebody.

Wlodek provided three names he'd gotten from Angelo—Rafael Rivera, Alphonse Bouvier and Cyrus Falcone. All three vampires' accounts had been frozen by the Council. I figured the vampire that had blown up the first convenience store had been pretty pissed about something. He may have discovered the exploding talent by accident, but he certainly had a weapon in his hands now, as long as Larry could keep supplying him with my blood. The questions were, what would they choose to destroy with that talent and how much of my blood did they have left?

"Why didn't I know about all these things you can do?" Winkler quizzed me later as we walked toward the van.

"I've learned these things as I went along." I wanted to elbow him in the ribs. It made me worry about what might have happened if I'd known all this from the beginning. Would Winkler or Weldon have tried to control my talents?

I still didn't know what the Council's intentions were toward me. They already had designs on Tony; I could see that from a mile away. What did they want from me? Would they take advantage of my youth as a vampire to get me to do as much for them as they could?

"Lissa, you have the biggest frown on your face," Tony said as he opened the van door for me.

"Just thinking," I muttered, climbing inside and scooting over on the bench seat so Gavin could slide in beside me. I wanted to yell at Tony. I didn't. That wouldn't solve anything, and both of us would feel worse afterward. We needed clear heads to deal with this problem.

"Lissa, I do not think Wlodek will be overly harsh," Gavin said. He was thinking back to Wlodek's words when he'd spilled the beans about my exploding mist trick.

"You two may be like this," I held up a hand with fingers crossed, "but he wants to yell at me every chance he gets."

Winkler crawled in on Gavin's other side and closed the door, Tony and René loaded into the third row. Bill was in the front passenger seat and our driver, who'd waited for us inside the van, put the vehicle in gear and drove us back to our hotel.

"Lissa, you should eat and then try to sleep," Gavin said when we reached our room. René was schooling Tony with the hours of night remaining.

"What are you planning to do?" I asked.

"I will assist René," Gavin replied. I waited until he left the room before misting into Roff and Michael's room. Roff murmured sleepily when I lay down beside him; he pulled my head onto his shoulder and fell asleep again quickly.

"Her blood does this?" Xenides hadn't felt like laughing with glee in a very long time. Some of the talents that Lissa bore were more than extraordinary. He would keep her alive and under his thumb for this latest reason alone. He'd intended to keep draining her blood for other reasons once she was his, but this—no other vampire had ever been able to do these things. Xenides had always envied the misters— all he had was mindspeech. With the little princess's blood, however, he could destroy anyone and anything.

"And the effects lasted for nearly half an hour," Rafael said. "More than enough time to do anything one might wish to do. It was a stroke of genius, my sire, to take Frazier. He gave us additional information we did not have before."

Rafael had no talents in misting, mindspeech or any other thing that might have made him special. For half an hour the previous evening, however, he'd been able to fly as invisible mist and had destroyed the convenience store when the clerk pulled a gun on his human puppet.

Rafael wanted that exhilaration again and was thinking of demanding the solution from the Frazier human. He had to rein himself in; he realized they might need every bit of blood left to accomplish their goals for Xenides.

"How much of her blood remains?" Xenides asked, causing Rafael to start and grip his cell phone tightly.

"Only five vials," Rafael admitted reluctantly.

"Then do not use any more for frivolous activities. I will see that you have a credit card to use quickly. No more robberies. You may be detected, and we cannot risk this. I want two vials of her blood sent to me. Make sure it is packed safely and securely."

"Of course. The package will be sent tomorrow, sire," Rafael felt chastened. "We have enough money to feed the humans and enough blood to feed us. It is fortunate the older human had an apartment that does not appear on any of his records," Rafael smiled. "We are staying there until our mission is complete."

"Remember, if you see the female, place compulsion immediately to do only as you instruct. I will come to retrieve her as quickly as I can."

"I will, sire," Rafael said.

CHAPTER 10

I dreamed of the High Demon's planet again, only this time there was a different king. The comesula addressed him as Raoni Jaydevik. The king was handsome, with thick brown hair that curled slightly, dark eyes and a sensuous mouth. A beautiful woman with a river of platinum hair hanging down her back stood beside him.

"Glindarok, avilepha, say you will have my children when this is over," Jaydevik put his arms around the woman after the comesula left them.

"Jaydevik, if we can defeat the Ra'Ak and the rogue High Demons, I will be more than happy to have your children," the woman sighed.

I knew, though I had no idea how I knew, that she was already pregnant. Not pregnant long—perhaps a month or two—but pregnant all the same, and holding that information back from the king for some reason.

What was she saying about the Ra'Ak and rogue High Demons? That sounded like a conspiracy of some kind. Dragon told me that only the High Demons' planet survived out of all the dark worlds, because the Ra'Ak could not defeat the High Demons. Yet it seemed that some High Demons had thrown their lot in with the Ra'Ak. What had they been promised? I couldn't imagine that High Demons would ally themselves with the enemy unless they wanted something very badly.

A phrase whispered into my mind; answering my question in the dream—*rule of the dark realm.* Was I looking at something in the recent past or something that had yet to come into being? That question wasn't answered for me as I was shaken awake by a frowning Gavin and hauled back to our room. He grumbled softly, even as he planted kisses on my brow.

Roff woke me this time; right at ten a.m. Winkler was with him, a standard Secret Service uniform in a plastic suit bag slung over his shoulder.

"Rise and shine, baby. We have to get you cleaned up and ready to go before Director Bill has an aneurysm." Winkler offered a wolfish grin.

"Raona, I was upset that you left me last night," Roff grumped.

"I didn't, sir schmuck over there came and got me," I sat up on the bed, rubbing my eyes.

"Ah," Roff said, nodding his acceptance. He wasn't about to argue with Gavin. Most people, vampires included, wouldn't argue with Gavin if they knew what was good for them.

"This is yours," Winkler handed the dark suit and white shirt over. I showered and dressed as quickly as I could. Winkler was dressed in a nice suit and was going as a guest—go figure. His name was recognizable; I guess Vampire Queen wasn't a title one could throw about at the White House, so I was going as hired help.

"Lissa, I want you to turn to mist or whatever it is you do and scout out the place," Bill told me later while we were going through an employee entrance. The reception was being held in the Blue Room at the White House.

I saw it from above everyone's heads; some of the biggest names in computer technology were there having tea and cake with the

President and the First Lady. Winkler fit right in, wouldn't you know?

There wouldn't be any other vampires there; my ability to walk in daylight had been given to me by Griffin and I hadn't been able to do that when Larry Frazier took my blood. He'd never get his hands on me again—not if I had anything to say about it. The reception was a bust, as far as attacks went. The worst thing I saw was one of the guests slipping a snack into a coat pocket.

Bill was waiting for me later in a hallway near the door, after the President and First Lady had gone back to their quarters. I materialized right beside Bill. "Nothing," I told him, shaking my head.

"Yeah. It was a long shot, anyway," Bill agreed. "We still have the one at five, and the dinner at eight." I didn't get a vibe off either of those things and figured it would be unimaginative of Xenides to attack the White House again. I didn't say that to Bill, though. He had enough on his plate to worry about.

Bill and I were served a light meal in the kitchen, where Winkler found us. The second reception was held in the East Room with a handful of foreign ministers from the European Union, who also represented member nations of NATO. That was over after an hour and a half. I didn't find anything during that one, either, but I misted into every nook and cranny anyway, just to check.

Gavin, René and Tony showed up for the dinner and it was a yawner. If I hadn't been mist, I think I would have cracked my jaws yawning. My long day and lack of sleep was affecting me. Bill had two of his vampire agents squirreled into the Secret Service for night duty, along with four werewolves for day duty. I'm sure the President had been briefed.

"It's all your fault, René," I teased him on the way to the hotel. "If I show up alone, all kinds of stuff happens. You come along and we get nothing."

Gavin shook his head but René laughed. "Little rose," he said, "you and Anthony make me feel young again."

"I hope that's a good thing," I said as we crawled out of the van at the hotel.

"We know where they are staying—our informant has given this information. You will go there tomorrow afternoon and kill the one in this photograph," Alphonse handed the photograph to Larry Frazier. They had everything they needed from Frazier now; he was expendable if he died. The Admiral was still under their control; his position of importance would become an asset very soon.

Larry Frazier stared at the photograph he'd been given and felt ill.

I'd slept through the rest of the night, waking around eleven. Roff was straightening the room—he'd gone downstairs to exchange our towels for clean ones and was restocking the bathroom when I woke.

Roff pulled me against him when I wandered into the bathroom and gave me a gentle kiss before letting me go. I was so attached to him now, and I think he felt the same way about me. He offered to help me bathe, but I shooed him out of the bathroom and cleaned up.

"I'm going down to the gift shop to see if there's a magazine or a paperback that looks interesting," I told Roff, who was now setting Gavin's dirty clothes in a neatly folded stack. He smiled and nodded so off I went.

One of Bill's guards was at the end of the hall near the stairs; our rooms were the last ones on the ninth floor. The guard nodded to me as I passed him on my way to the stairs.

Winkler was in the coffee shop, typing away on his laptop; I caught his scent on my way to the gift shop. Taking a detour from my intended target, I walked inside the coffee shop instead and sat down at Winkler's table.

"Want another cinnamon roll?" Winkler looked up and grinned at me. Honestly, that grin alone could make just about any female heart flop like a landed fish.

"I may have one," I smiled back at him and went to the counter to order it. I set my latte and cinnamon roll on the small table while

Winkler finished sending e-mails. "What's the status on little Winkler and Winklerette?" I asked, using my plastic knife and fork to cut into my cinnamon roll.

"Everything seems to be fine," Winkler looked over the lid of his laptop. "I think Kellee snapped at Trajan, so he refused to let her go shopping for a day."

"A fate worse than death," I nodded, stuffing a generous bite of frosting-coated cinnamon roll in my mouth. "What about Whitney and Sam?" I asked about Winkler's sister and her husband—they'd been married a year and a half now.

"Whitney wanted to drop out of school and get pregnant," Winkler grumped. "I told her she had plenty of time for that later. Sam doesn't know how to say no to her, so I had to be the bad guy."

"I'm surprised you said no to her," I pointed my plastic fork at him. "I thought she was spending your money faster than you could earn it when I first met her."

"She does have a tendency to wear out credit cards," Winkler chuckled.

"Whitney can wear out a credit card in a single mall," I teased Winkler. "I should know—I've seen her do it."

"Then it's a good thing I have money, isn't it?" He closed his laptop and slipped it into the case he'd brought with him.

"I'm thinkin' it is," I said, eating another bite of cinnamon roll.

"Roff told me you have no money," Winkler wasn't looking at me as he took a sip from his coffee cup.

"Baby vamps aren't allowed to earn money," I grumped. "I'm a dependent until my five years are up, which pisses me off no end. I'm supposed to have a trust fund somewhere, but I haven't seen the financials. Merrill is handling that for me. I inherited my real sire's holdings when Gavin offed him after he was sentenced by the Council."

"Gavin killed him?" Winkler's eyebrows lifted in alarm. I snorted.

"I thought he was going to kill me, too," I said. "Those two twits who turned me had done that sort of thing before. They thought it was a game. I was the only one who lived over it," I set my plastic fork down with a sigh. I'd only gotten halfway through this cinnamon roll, too.

"I didn't mean to bring up bad memories," Winkler said, covering one of my hands with warm fingers.

"Both times I've stood before the Council haven't been good memories," I agreed. "And those holding cells they have suck."

"I guess you can't let vampires out on bond, huh?" Winkler was trying to steer me away from the subject.

"They won't ever put this vampire back in one of those cracker boxes," I said. "And I think they know that, now. If they ever have a problem with me, they're gonna have to kill me quickly while I'm unsuspecting."

"Lissa, if I didn't see pure worship in Gavin's eyes every time he looks at you while you're not watching, I'd take you out of here today and they'd never find you again. You'd be raising my kids, baby, if you wanted to. Kellee is already saying she's leaving as soon as she can get up and walk after the twins are born."

"Life is just way too complicated, isn't it?" I squeezed Winkler's fingers and took my hand away. The thought of having kids that I could bring up? That was an old wound. Howard Graham made sure I'd never have any of my own and that wasn't anything that vampires got, either. "Your twins will just have to settle for having Auntie Lissa, who sends them birthday and Christmas presents."

"Don't forget you'll have a house next door—they can come over and play. Surely Gavin can't control you every minute after the five years are up, and you only have three more to go."

"Yeah. I hope I make it through the next three years."

"It won't be forever," Winkler said. "You can come to Whitney's graduation. She should be finishing her master's at the same time."

"That'll be nice. I'll look forward to that," I sighed. Winkler and I both got up and headed toward the elevator; it was already two in the afternoon.

Halfway up to the ninth floor, my skin began to itch and then it was on fire. Winkler grunted when I grabbed his arm and hauled him out of the elevator as mist, and we were zooming upward through the remaining floors. The guard was already down and dead when we reached our floor and Larry Frazier was kicking in René and Tony's door as we sped toward him.

The door splintered before we got there and I wanted to scream at the sharpened stake that Larry held in his hand as he walked into the room. Winkler was almost thrown to the floor as I let him go; I intended to mist in front of Larry, take the stake away and maybe toss him into a wall a time or two before I let Bill have him.

The first part of my plan worked flawlessly; I materialized right in front of Larry and snatched the stake out of his hand before he had time to blink. The rest of my plan should have gone well, too, but it didn't.

I hadn't been thinking, other than to protect Tony and René and corner Larry. I could only imagine that Larry had the wrong room and intended to stake Gavin and perhaps haul me off. Who knew if I was right or not?

I should have realized that a mere wooden stake couldn't have been used to kill the guard. It wasn't enough, as it turns out. The gun was, though, and after I snatched the stake, Larry let me have it with the .38 he was carrying. Twice.

Still intending to take him down, I reached out—but he was now farther away and I was falling. Pain bloomed in my chest and the room went spinning about me. The last thing I saw—before the room went dark, that is—was Winkler in wolf form, viciously snapping Larry's head from his shoulders with powerful jaws.

The room itself was suddenly boiling with people of all kinds. Voices were calling my name, asking me questions, and hands were on me; I couldn't really say whose at the moment. All I know was that at least one pair of those hands was huge and blue.

CHAPTER 11

"What the fuck was he doing breaking into that room?" Winkler was pacing and growling. In the past hour, he'd seen things he'd never thought to see, including an eight and a half foot blue giant, Lissa's father Griffin, Kifirin, another man who claimed to be a healer, Lissa's father's wife and a man with Asian features who had a thick braid down to his waist.

Winkler and Bill had been shoved aside as Lissa's body was lifted up; all while Lissa's father was handing out instructions for her to be placed in stasis so she wouldn't bleed out. The healer and the blue giant had taken over, Tony was moved to Roff's bed and Lissa was now in Tony's spot, getting attention.

"Frazier must have been given the wrong room number by a member of the staff," Bill muttered. He was just as frustrated as Winkler; poor Roff was nearly in tears and Michael was berating himself for going to the pool instead of hanging around the room all day. He'd thought the agent Bill left to guard the rooms was enough. Roff hadn't heard the shots that killed Bill's agent; Larry's gun had a silencer on it.

"How long until sunset?" Two of Bill's werewolf agents had been called in and one was asking questions. He knew the vampires would be rising at that time. Winkler frowned. He had no idea what would calm Gavin if he woke to find Lissa wounded or dead. Larry Frazier had hit her twice in the chest from close range. A human would be dead already.

"We have another twenty minutes," Bill replied, checking his watch.

"I'd pay money to know who or what that blue guy is," the other werewolf said softly.

"I don't think he's local," Winkler muttered.

"I am Griffin, Lissa's father," Griffin held his hand out to one of the werewolf agents as he walked over. The werewolves shook the offered hand and introduced themselves as Agents Renfro and Delgado. Griffin acknowledged their names as if he already knew who they were.

"We've got her stabilized; she'll be ready to move as soon as the vampires waken," Griffin went on. "Two bullets, one through the heart. Her heart beats now, since she received my blood, but I muted her heartbeat so the vampires wouldn't become alarmed. If we hadn't come, she might have died." Griffin rubbed tension from his forehead with strong fingers.

"How did they find out where we were?" Winkler asked.

"I cannot answer that as it would be interfering," Griffin answered. "I will give advice, however, since this involves my daughter. Have no contact with anyone other than Merrill or Wlodek as far as vampires are concerned."

"Who's the blue guy?" werewolf agent Renfro took the opportunity to ask.

Griffin almost smiled. "That is Pheligar of the Larentii. You may never see another like him. Lissa will live over this," Griffin turned to Winkler. "She will be down for perhaps a week or so; that's what Pheligar and Karzac say. Karzac will stay for a day or two until he is assured that nothing is amiss. I am telling you now, for your own safety, not to argue with him. There is not a more autocratic physician anywhere, I do not believe. He is also the most powerful of our healers, so you will not get far if you do argue." Griffin nodded at

Winkler, Bill and the two werewolf agents before returning to the knot of people surrounding Lissa's bed.

~

"Lissa, wake up little girl." Those were the first words I heard as I blinked my eyes open. Griffin was sitting at the side of my bed, only I didn't recognize any of my surroundings.

"This house belongs to the Council," Griffin said softly, reading my mind. My chest ached—I realized that now. Larry Frazier had shot me. I hadn't dreamed or imagined that.

"The tissue has been healed and Karzac gave you a transfusion," Griffin said, patting my hand that he held in both of his. "Pheligar and Karzac managed to do that quickly. They kept you from dying, baby." Griffin was smiling, though his eyes looked a little misty.

"Are they still here?" I asked. I wanted to thank them.

"Pheligar has gone, but Karzac is having a meal somewhere. He'll be back and staying with you for a day or two to make sure everything is all right. I had to order the vampires and the werewolves out of your room; they've been hovering since we brought you here."

"What happened with Larry? Why was he doing this?" I almost hissed his name.

"He'd been placed under compulsion and ordered to attack your party, sweetheart."

"I thought Xenides wanted me alive." I raised a hand to rub my forehead and discovered that an IV was in it. A bag of IV fluid hung from a pole at the side of the bed.

"Karzac," Griffin explained the IV. "And Xenides does want you alive. The ones who sent Mr. Frazier gave him a specific task and didn't instruct him not to protect himself or not to shoot at you if you attacked him. As you can see, it could have turned out very badly."

"It did turn out badly—for him," I muttered. I'd seen Winkler snap Larry's head off before I lost consciousness.

"Yes, it did turn out badly for him. Pheligar cleared away the blood from the hotel room and the Director had the body hauled away. I must go and allow the others in here before Gavin attempts to remove my head," Griffin sighed, raising my hand to his lips and kissing it. "Try to stay out of trouble, baby girl." He smiled at me before disappearing.

Gavin was growling the minute he entered the room, closely followed by Winkler, Roff, René and Tony. We were in a safe house. A large one, as it turns out.

"Do not upset her or I will have all of you removed!" Karzac appeared and snapped out orders. Gavin stopped growling immediately. He was allowed to sit down on the side of my bed while Karzac glared; the others had to stand. Karzac was now checking my IV and still frowning at all of my visitors.

"Cara, how are you feeling?" Gavin asked.

"My chest aches," I said. "Not bad for somebody who got shot twice, is it?"

"Cara, you might have died," Gavin grumbled.

"It's my fault. I was reaching for the stake he had in his hand, not even thinking he might have a gun," I sighed. "If I'd stayed mist and just taken his head with my claws, the bullets would have gone right through. I wanted to capture him so we could ask questions. You see how that turned out." I waved the hand that held the IV. Karzac didn't say anything; he just grabbed the hand and set it on the bed.

"Lissa, I have informed Wlodek and Merrill. I think Charles is in need of oxygen," René said over Gavin's shoulder. René's blond hair looked like it had been finger-combed multiple times, and his warm brown eyes held a worry I couldn't define. It was probably just as well that he'd made the call to Wlodek instead of Gavin. Gavin looked like a wreck.

"I'll call him," I said.

"Not until tomorrow," Karzac informed me. "You will ease the hearts and minds that are here at the moment, and then I will place you in a healing sleep and administer another transfusion. You will be weak for several days. I may allow solid food after tomorrow if you are healing well."

"Karzac, have I told you how nice it is to see you?" I turned to look at him.

"I prefer to see you when you are not bleeding all over hotel rooms," he grumped.

"That was an unscheduled bleeding, I assure you," I wrinkled my nose at him.

Do not wrinkle that pretty nose at me, young woman, Karzac sent. *Had it not been for the Larentii helping me, this might have turned out quite differently.*

Thank you, I returned. *And tell Pheligar thanks, too.*

Send him mindspeech and tell him yourself, Karzac instructed. I did.

Pheligar, thank you—you didn't have to, but I'm glad you did, I sent.

Little one, you are more than welcome, came the reply. How about that? I could talk with Pheligar if I wanted!

"He's so polite," I said aloud.

"Who is polite, Cara?" Gavin was kissing my free hand, now.

"Pheligar. Did you see him, Gavin? He's Larentii."

"The tall blue one?" René asked.

"Yeah. His skin is like a summer day," I said. I felt tired.

"Say what you must, I will be placing the healing sleep soon," Karzac said.

"Cara, we will talk tomorrow, love. Gavin stroked hair away from my face and smiled as best he could. I knew the worry and fear in his eyes. I'd felt a little of it myself.

"Lissa Beth, wake now," Karzac's fingers trailed down my cheek after touching my forehead. I gasped in a deep breath, I couldn't help it. My eyes felt like they were glued shut. "Take your time," Karzac said softly. I blinked at him eventually, bringing his face into focus.

"Hi," I said. My mouth felt like sandpaper and my voice wasn't much better.

"Would you like some water?"

"Yeah. What time is it?" I asked. I was completely disoriented.

"Nearly sundown," Karzac answered my question as he helped me sit up. I was handed a mug of ice water and he helped me hold it while I gulped thirstily. "I had to place Roff in a healing sleep as well, he was fretting and wouldn't go to bed," Karzac said when I was done drinking. "I removed the IV—your body heals quickly on its own, although you will be sore and weak for another four days or so." I nodded at his words. "I will also leave as soon as the vampires are awake. I must get home in case I am needed elsewhere."

"I hope I didn't take you from anything important," I said, feeling worried.

"Do not fret, little vampire. I had others volunteering to watch over you. I wanted this for myself."

"I feel special," I smiled at him. He gave me a quick grin. Honestly, I hadn't seen Karzac smile that often so a grin was worth its weight in gold.

"You may get up now and bathe if you want," Karzac said. "If you tire before you are done, I will help." He did help me out of the bed and I only wobbled slightly on my way to the bathroom. My suite had a nice bath plus a small sitting area, and I was betting I had the best bedroom inside the safe house. The bath took longer than normal, but I was clean and feeling better afterward.

Karzac had fresh sheets on the bed when I left the bathroom. He also did something I hadn't even thought about before. I'd washed my hair, and it was still wet. He put his hands on my head and dried my hair with some of the power he has. That was outstanding in my book. Too bad I couldn't do that for myself.

"Tomorrow you may get up and wander around the house, but do not tire yourself," Karzac warned as he plumped the pillows at my back. "And you may eat anything you wish beginning then. I do not recommend chili, however," he was smiling again.

"Yeah, I think that would be asking for trouble," I agreed.

"Dragon sends his regards," Karzac added.

"How is he?" I asked.

"As enigmatic as usual," Karzac informed me. I could picture the scowl on Dragon's face. He'd once been Warlord on Falchan and I figured that scowl came in handy when he didn't want everybody to know what he was thinking.

"You know, Karzac, even though it was dangerous as all get out when I was on Refizan, it was one of the happiest times of my life. I got to make my own decisions and I didn't have the Council breathing down my neck or yelling about what I'd done. That was so nice. Gabron, too, didn't try to control me, even though he was a King Vampire and head of the Council there."

"Dragon worried about you having to clean his dojo," Karzac sat on the edge of my bed.

"Hmmph, that was nothing," I said. "I've cooked meals for werewolves. They can eat twice what any normal human can eat," I laughed a little over that. Winkler could still put it away.

"Are you talking about me?" Winkler walked into my bedroom.

"Your name wasn't mentioned specifically," I pouted at him.

"Damn," Winkler grinned. "Feeling better?"

"A lot better. I still feel like somebody kicked me in the chest, but it's not enough to worry over," I said. Winkler leaned down and kissed me on the forehead, then pulled a chair closer to the bed.

"How do you two know each other?" Winkler asked.

"Lissa came to my homeworld not long ago and helped one of my associates clean out a nest of Ra'Ak," Karzac said.

"If I hadn't seen the blue giant, I'd be questioning your words," Winkler said. "As it is, I think I'd believe just about anything, right now."

"My kind cannot tell an untruth," Karzac informed Winkler. "It is the way we are made."

"Everybody on your planet speaks the truth?" That had Winkler's interest.

"You misunderstand me," Karzac replied. "I am a healer for the Saa Thalarr. That race is the one that cannot lie. You must be invited to become Saa Thalarr or one of their healers. I am Dragon's healer."

"Dragon?"

"You should see him when he is a Dragon," I said, smiling at the memory. "He's huge, with red scales tipped in black."

"You saw him in his normal shape yesterday," Karzac explained to Winkler. "He was the one with the long braid down his back."

"That guy?" Winkler asked.

"You should see his tattoos, they're everywhere," I said. "Chest, back and arms. Anyway, that's what I saw." I had no idea if Dragon had tattoos elsewhere and I wasn't about to ask.

"I find myself wishing you could go out with him again on his assignments," Karzac said. "I never felt as safe in my life as I did when you were guarding the nights on Refizan."

"She used to do that for me," Winkler agreed amiably. "I slept better, knowing she was out there, patrolling the grounds."

"And yet I was stupid enough to let Larry the dickhead shoot me," I muttered.

"Lissa, that could have happened to anyone," Winkler reached out to touch my cheek. "I was about to jump him myself and he would have shot me, too. I focused on the stake just like you did."

"I still feel like an idiot and Wlodek already has it in for me when I get back. I'm sure he'll yell about this, too." I blew out a breath. Gavin, René, Tony and Roff chose that moment to walk in—the sun must have gone down.

"Cara, are you well?" Gavin waved a hand imperiously at Winkler, who got up from his chair and allowed Gavin to sit down.

"I'm all right. Karzac let me have a shower so I feel pretty good."

"She may rise tomorrow, but she may only walk about the house," Karzac was preparing to leave. "Nothing strenuous for the next four days." He was gathering a few things he'd brought with him, including the IV pole. "Lissa, be well and happy," Karzac said, giving me a smile.

I love you I sent. Yeah, I don't know why I said it either, but it was true. I loved him, just as I loved Roff, Winkler, and Tony, even. Karzac raised a hand in farewell and he was gone.

"Raona, do you want something to eat?" Roff asked.

"Karzac said I couldn't have solid food until tomorrow, so I guess I'll have some blood," I told him. He came back with a bag in a few minutes and I drank what I could, giving the unused portion back to him.

"Does anybody have anything to read?" I asked. I'd never made it to the gift shop two days before—I'd sat down in the coffee shop to talk with Winkler instead.

"My child and I have purchased an e-reader for you," René smiled. Tony left to get it while I stared at René. "It is much easier to carry than many books, and Anthony and I have already selected several titles for you." René's smile widened.

"I think I love you," I smiled back at René. Gavin never turned a hair at my statement.

"How are they explaining Larry Frazier's death?" I asked while Tony was gone. Bill was noticeably absent, as was Michael.

"Bill decided to connect Frazier to the convenience store murders and robberies," Gavin sighed. "They've manufactured evidence of unstable behavior, culminating in a mental episode of some sort."

"They still have Hafer," I pointed out. "So he must be useful to them in some way. Does everybody know to call Bill if the esteemed Admiral just shows up somewhere?"

"I do not know that, cara," Gavin shook his head. "When Director Jennings contacts us again, we will ask about it. Wlodek dislikes the idea of any humans knowing where this safe house is located. Bill agreed to have compulsion laid not to reveal it before he was permitted to come. Wlodek stretched the rules to allow our werewolf, here, to stay."

That made me smile again—Gavin was calling Winkler *our* werewolf. I thought of him as that too. Not that Gavin didn't feel the bite of jealousy now and then—he did. Winkler had joined the family, I think, as had Tony. Gavin at one time might have been willing to remove Tony's head. Now, as René's vampire child, Gavin accepted him completely.

Gavin pulled out his cell and dialed as we talked. Charles was on the line quickly. "Charles, hold for a moment," Gavin passed the phone to me.

"Charles?" I said.

"Thank goodness," Charles heaved a huge sigh. "How are you feeling?"

"Much better. The healer that came said I can't do much for the next four days but we're moving in the right direction, I think."

"Gavin said your blood was everywhere, Lissa," Charles scolded. "You need to take it easy. It'll take a while to come back after that."

"You need to stop fretting, honey," I said.

"Does that include me?" Wlodek was now on the line. I drew a shaky breath. "Lissa, will you ever stop being frightened when I speak with you?" Wlodek asked.

"I don't know," I answered truthfully.

"Moro mou, I am not going to chastise you over the phone. You merely need to let me know when there is information that should be shared with me. Gavin had difficulty with this at first, as did many others. I did not punish them or lock them up for it."

"They're not female, either," I muttered.

"Is that upsetting you? I am worried over you because you are female, it is true," Wlodek sighed. "You are so precious to us; something that we cannot replace if you are lost. I know that any sort of confinement is a cage to you, child. When we gave you to Gavin in your absence, we were looking for ways to make your cage a comfortable one. You must forgive us our mistakes. I beg you to not give us a scare such as this again, daughter."

"I'm right there with you on that one, honey," I muttered. Wlodek chuckled, more than likely over the fact that I'd called him honey. That always seemed to amuse him. "How's Flavio doing?" I asked to change the subject.

"Much better," Wlodek replied. "He wishes to entertain you and Gavin when you return."

"I'll probably drive him crazy," I said. "I make Gavin crazy on a daily basis."

"Lissa, I think you may have that effect on any vampire more than five hundred years of age," Wlodek had a smile in his voice.

"Maybe you need to include mental health leave in the vampire package of benefits," I teased. "I'm sure that vampire doctor you have can name a mental illness after me. Then Gavin can call in sick with Lissa syndrome." Gavin was now frowning—I'm sure I'd stepped over some sort of line. Nobody treated the Honored One in this manner.

"Lissa, I think we are all afflicted with that," Wlodek replied and I laughed. Gavin attempted to pull the phone away from my hand. After a brief tussle, I ended up in Gavin's lap; my arms were wrapped tightly around his neck as he stroked my back gently with one hand and held the phone to his ear with the other.

"She is still recovering, Honored One," Gavin said and I muffled more laughter against Gavin's neck.

"Gavin, this is good for her," Wlodek informed him. "It gives me pleasure to make her laugh."

Gavin got off the phone shortly afterward and our audience disappeared as Gavin pulled my arms away and held my face in his hands. "Cara, I was so frightened," he said and kissed me as carefully as he could. "Your father tells me you have a muted heartbeat since he gave you blood. You could have died, my love." I was placed in my bed and Gavin crawled in beside me, holding me until I fell asleep.

"Listen to me carefully," Xenides struggled to hold his anger back. Lawrence Frazier, his human pawn, had not received the best of instruction and had almost killed the little princess. His spy informed him of this, although he hadn't been able to get updated information on where she'd been taken. The fools in the U.S. had botched this completely. Xenides would see that they paid for this mistake later. In the interim, he still needed them. "You will instruct any others to protect her life, not take it," Xenides' anger came through in his voice.

Rafael hadn't been the one to give Larry Frazier instructions, but he was bearing the brunt of Xenides' wrath. He knew not to make excuses—that was extreme foolishness and the punishment when it came would be harsher if he attempted it. He held his tongue and accepted the verbal abuse.

"I'm not going to argue if she wants to go eat," Winkler said. We had very little in the house other than blood to consume and I knew Roff was tired of sandwiches. Winkler, too, actually. I was trying to talk Gavin into going out so some of us could enjoy a decent meal. I know he didn't like letting me out of the house, but it had been three days since Karzac left and there was only one more day that I had to take it easy anyway.

"Cara, if this is what you want, then we will do this," Gavin finally caved. "What do you wish to eat?"

"Is there a good prime rib nearby?" I asked. Bill had come to the safe house, after making sure he wasn't followed.

"I know a restaurant," Bill nodded. He'd dropped by to give us updates—there still wasn't any word on Admiral Hafer, although everybody was looking for him, now.

"How did Larry get to the hotel?" I asked Bill later.

"He had a stolen car," Bill said as we climbed out of the van at a restaurant. "We're checking the area where the car was taken, but we haven't found anything yet."

Gavin, René, Tony and Winkler were all scanning the area as we walked toward the restaurant. I discovered that all of them were forming a circle around me, Bill included. Roff walked alongside me; Gavin had one of my arms, Roff the other.

Winkler ate half my prime rib, since it was too much food. It was good, though. I hadn't had anything like it in a long time. "What I can't figure out," I said, pushing half my baked potato in Winkler's direction, "is why they let Larry go to the hotel to do what he did. Surely they didn't think he was just going to walk away afterward with his life. I thought he was valuable to them, giving them his expertise along with what he took from me."

"I am concerned about this as well," Gavin agreed. "What changed to make him expendable?"

"We still don't have a line on the three humans that Lissa scented," Tony gestured with the swizzle stick from his obligatory drink. "Who are they? Did they work with Rahim, or did Xenides pick them up somewhere and force them to work with his vampires?"

"Maybe they have medical training, too," I suggested. "Larry was too well-known, and maybe these three were there to learn what they could from him before Xenides dumped him." Bill jerked his phone out of a pocket and punched a button.

I was thankful we'd gotten a private alcove at the restaurant since there were so many of us. Bill was asking questions the moment somebody picked up on the other end. Questions about doctors, medical personnel, EMTs or such that may have gone missing recently.

Bill was on the phone for maybe ten minutes while somebody did research somewhere. We were all listening in except Roff, whose hearing wasn't quite as good as everyone else's. I was leaning my forehead against Gavin's arm when the conversation was over.

Three research biologists had disappeared from the Atlanta area just before Tony and I had gone there to check things out. The official story was that they were friends and had gone camping together. They'd been lost somewhere in the Appalachian Mountains. The three men still hadn't been found, although their campsite had been searched thoroughly.

"Let me guess—they worked for the company in Atlanta that manufactured the flu vaccine." I mumbled against Gavin's arm; I didn't want to pull my head away. Honestly, I wanted to be somebody else, right then. Anybody would do. It just had to be somebody who didn't know what I knew and wasn't worried about what Xenides might be able to do from this point forward.

"Yes." Bill confirmed my worry after Gavin repeated my words to him—his hearing wasn't very good, either.

"At least we have names, now," Tony said. He was upset about this too, I could tell. René was rubbing Tony's shoulders.

You're such a good parent, I sent to René. He smiled, although he wasn't looking at me. He could receive, just as Gavin could. They just didn't have the talent to send back. Not normally, anyway. If Gavin got my blood, though—I sighed, thinking about the blood that Frazier had taken from me and handed to Xenides.

"So, have we done any more research on Hafer and Larry Frazier?"

I asked pulling my mind away from more frightening thoughts. "Since Larry did his hip replacement and heart surgery?" Bill's fork stopped halfway to his mouth.

"Lissa, I completely forgot about that," Winkler said. "Too many things happened and it went right out of my head." We hadn't mentioned it before—we'd speculated about Larry Frazier, figuring he'd pointed a finger in Hafer's direction as someone Xenides might target for information and state secrets. We'd never done any speculation on Hafer himself.

"Yeah, well, we got privileged information from a mutual source I can't name who said Hafer got Larry to do a hip replacement a few years ago and that he had some heart surgery done, too, but all of it was hushed up for some reason." I grimaced and knotted the napkin in my hands beneath the table. Things were starting to fall into place, and I didn't like the picture it presented.

"More than likely so the president wouldn't ask Hafer to retire— we always suspected he had other health issues and shouldn't have been involved in national security," Bill said, hauling out his cell again. "If Frazier was treating him and keeping it under wraps, that would keep Hafer in the thick of things, wouldn't it?" Bill was repeating exactly what Daniel Carey said. "Frazier might know exactly what kind of information Hafer might offer to Xenides, but there's another way this could go as well," Bill muttered.

"You don't think—oh my gosh." I wanted to slap my forehead again.

"I'm thinking the same thing, I'm sure," Bill said and punched a number on his cell.

"You think Hafer was spying, don't you Lissy?" Tony leaned around René and gave me a look. That would explain why Hafer was after me —I could get in anywhere and find any information.

"Hafer probably knew Larry was on that boat, didn't he? And even if Rahim or one of the others didn't get that information from Larry, they may have gotten it from Hafer. Which explains why he wanted me so bad."

I wanted to get up from the table right then and go looking for the bastard. We had to shut up when the President came on the line. Bill outlined his suspicions and asked for help from the FBI and CIA to pull financial records and such, including any aliases that Hafer might have used. The wheels were turning before Bill stopped talking.

"Lissa, I should have dinner with you more often; I get more work done that way," Bill sighed, slipping his phone in a jacket pocket.

"I remember when you were looking at me like I was the demon from hell du jour when Tony spilled the beans before," I lifted my wineglass in a toast.

"First impressions are often misleading, don't you think?" Bill smiled at me and held up his own glass. "I had no idea what Director Hancock was thinking when he dragged you along with us to Atlanta. You obviously weren't an agent; I could see that from a mile away. I was worried that Tony had developed an infatuation."

"I did, but Lissy wasn't having any of it," Tony grumbled. Gavin gave a satisfied grunt.

"Did you put Tony under compulsion and ask him?" I was now giving Gavin a hard stare. He was deliberately ignoring me. "You did, didn't you? You slime." I slapped him on the arm.

"Cousin, she just called you slime. Are you going to retaliate?" René was enjoying himself. So was Winkler; he was grinning. Our waiter came over and Winkler and Bill ordered dessert; I was too full even to think about it.

Too bad Gavin hadn't heard the conversation Winkler and I had in the coffee shop of the hotel before I'd been shot. If Gavin knew that Winkler had offered to take me somewhere so I couldn't be found, I figured the fur would fly.

"I will see about retaliation later," Gavin huffed.

"Uh-huh." I was contemplating misting away, but that would cause chaos, so I left things alone for the moment.

~

"I don't think we can save him." The physician was trying to tell

Franklin as gently as he could that it was only a matter of time. Greg was dying and there wasn't anything anyone could do.

Merrill's arm was around his human child's shoulders and he was doing his best to comfort Franklin. "Give us a moment, please," Merrill said. The physician nodded and walked out of the counselor's office, leaving Franklin and Merrill alone.

"Son, now is the time if you wish for me to take him and make him vampire," Merrill said softly, pulling Franklin's head against his shoulder.

"I want to but I promised I wouldn't," Franklin sobbed.

"Son, look at me," Merrill lifted Franklin's face. "If I turn him, then you'll have to agree to it, too. It won't do either of you any good if I do one and not the other. That's the way this works. Franklin, decide now if this is what you want."

"I can't do it, father. He said no. I promised."

Merrill sighed. "Child, we will get through this." Merrill kissed Franklin's forehead and pulled him closer. "Come, my child. We will sit with Greg." Franklin wiped his eyes when Merrill handed the handkerchief over, and then Merrill helped him stand and held him up as they made their way down the hospital corridor toward Greg's room.

"Lissa, I do not call you names when we are with others." Gavin was pointing out something I already knew.

"I know. I didn't mean to hurt you."

"Lissa," Gavin sighed. "I know I deserve most of what you level against me, but I would prefer that you do it when we are alone so I feel free to discuss these things with you."

"Are you going to listen or are you going to pretend to listen while you go through baseball stats in your head?" I asked tartly. "Just let me run down until I lose steam, pat me on the head and say that's nice, dear and go on about your business?"

"Lissa, please."

"Please what, Gavin? If you want me to do something or treat you a certain way, then you need to say something. I can't read your mind, you know. All I can do is send mindspeech. Not the same thing."

"Lissa, I am old. Sometimes I do not know how to deal with your youth or your humor. Mostly I have worked alone in the past, only occasionally working with other vampires. Even the ones three or four hundred years of age irritate me at times because they are so young."

"Gavin," I held up my left hand, wiggling his rings with my thumb. "You did this to yourself. Not that I don't love you—I do. I never thought that forty-nine would be young to anyone. In the human way of thinking, that's definitely on the down side. I'm sorry I can't add a thousand years to my life and behave in a more circumspect manner."

"Lissa, I know I am asking the impossible. How can I expect you to force that much time and experience into less than fifty years? I must be the one to develop patience, I think."

"I'm sorry I disappoint you," I muttered and misted away.

CHAPTER 12

hy pay for an aerial tour of our nation's capital, when you can mist? I might have been brushing away the occasional tear if I'd been anything other than mist. As it is, I got a good view of everything. I saw the Washington Monument, the Lincoln Memorial, flew over the Smithsonian (which I still wanted to see, someday) and breezed over the National Mall.

I saw all sorts of things until I got to the White House. *Been there, done that,* I was thinking, until I saw the helicopter out on the helipad and Secret Service surrounding the President. Director Bill Jennings was walking alongside said President.

Bill, I'm misting overhead, I sent to him. *What's going on?*

Bill broke away from the President's side as soon as I sent mindspeech and he was waving his arms, shouting, and then making gestures toward the sky, motioning me down. I went. I didn't know what those Secret Service guys thought when I suddenly appeared right next to Director Bill, but a barked "stop" from the President kept me from being shot again.

The helicopter was making a bit of noise—it was revving up. "Lissa, please say you can come along!" Bill's jacket was whipping about in the winds created by the rotor blades and he was shouting to make himself heard. "I wanted to bring you, but I couldn't get the others to agree or stay behind and the President didn't want a committee."

"I'll come," I nodded. Gavin and Wlodek would make sure there was hell to pay later, but then there was always hell to pay, no matter what I did. "Where are we going?" I thought to ask as Bill hauled me toward the President and the waiting helicopter.

"Camp David!" Bill shouted as I was hustled on board the helicopter, right behind the President.

We were flying along at a fast clip and I was still getting odd looks from the Secret Service guys. Maybe they'd never ridden in a helicopter with a vampire before. How was I to know? We were almost to our destination when I got mindspeech from Tony.

Lissy, Gavin is about to take the house apart. Where are you?

With the President and Director Bill, I returned. *Tell Gavin he can have his hissy fit when I get back.*

Lissy, I just told him where you were and I think it's a good thing you can't see his face right now.

Tony, find out if vampires can have a stroke, I sent back.

René says no, but apoplexy might be an option.

Is he yelling yet or calling Wlodek?

The phone is in his hand; I think he's waiting to calm down, first.

That could take a while. Tell him this is all my idea—I didn't know Bill wanted to take me; I just happened to be misting over the White House while they were revving up the helicopter.

Lissy, telling him this is all your idea may be a mistake right now.

Tony, you tell him and Wlodek too, that they'll never put me in one of those holding cells again.

Lissy, I don't have enough clout to tell anybody anything. I can give the info to René, but that's the best I can do.

I know. I hate being treated like a six-year-old.

Yeah. I'm right there with you on that.

∼

"What did she say?" Gavin snapped. René was right beside Tony in case Gavin became violent. He didn't want to fight Gavin, but he also didn't want Gavin attacking his newest child because he was the one receiving Lissa's mindspeech. Winkler and Roff had left the safe house the moment Gavin became angry.

"She said something about not liking the holding cells," Tony said, watching Gavin carefully.

"Inform her, please, that she is still recuperating from two gunshot wounds to her chest. Inform her please, that I am about to lose my mind. Inform her, please, that I have already lost my temper and I have been commanded by Wlodek to let him know if she goes off on her own at any time. Inform her, please, that the hole I am about to put in the wall is her fault and no other's."

Gavin set his cell phone carefully on the tiny kitchen table and then punched his fist through the cinderblocks of the wall so swiftly even Tony couldn't follow it. Bits of crumbled concrete followed Gavin's fist as he withdrew it from the newly formed hole in the wall. Tony could see the thick steel plate behind the cinderblocks was dented severely.

"Gavin is not angry with you," René assured Tony. Tony was worried about Lissa more than himself. Gavin lifted his phone after brushing bits of concrete off his hand and dialed Wlodek's number. It would be day soon in England, so Gavin was making the call as quickly as he could. Charles picked up immediately.

"Charles, I need to speak with the Honored One," Gavin growled. Charles wasted no time, getting Wlodek on the phone immediately.

"Gavin?" Wlodek's voice held a question.

"Our little Queen has gone off the reservation," Gavin snapped. Tony stood by and listened while Wlodek cursed fluently in Greek.

"How did you like the helicopter ride?" The President gave me a big smile as we climbed out of the SUV that had taken us from the helicopter pad to a nearby building. The sign out front said it was

Aspen lodge and I learned that all the cabins and buildings had tree names. There were guards everywhere—all Navy, I learned.

"It was fine except for the noise," I answered the President's question. Bill was right beside us, so I wasn't completely uncomfortable. I was dressed in jeans with a nice blouse and flats. Hey, I didn't know I was going to end up next to the President.

"You really do have sensitive ears?" The president was grinning as we walked inside Aspen Lodge.

"I can hear the other end of a cell phone conversation, even if you were standing over in that corner," I pointed to the corner farthest from us.

"That's outstanding," he said. "Come on; let's see what we can do about hammering out some peace." Bill and I walked behind the President; Secret Service agents and elite Navy guards drew in and surrounded us as we made our way into another room.

I recognized the Russian President right away and thought I knew who the other two were—Pakistan and Afghanistan came to mind. I was getting to see something I'd never thought to see; world leaders talking about what could be done concerning the current situations. Things might have come to some sort of congenial conclusions, too, if Admiral Hafer, five vampires and three former research biologists hadn't come to call.

The vampires had placed compulsion; otherwise, they'd have never gotten past the guards and Secret Service. What was I supposed to do? When Hafer and his newfound cronies rushed in with claws out or guns blazing, I gathered all four leaders and Director Bill inside my mist and got the hell out of there.

Camp David is located in the Catoctin Mountains in Maryland, and let me tell you, I was just about to have a meltdown, hauling the President and three world leaders along, all of them having a conniption in a different language. Bill was the only one remaining silent. I had to take these guys somewhere and then get back to Hafer and his posse.

The Visitor's Center down the mountain was closed when I dropped my cargo inside it, and I then did my best to place compulsion on three guys whose first language wasn't English.

I finally got things under control and felt very thankful that Bill had his cell phone with him. He was calling for a helicopter and as much firepower as he could get as I left him and the others behind. *Sorry, Mr. President,* I sent as I turned to mist and flew upward through the ceiling.

I discovered why three kidnapped research biologists had been dragged along on this little attempt at murder and espionage; they were there to inject my blood into three vampires. I saw three distinct spots of mist when I returned to Aspen Lodge. I was hovering in a corner of the ceiling, watching as three patches of mist floated closer to the floor. They weren't used to flying high overhead yet, so that might give me a bit of an advantage. I also didn't want to kill Hafer unless I had to—I figured Bill would like to get his hands on Mr. Spy Pants.

Hafer was ordering the remaining two vampires, the Secret Service and the Navy guards about, making me think they hadn't been alerted to his new status as a spy. Hafer was shouting at them, telling them that the President and his guests had been abducted and the entire compound needed to be searched.

He also told them to be on the lookout for a female spy (I'm assuming that meant yours truly). Hafer was also instructing them not to shoot at me or damage me in any way. At least he'd been briefed, whereas Larry Frazier hadn't. They still thought the President and the others were somewhere on the grounds. Hafer wasn't asking anyone to search anywhere else.

Winkler had his cell glued to his ear as he punched the code to get back into the safe house. Bill had called out the National Guard, in addition to anybody else available, including all four branches of the military.

Then he'd called Winkler, asking him to pass the message to Gavin and the others—he wanted their help. Camp David had been taken over by Admiral Hafer, a contingent of vampires and their human sheep.

Bill did explain that the President was safe and on his way back to the White House, along with three foreign dignitaries, but didn't elaborate past that. Gavin was growling as Winkler appeared in the basement of the safe house just as he was ending the call. Roff was directly behind the werewolf, his eyes huge and frightened.

"Hafer and those vampires tried to take the President and now they have control of Camp David," Winkler muttered. "Bill is sending a helicopter for us but we have to be at a helipad nearby as quickly as we can get there. Lissa saved the President and three others—they're safe at least, but she went back into the whole mess as soon as she got them away from there."

Gavin started cursing again until René intervened. "Cousin, she is doing what she can in a volatile situation. I know you worry for her, as do the rest of us. Let us go and see if we can offer assistance." Gavin quieted after that, nodded at René and motioned for Winkler to lead the way out of the safe house.

"Roff, do you wish to go?" René asked quietly. "I warn you, it will be extremely dangerous."

"I will stay here. Please keep the Raona safe," he whispered.

"That will be our top priority," René smiled at the comesula and followed the others out of the basement.

"You look an awful lot like Director Hancock," an FBI agent commented when Tony, Gavin and the others piled out of the van near the helicopter.

"He looks like no one you know," Gavin growled out compulsion. The agent nodded, his eyes going blank for a moment before leading them to the helicopter, its blades already whirling swiftly in preparation for takeoff. There were headsets for all of them as they climbed aboard and settled in.

This had turned into a waiting game—at least fifteen minutes had passed while Hafer and his cronies, surrounded by elite Navy guards, combed through the main building and then went on to the next, and the next after that. I hovered over their heads; they were frantically searching for the President and the others, sure that I'd be with them.

It was likely they intended to kill the President and the others, in order to cause an international incident. They'd made an attempt on the Vice President already; if that had succeeded, and then they'd succeeded in this attempt on the President and the others, the entire country would be in chaos. Gavin had been correct—Xenides wanted to destroy countries, along with getting his hands on me.

It was fortuitous that I'd sent mindspeech to Bill as he and the President were preparing to fly to Camp David. The fact that I'd agreed to come along with them was almost too good to be true. Too bad I couldn't get inside Hafer's brain to see what he or the two vampires who weren't mist were thinking. As it was, I was afraid to go lower, not while the other three were still mist. I wondered how long they could remain mist. I think I was about to find out.

One of the vampires began to rise higher inside the building currently being searched, so I was forced to hover next to a fluorescent light, hoping he wouldn't be able to distinguish my white mist from that of the artificial light. He couldn't, and I heaved a mental sigh of relief. He did search out every corner of the room, though, carefully checking to see if I was there.

There was sudden shouting and a commotion outside—evidently the cavalry had arrived and more compulsion was about to be placed for the Navy guards to fire on their fellow soldiers. I misted through the ceiling while the others rushed for the door—they hadn't discovered that they could mist through walls—another advantage I held over them.

The two vampires that weren't mist were shouting out orders laced with heavy compulsion for the guards to start shooting. They did. And if something wasn't done soon, then this would likely turn into a bloodbath.

Hafer was hiding behind his two vampires as well as he could, the jerk. He was doing his best to get honest, loyal soldiers killed just so he and Xenides could get what they wanted. Bullets were now flying indiscriminately, several of which zinged right through my mist. Yeah, I wasn't crazy about being shot at again, even if the bullets didn't do any damage. I heard a helicopter in the distance and figured more troops were coming.

I misted toward the ground troops that had just arrived to see if I could help them in any way. They were down low, completely puzzled over why their own were shooting at them. I found Bill and a few other important people at the back of that crowd. I dropped toward them at an incredible rate of speed.

Bill, I'm right beside you, I sent.

"Lissa, come on out, we'll cover this up," Bill said, still bending low with the three others with him. Bullets were still flying overhead.

"I sure hope you can cover this up," I muttered dryly, materializing next to him in a kneeling position. "Three of theirs are invisible right now."

"Can they hurt any of ours?" Bill was worried, and I now had three sets of eyes trained on me. Looked like bigwigs from the Army, Navy and Marines. I figured the Air Force were the ones flying around the perimeter of the camp.

"If they figure out what they can do before the effects wear off," I grumbled while a bullet cracked into a tree limb over our heads. Honestly, I was about to get pissed and go after those schmucks anyway, mist or no mist.

"Lissa, what will they do to you while you're mist?" Bill asked while more bullets whacked into the tree over our heads. Somebody had our location, looked like.

"You know, I don't think they can do much at all." I smiled sweetly at Bill, gave him a kiss for pointing out the obvious, (which shocked the hell out of him, I'm sure) and misted away in a heartbeat.

Two vampires died swiftly, their heads and bodies separately turning to ash in seconds. Three research biologists under compulsion were then gathered and dropped in the midst of the advancing soldiers; they were disarmed and restrained quickly.

Admiral Hafer was then jerked up and hauled straight to Bill; I dropped him from ten feet overhead, breaking a few bones when he hit the ground like a sack of bricks. Hafer's gun flew out of his hand and he yelped as he fell.

Now, the three that were mist were chasing me; they'd seen me finally and I was about to see how long they could remain mist. I flew straight east as fast as I could go while they tried their best to keep up with me. I had experience being mist—they didn't.

After ten minutes, we were over the Atlantic. I didn't want them dropping into the ocean and possibly living over this, so I turned and headed toward land. Good thing, too—the injection of my blood wore off and the first one materialized, dropping right out of the sky, screaming all the way down.

I swooped in and gathered him into my mist. Let me tell you—he could curse in as many languages as Gavin. The second one rematerialized and dropped. We picked him up as well. The third one was misting toward the ground when he turned and I still managed to get him. Now, what to do with them?

Tony, is Gavin still having a rant? I sent. My mental voice sounded weary, even to my own ears. Karzac had been correct—I hadn't waited the extra day to get over my bullet wounds to the chest and I was tiring.

He is, but we're here at Camp David, now, Tony replied.

Tell me where you are, I have the three misters, I informed him mentally. *You guys need to be ready; we need these dead as soon as I dump them on the ground.* Tony described where he, Gavin and René were, so I headed in that direction.

I didn't dump the vampires gently, either, opting to fling them onto the ground. Gavin, Tony and René didn't take long to remove heads from bodies, and Bill and his buddies were there to witness the entire thing. Gavin was growling and had my upper arm in a tight grip as soon as I appeared. I didn't expect anything else, to be honest.

I heard René placing compulsion on humans as Gavin hauled me toward a nearby stand of trees. "Lissa, I want an explanation and I want it now," Gavin's eyes were dark and his fangs were showing.

"Gavin, I don't have any excuse. You're right as usual. I'll try harder next time." I'm not sure what he wanted to hear, if anything. I was terrified and exhausted at the same moment. Anybody else would be terrified, too, with Gavin like that.

I'd seen anger before—killing anger. Alcohol-induced, crazed and irrational. Watched my mother die as a result, and then took blows meant to kill me afterward. I had no desire to wait for Gavin to deliver any blows of his own, so I was shaking and prepared to go to mist in a blink.

Yes, I was watching Gavin's hands, now, and not his face. That would be my signal—when those fists clenched or the claws formed. I took a step backward. Gavin followed, still shouting and cursing. I'd stopped trying to translate the words; I was watching his body, waiting for the blows to come. When I saw the fists clench, instinctively I raised my arms to ward off the inevitable punch. I think I was crying by that time.

"Lissa, stop crying. Please." Winkler was kneeling beside me, an arm around my shoulders. I don't know what happened—I'd dropped to the ground while Gavin had been shouting, expecting him to hit me at any moment, he was so angry.

And then I couldn't stop sobbing. Couldn't. I heard someone nearby, telling someone else that drugs had no effect on me so the tranquilizer should be put away. I heard René's voice, quietly talking to Gavin, who wasn't saying anything, now.

"Lissy, you can't have a breakdown now," Tony was kneeling on my other side. "Baby, we need you. We can't do this without you. He didn't mean it, he was just upset. He wasn't going to hit you, pretty girl. I promise."

"Come on," Winkler coaxed softly, drawing my arms around his neck and lifting me up. I was sobbing against his neck, now. He carried me toward Gavin, René, Bill and a few others standing there on the leaf-strewn grounds of Camp David on a September night, quiet now except for my sobs.

Gavin and René were on a conference call with Wlodek. Gavin was a wreck. "I have not seen this before, not in a vampire," René sighed. "She believed that Gavin was going to strike her. As soon as his fists clenched, she dropped to the ground and we could not stop the weeping. She cried herself out after four hours, when sunrise came."

Wlodek's fingers stilled on his gold pen. Gavin and René were in Director Bill Jennings' office. He'd set up the conference call for them. Charles had set up the webcam from their end and Gavin and René both watched Wlodek's face. It held no expression, as usual. "I can do nothing about this from so far away," Wlodek said after several moments of silence.

"We were hoping that Merrill, perhaps, or even Lissa's father, if he could be contacted," René suggested.

"No, Merrill cannot be disturbed at this time," Wlodek sighed. "Gavin, I have never seen you allow your temper to run away with you like this," Wlodek went on. "This is your mate. You know how fragile she can be in this respect. What were you thinking?"

"And I did this in a public place," Gavin reluctantly admitted.

"He didn't say anything that would reveal the race," René offered. "He was shouting as an angry husband might. Well, as some angry husbands might," he amended.

"Will she be able to function after this?" Wlodek asked quietly. "Where is she now and what is she doing?"

"I left her in bed at the safe house. I wanted her to sleep as long as possible. I think the recent injury as well as exhaustion may be playing a part in all this since she has been awake so much during the day," Gavin muttered. Wlodek had already been advised regarding Lissa's adventures during the day. He understood now what Griffin's blood had done for her.

"At least she was able to eliminate Xenides' minions," Wlodek remarked, staring at the gold pen in his hands. "But there are others still out there and the threat in Kansas has not been dealt with. We need her help with this. If this is not possible as a result of this breakdown, I expect to be alerted immediately."

"We will let you know," René promised and terminated the call.

My head was pounding when I woke and Roff was there, waiting for me to wake, a glass of ice water in his hands. "Roff, I feel sick," I scooted up in the bed, my head in my hands. It felt like a migraine, to be honest, and I wished that aspirin or something actually worked right then.

"Raona, will a bath help?" Roff was trying to coax me off the bed.

"Roff, my head feels like it may explode," I muttered.

"Weeping will do that," he pulled my head against his chest and stroked my jaw. Roff pushed and pulled, coaxed, begged and cajoled until he had me soaking in a bathtub full of hot water, a cool compress over my forehead and eyes.

That's where Gavin found me when he came in. I don't know where he'd been and at the moment, I didn't really care. He'd frightened me the night before, causing something to happen that hadn't happened in a long time.

Don was the only one who'd ever seen one of those—some sort of breakdown. I'd had several in the first few years after Howard Graham nearly killed me, but nothing in the past decade or so—until now, that is. I suppose it was the injury, the stress and the exhaustion, all weighing in at once. Roff left the bathroom quietly. I didn't make a move, leaving the compress over my eyes. I knew Gavin was there by his scent. He knew I knew as well.

"I'm not going to apologize," I said right off. "That hasn't happened for at least ten years. Hopefully it won't happen again."

"Cara, what hasn't happened in ten years?" Gavin's voice was gentle. Where did that come from? It was as far from what he'd been last night as it was possible to be.

"Don called it crying jags. It happened a lot in the first five years after Howard Graham, well," I didn't finish. "Only once in a while after that before it finally went away. Until last night."

"Cara, I am not Howard Graham."

"I know."

"Cara, I will not touch you in anger."

"Gavin, you say that now. What if I make you mad again? Howard Graham always promised my mother that he wouldn't hit her again. Until he'd get drunk the very next day and break his promise," I pulled the compress off my eyes. The light in the bathroom made me squint and ramped up the headache.

"Headache?"

"Migraine."

"Worse."

"Yes."

"He yelled and cursed, didn't he?" The subject had changed again. Gavin now knelt next to the bathtub, taking the compress out of my hand and settling it over my eyes again. "While he beat you and your mother."

"And before and after, don't forget that." I slipped down farther into the water. There was no bubble bath in this water, it was perfectly clear. Gavin could see every bit of me. I felt a little embarrassed, but then he'd seen every bit of me for a while, now. Gavin took the mesh sponge, dribbled body wash on it and proceeded to give me a slow and lazy bath.

After a while, he began to talk. First in Italian, then switching to French. Telling me how beautiful I was. He kissed my hands and my fingers. Traced my collarbone and nipples with the sponge, and then with his fingers. Said he loved my ankles and kissed those when he lifted them out of the water. And then he started to talk about Howard Graham.

"How could he harm this?" Gavin ran fingers down my ribs. "Could he not see how fine and beautiful it was? Why would any man harm a child, even if it were not his?" Gavin leaned in and placed a kiss—the first of the evening—on my mouth. "Cara, when you are away from me, I dream of your mouth." He kissed me again. Eventually he pulled me out of the tub after the water had cooled, wrapped me up in my robe and carried me out of the bathroom.

"There is our little rose," René said when Gavin carried me into the kitchen to feed me a bag of blood. At least two-thirds of a bag, anyway. Winkler, Roff and Tony watched as I had my meal.

"Our girl is fine except for the terrible headache," Gavin put the rest of my blood back in the fridge. I think they all heaved a sigh of relief.

∽

"We have records of deposits, as well as the aliases and the addresses of several homes across the globe connected to those aliases," Bill thumped a thick folder down in front of Admiral Hafer. "Along with names of contacts. Rahim Alif has no loyalty to you, Admiral. He's been handing out information right and left about you. Now, suppose you tell us what you know and which information you've handed to the enemy, or so help me, I'll see you crucified."

Admiral Hafer sat in one of the interrogation rooms at FBI Headquarters, casts on one arm and both legs. He'd been inside those rooms before, only on the other end of the questioning. He knew the drill. He also knew exactly what was going to happen to him.

His ex-wife and his son would be crucified with him and they hadn't even suspected. Alif hadn't been the only one pulling his strings, he now knew. The powerful vampire Xenides had gotten Alif involved to begin with.

It was a game to Hafer in the beginning. He just hadn't realized how far it would go or how deeply it would wound the country. He suspected now that he'd been under some sort of compulsion all along, but Director Jennings wasn't going to accept that as an excuse. Admiral Hafer's career—and his life—were over.

I was huddled against Gavin's side as we watched the early news before dawn. The news crews had gotten word that something had gone down at Camp David two nights before and were pressing the White House for information. Eventually the White House Press Secretary held a press conference, explaining that campers had gotten lost and wandered into the space normally off-limits to visitors. He denied any altercation and said the situation was resolved amicably. That made Gavin snort while I laughed.

"How is you headache, cara?" he leaned down to kiss my forehead.

"Better. I hope it goes away when I sleep," I yawned.

Xenides had seen the misdirected information released by the White House and wanted to shout and tear the hotel down. Alif captured, Hafer captured or dead, five of his vampires dead—he hadn't gotten an answer when he'd tried to call and the three research biologists Frazier had trained were likely dead as well.

Xenides' anger was at a dangerous simmer, but he still had several trump cards up his sleeve. He'd see about putting those into play very soon. Meanwhile, he cursed the vampires who'd died; they'd failed him for the last time.

CHAPTER 13

"Wear this, cara." Gavin had packed for me, with Roff's help, when we'd left Oklahoma City. Now he was holding up the dark green dress that he'd paid a fortune for last year in Dallas. It was V-necked with long sleeves, hugged my breasts and waist and had a flared skirt that came tastefully to my knees. There was a pair of brown designer heels to go with it.

We had an invitation to the White House and Bill told Winkler that the President wouldn't accept no as an answer. Therefore, we were going. Bill sent a limo for us so we packed into it; Gavin, René, Winkler and Tony all dressed in expensive suits.

I hadn't seen Michael in days, only now learning that the werewolf agents Renfro and Delgado had taken him with them to do a bit of moonlighting. I hoped he was happy and impressing Director Bill.

Roff had no desire to go with us to the White House and Bill said it was all right if he didn't come. Just as well, I wasn't sure how to explain to the President that not only was he entertaining vampires and a werewolf but a genuine alien as well.

We almost had a private audience with the President and First Lady—Bill was there, the Vice President was there, and the Speaker of the House. Apparently, he was in on the secret too, though I'd never met him before. He knew Tony; that much was certain.

Secret Service agents led us into the oval office, the doors were closed and we were offered drinks. We were all seated comfortably while we talked with the President, the First Lady and the others.

"Lissa," the President finally said, "I can't begin to tell you how much I appreciate what you did for me earlier. If you hadn't come along, things might have turned out badly."

This sort of thing always embarrassed me, and I discovered that I could now flush, which embarrassed me further.

"It was nothing," I mumbled, attempting to wave off the praise.

"It might be nothing to you, but it means a great deal to us. That's why you'll join a select few in receiving a second Medal of Freedom tonight. Lissa, will you stand to receive this honor?" The President stood and Gavin had to help me stand as everyone else in the room stood as well.

My knees were knocking together, I was so nervous. The Vice President handed the velvet case to the First Lady who opened it, allowing the President to lift the medal out so he could place it around my neck. He leaned down and gave me a peck on the cheek, too, as he shook my hand.

"Thank you," I barely got the words out while dipping my head in respect. Thank goodness our group was small; I was obligated to wear that thing for another hour as we made small talk.

The First Lady admired my ring, so of course I had to tell her that Gavin was my husband. Surprisingly, he was quite smooth about the whole thing when she started asking questions, such as how we met and how long we'd been married. He only gave the facts, stating that we'd met in Texas and had only been married a short while. She might have been shocked out of her shoes if she knew all the particulars in between.

"Will we see other female vampires?" The Vice President joined the conversation. Gavin cleared his throat.

"Most female vampires are much too shy," René offered a

disarming smile as he and Tony came to the rescue. Winkler grinned and winked at me from his place at Bill's side.

"Lissa is the only vampire I know that could do this sort of thing," Tony added. That much was certainly true.

"How do you feel about joining their ranks?" The President asked Tony.

"I like it very much," Tony replied. "Although it does have its drawbacks." The First Lady found that amusing.

"I take it you were near death after the bombing in Paris?" The Vice President wanted to know.

"That is correct, otherwise it would not have been considered," Tony inclined his head. René placed a hand on Tony's shoulder as a warning—not to give too much away.

We finally were allowed to leave, after assuring the President that Bill had our number. Bill walked out with us and got us loaded into the Limo. "The President wanted to meet with you alone, Lissa," he told me before shutting the door on my side. "The Secret Service wouldn't allow it."

"Are the other three all right?" I asked, meaning the foreign heads of state I'd hauled away from Camp David.

"They're fine; perhaps a bit disgruntled over their shuffling off to the White House for the meeting. Camp David is being put back together as we speak. Hafer won't ever see the free light of day again." Bill closed the door and our driver pulled out.

"We will leave tomorrow evening for Oklahoma City," Gavin said after we got back to the safe house. He'd gone outside for a while to have a private conversation with Wlodek and came back in with a grim expression on his face.

I had no idea what the conversation entailed, but I'm sure it involved me, somehow. I packed up Medal of Freedom number two and placed it in the bottom of my suitcase, along with the green dress and heels. It was unlikely I'd be wearing them again before this trip was done.

September was nearly over when we landed in Oklahoma City; Roff pointed that out to me. His watch was working just fine, thank you, and once again, I contemplated smacking Gavin for giving it to him.

"We have two days here and then we must travel to Kansas City," Gavin informed all of us on the drive from the airport to the house in Nichols Hills. Something about that bothered me, but I couldn't put my finger on it.

Gavin wasn't talking much, either, for some reason. Normally he didn't talk much, but he was bordering on complete silence now and that worried me.

Winkler was eating in the kitchen the following evening with Michael, who'd flown in separately. I'd made spaghetti for them—with meatballs, of course, when Winkler's cell rang. Trajan, Winkler's Second was on the other end; I recognized his voice.

"Boss—it looks like Kellee's in labor. No false alarms this time," came through loud and clear. Winkler was standing up as soon as the words were out of Trajan's mouth.

"I'll be there in a couple of hours," Winkler said and terminated the call. "I'm going to the airport," he said. "I'll leave my things here; I can pick them up later. Michael—Bill said to tell you to give him a call when this is over and he may have a job for you. Lissa, gotta go."

I stood there, gaping like a fool at Winkler. What else could I do? I thought Winkler was going to be with us through this whole thing. I should have known better. Multiple births tend to come early and not the other way around. Somehow, I wished I could go with him, just so I could see the babies when they were new.

"Winkler, you're gonna be a good father," I came over and hugged him, trying not to cry.

"Lissa, I'll make sure the twins know they have an aunt. I hope I see you again really soon." He leaned down and gave me a kiss—he didn't care that Gavin had just walked into the room. Winkler waved as he strode swiftly toward the front door and then he was gone. I wanted to run after him, but that wouldn't do. I stayed right there, rooted to the spot, while Gavin came to put his arms around me.

"Children on the way?" he asked softly.

"Yeah," I nodded against his shoulder.

"If there were any way, I would take you," he murmured against my hair.

"I know," I said, reaching up to wipe away the tear that insisted on falling. Gavin led me out of the house and I went with him, climbing the steps to our second-floor guesthouse. Kifirin was there when we opened the door and Roff stood beside him, his bag packed. He looked as miserable as I felt.

"I am sorry, avilepha, but I must take Roff back to his home, now. Giff has already been taken there, earlier today. I regret that I must take him at such a difficult time for you, but I have no choice. Roff must go home."

Kifirin's dark gaze held torment, and I had no explanation for it. Gavin held me up when my knees threatened to buckle. I wanted to fall to the floor and weep. I thought all my tears had been spent five nights ago, but I was very wrong. I knew if I said the word that I wanted to say—*why?*—that I would break down again.

"M'hala, it must be so. Do not forget that my love is forever," Kifirin sighed and he and Roff disappeared before I could reach out to touch either of them.

"Mr. President, do you think I haven't asked already? That Director Hancock didn't ask before me?" Bill huffed as the President looked at him across his desk, fingertips together and a slight frown on his face. "The ones we deal with—the ones in charge—will not allow her anywhere near the Middle East. That was a stipulation in order to get her help at all. In fact, when Director Hancock took her on that trip to the Arabian Sea, he was breaking his agreement with them."

"Why are they insisting on this?" The President lowered his hands but his gaze remained fixed on Director Jennings' face. "She could do so many things if we could just get her over there to work with our field agents."

"Mr. President, the information I have gathered I am not supposed to know. In fact, if her superiors knew that I hold such information, my life might be in jeopardy."

"What information is that, Director?"

"That there are only a handful of female vampires. They are nearly impossible to turn, as I understand it. As for Lissa, well, she isn't like any of the others. You've seen a little of what she can do. They have a name for what she is, Mr. President."

"And what is that?"

"They call her Queen, sir."

We didn't speak, Gavin and I. We just sat on the roof of a mansion in Nichols Hills, Gavin staring at the Oklahoma City skyline while I examined the toes of my athletic shoes. I shivered now and then, though I wasn't cold.

All at once, it had happened. One blow after another. Experiencing one of those moments in my life when I might have given just about anything to crawl out of my skin and into someone else's, in order to leave the suffering behind until it reached a more bearable level. My forehead was against my knees and Gavin, wisely, didn't touch or speak.

"He's gone." The doctor and a nurse stood before Franklin as Merrill slipped an arm around his shoulders. Franklin turned, placed both arms around Merrill's neck and wept. Greg had left him; only the machines had kept his body alive until Franklin gave permission to turn them off. That had been bare moments earlier. Greg had taken three breaths after the ventilator was shut off, each slower than the last until there were no more.

217

"Leave us," Merrill commanded and the doctor and nurse left the room quickly. "Child," Merrill held Franklin away from him gently, "we must say goodbye to Greg. If there is anything else you wish to say to him, then now is the time."

"I love you, Greg," Franklin's voice was agonized. Merrill led him to the bed, and Franklin collapsed against it, holding Greg's hand one last time.

∾

Kansas City always looks so green to me, with trees everywhere. Oklahoma City generally turns brown toward the end of summer. Don and I used to go to Kansas City now and then—they have nice museums there to visit and we could get there in five or six hours. The Nelson-Atkins Museum of Art was one of my favorites. There would be no museum visit on this trip.

"Gavin, do you ever go to art museums?" I asked as he drove our rental toward a hotel. It was Sunday night—the twenty-sixth of September.

"If there are any open late enough for me to visit. I have been to the Louvre several times, as well as the Rijksmuseum. I am glad you kept the Vermeer, cara. Of all the works collected by Sergio, that would have been the one I would have kept as well."

"Yeah. Someday, I want to hang it in my own home."

"Cara, that is the first time you have said such a thing to me." Gavin turned to study my face. "I know my apartments are not suitable, even if they were updated. I have never taken the opportunity nor held the desire to change my address for a very long time. When your five years of training are over, love, I will buy any home you want and we will hang your painting in a place of honor."

"All right," I leaned back in my seat with a sigh. René and Tony sat in the back seat, listening to us. Michael had been willing to come, but Gavin told Wlodek he didn't think it was necessary, so the werewolf made his call to Director Bill. He'd be leaving in three days for D.C. and an interview. I hoped things worked out for him.

I missed Roff and I missed Winkler. Why hadn't Kifirin stayed to explain why Roff had to leave, or at least given me a chance to hug him before he left? Winkler called just before dawn after he left, saying that William Wayne Winkler, Jr. and Wynter Willow Winkler had come into the world, both beautiful and exercising their lungs. Winkler had even sent photos through his cell. I'd shown them to Gavin, who smiled.

"How did you get a Vermeer?" Tony's curiosity got the better of him and his question pulled me away from my thoughts.

"Lissa's original sire, now deceased, had quite an art collection," René said. Neither Gavin nor I wanted to talk about that.

I asked Gavin if I could borrow his laptop when we got to the hotel, but he informed me that he had work to do so I left it and flipped through the titles on my e-reader, searching for a good book to read.

I'd intended to email Franklin and Greg—I was worried since I hadn't heard from either of them in several weeks. I hoped everything was all right, but I figured Merrill would let me know if they weren't. Maybe they'd gone to Monte Carlo, this time; they seemed to enjoy the gambling in Vegas. I sure hoped somebody somewhere was having a good time.

I hadn't truly felt good, either, since Larry Frazier shot me twice in the chest, but I didn't want to tell Gavin. There wasn't any way to gauge what his reaction would be. Honestly, I just wanted to go home and realized that England was home. With Franklin and Greg. And Merrill, when he wasn't making me crazy.

I wanted to have a sit-down with Griffin, too, and ask a lot of questions. About his side of the family. He'd said he was more than a hundred thousand years old—surely, he had family somewhere. I wanted to know about them. Who they were, where they lived, what they did. So far, he hadn't offered anything, other than the information that he was my father and that he'd been punished and kept from seeing me. I wanted that explained fully.

Gavin packed up his laptop around dawn and hauled me off to bed without even letting me finish a chapter in the mystery I was reading. And I had another dream—the first one in weeks, I think.

I was standing in a small clearing, thinking I recognized it somehow—as if I'd seen it before. Trees surrounded me on all sides and it was dark beneath their withering leaves. The air inside the clearing began to shimmer and I realized, even though I was dreaming, that this was another gate—just like the one I'd seen before when a young Xenides and others had walked through it. Only this time, I was close enough to feel the power of the gate—to feel the pull it exerted on me.

I stepped closer and heard conversation—laughter even—as the Elemaiya came through. The energy of the gate whispered through me, luring me, coaxing me. Telling me what I needed to know to walk through it and go anywhere I wished to go. Anywhere. As long as a gate existed there, I was free to travel. That fascinated me. Called to me. Offered itself to me.

I had to borrow a couple dollars from Gavin's money clip. I hadn't replenished my cash since I'd handed what I had to Winston Byrnett and his female companion. Hadn't needed any cash, either—someone else always paid or I used my credit card. Now, here I was, up again during the day and standing in front of the hotel's soda machine. An orange soda had my name on it if I could get one of my dollars to straighten up and go through the machine properly.

"Here, try this." A very tall young man was there, his light-brown hair combed neatly and a smile in his blue eyes. He offered to trade a better single for the one I had. I gave him my best smile and accepted the trade. It worked, so I thanked him again and walked down the hall drinking orange soda as I went. I was sitting up in bed, finishing off my soda and reading when Gavin woke for the evening. I don't think I'd ever seen him wake before. His eyes popped right open.

"I wish I could wake up like that," I said.

"Lissa, what are you doing awake?" he was growling at me and eyeing his laptop case immediately after. That worried me for an instant, until Gavin pulled me down next to him and proceeded to make me forget everything except him for a while.

While we cleaned up afterward, Gavin informed me that we were checking out a location later. "Cara, I want you to go to mist and if you see anything or notice anything strange or out of the ordinary, I expect you to send René, Tony and me mindspeech immediately. And, if we are in danger, you know to take us up as mist and get us away." Gavin held my chin in his fist and leaned down to kiss me in the shower.

"You don't have to tell me twice," I huffed.

"Where are we going?" I asked, as Gavin led the way out of the hotel later, René and Tony right behind us.

"Lissy, there are caves around here and we've had people checking them out," Tony was the one to answer. "We got the idea that some of Xenides' spawn or allies might be using the caves to hide out if they decided to go after your cousins."

My two remaining relatives lived in the area and that's why I thought we'd come to begin with. Kansas City had a warren of caves—in fact, they'd used some of them to house businesses and such. It made sense that vampires might use them as well. I turned in my seat to look at Tony, who sat right behind me in the rented SUV. Gavin had gotten it because he wanted something with four-wheel drive. Now I knew why.

"Bill was going to meet us here, but something came up," Tony went on. "He had to take his vamps and wolves out of the country on some secret mission." Tony sounded grumpy over that—more than likely because he hadn't been included in the information handout.

"You think things might be in an uproar since Rahim got caught?" I asked.

"Lissy, I think that's exactly what happened. We caught one of theirs, so now they want to retaliate. Rahim was a hero to some of those people."

"Yeah, that's what I thought, too," I turned around and leaned back in my seat.

"Cara, you cannot take responsibility for the unrest in those countries," Gavin said. I wasn't sure what I could take responsibility for, but I didn't mention that to Gavin.

Tony pulled some sort of GPS device out of a case when we parked near a wooded area a few minutes later, flipped it on and started walking. Gavin, René and I followed, after I turned to mist.

We walked for perhaps a mile and a half before Tony started pointing—we'd apparently come to some sort of prearranged spot. I wondered then where the information had come from and what it included. I was so busy trying to hover over Tony's shoulder now, attempting to decipher what was showing on the little screen he was studying that I failed to notice my surroundings for a few moments.

When I eventually gave up on the little numbers on Tony's tracking device, I did look around and gave a mental gasp. It was the clearing from my dream. We were right in the middle of it.

Tony, there's a gate here, I sent. That puzzled him—he didn't know what a gate was. He'd walked ahead of me, leaving me behind to consider the situation.

Lissy, what are you talking about? I don't see any gate. Tony was looking for a physical gate and there wasn't one. The light at the center of the clearing shimmered—I could see it as mist but the others couldn't.

Gavin, I think we need to get out of here, I warned as the light began to glow brighter.

"Cara, I don't see, hear or smell anything," Gavin said aloud. Crap. They didn't see it for sure.

"What is wrong?" René asked and then he froze. René was old, as was Gavin. They both recognized the sound, brief as it was, although they hadn't seen what I had. Gavin was already mist and I was rushing toward Tony and René at blinding speed but they'd wandered too far ahead of Gavin—Tony following the directions of his little device instead of paying attention to any of his surroundings.

René knew before any of us; he flung himself forward, shoving his youngest vampire child to the ground as the gate opened and the Dark Elemaiya opened fire with bows and wooden shafts.

I lifted René and Tony into my mist and following my instincts, misted right through the gate, picking up a dozen Dark Elemaiya as I did so. Remembering my dream from the night before, I focused on where I wished to go—which was the only other gate I knew. The one on Merrill's property. The one Griffin had closed to all except those of his kind and a few others. I was hoping—no, praying—that I was one of the few others.

It all happened in a blink or two. The second gate was before me and I opened it with a mental flick of power, hoping right then that it would allow me passage. It did. I went right through, Gavin, René and Tony with me.

Somehow, the Dark Elemaiya I carried were filtered out of my mist and died as I flew through the gate on Merrill's property; frying on a grid of power erected by my natural father, who knew how long ago. They shrieked and screamed as they died, too, but I didn't have time to worry about that. I'd seen the arrow aimed right at Tony and I had to make sure he was all right.

After setting my burdens down as gently as I could on the damp grass and leaves that littered the area surrounding the gate, I found the damage that had been done. Tony was fine, as was Gavin. Somehow, though, my mist had only delayed the inevitable for René.

A black shaft protruded from his chest and his eyes were wide and filled with pain. "No!" I heard my own harsh cry and I was on my knees next to René in a flash. I'd lost too many people lately. René couldn't leave me, too. Tony loved him. Looked to him as a father. And René was an exceptional parent—kind and loving.

"René, don't leave me," I begged. I was weeping by that time and clutching René's hand in mine. Tony was kneeling beside me and begging as well. Gavin was crouching on René's other side, looking gray.

"Little rose," René whispered, squeezing my hand. "The bloom is on your cheeks, my pretty one," he told me. "I thought you would never come to me." His hand turned to ash inside mine and I sobbed as rain began to fall around us.

~

I don't know how Gavin managed to haul Tony and me to Merrill's—

it was half a mile away and neither Tony nor I were in any shape to walk. We were sobbing the entire time and Gavin had his own sorrow to deal with.

The door was locked and the lights were dim inside the manor, so Gavin had to work to get me calm enough to mist the three of us through the door. I did it finally, but it was painful.

The house was completely deserted for some reason and it was near dawn, too. Gavin pulled Tony and me upstairs, tending to Tony first while I wept on Tony's bed. Gavin shoved Tony into the shower, turned it on as cold as it would go, got him out of his clothes and eventually calmed him down.

"Lissy, what am I going to do?" Tony was wrapped in a robe and shivering as he crawled onto the bed beside me. I'd never seen him like this.

"Anthony, should the Honored One allow it, I will take over my cousin's teachings," Gavin's voice was rough with emotion as he sat on the edge of the bed.

"I'm so sorry," I flung my arms around Gavin's neck, shedding even more tears.

"Cara, don't," Gavin wrapped me in his arms. Tony hugged up against my back and that's where dawn found us.

I got Tony situated on his bed and then carrying Gavin easily, took him down to our shared bedroom, undressing him and covering him up. After that, I wandered listlessly through the house.

Deryn and Paul—the two werewolves, were gone. Their rooms were empty on the third floor and their scents were only a memory. Giff's things, too, were all gone, just as Kifirin said. Franklin, Greg and Merrill were also gone, and Merrill hadn't mentioned that they were going anywhere.

I wasn't about to go to the basement. It would be weird to find Wlodek sleeping the sleep of the dead so I left that alone. I wanted to call Merrill but it was daylight. I thought about calling Charles and the same reason reared its ugly head. That's why I ended up calling Weldon, who quickly put me on a conference call with Winkler.

"They killed René," I was trying not to cry again.

"Lissa, baby, it's all right," Winkler was trying to soothe me from thousands of miles away. He didn't need to be handling a vampire basket case right now—he was a new father and had his own set of worries.

"Lissa, there's nothing we can say right now that will lessen the pain. All we can tell you is that we love you and we'll support you through this in any way we can. If you need someone to come, then someone will come." Weldon always knew the right words.

"Weldon, I'll have to let you know. Right now, I don't know where Merrill is. And Tony's worse off than I am, I think."

"René was his sire. I figured that out," Winkler sighed. "This is bad."

"Yeah," I wiped a tear away. We talked for a few more minutes and Weldon convinced me to lie down.

"Try to get some sleep, sweetheart. Just close your eyes for a while, all right?" We said goodbye and I huddled on the sofa inside Merrill's large media room on the first floor. That's where Charles found me later when the sun went down.

I jerked awake when his fingers touched my cheek. "Lissa, how are you here?" he asked, stunned wonder in his voice.

"Charles," my heart was pounding now with remembered pain. "René is dead. He was killed with a wooden arrow."

Gavin was shouting my name only a heartbeat later, and he and Tony were both racing downstairs, searching for me.

"I'm here, honey, I'm fine, I just fell asleep on the sofa," I brushed more tears off my face. Wlodek and Rolfe found us there; Gavin sat next to me and crushed me against him while Tony sat on the other side.

"René got killed," Charles passed the information off to Wlodek.

Wlodek sat down heavily in a chair nearby. "Explain, please," he sighed. Gavin was the one to tell the story.

"They came through a gate?" Wlodek asked.

"Lissa saw it, I did not," Gavin said. "Nevertheless, René and I both heard the bowstring as it was drawn back. Lissa tried to gather us up as quickly as she could, but René rushed to protect his youngest. That is how he died."

Tony was the target, I'm sure of it, I sent directly to Wlodek. He never twitched, although I know he heard me.

"Gavin, Anthony, come with me. There are arrangements to be made," Wlodek said after he'd gotten the whole story, asking questions here and there and going over parts of it two or three times. Gavin and Tony rose and followed Wlodek and Charles as they made their way toward Wlodek's temporary offices in the basement. Rolfe stayed upstairs—he would be guarding the house.

"Rolfe, where is Merrill?" I asked.

"Your surrogate sire is in New York at the moment," the tall vampire replied. "He will return tomorrow, I believe." He walked out of the room, leaving me alone with my thoughts.

If Merrill was in New York, then Franklin and Greg were with him. I climbed off the sofa, feeling cold and out of sorts. Nothing was going to make me feel any better—not for a while, anyway. Time was the only thing that would make grief easier to bear.

In the meantime, I headed toward the hot tub, and throwing caution to the winds, I dropped my clothes beside it and crawled in naked, doing my best to get rid of the chill that wouldn't leave.

"Anthony, René's assets will be divided between you and René's other living child, Devlin. Meanwhile, I will be granting temporary custody to Gavin. His claim is strongest—Devlin has never expressed any desire to have a vampire child and in my opinion, he is a bit immature, although he is nearing six hundred. Therefore, pending the Council's approval, your lessons will be with Gavin from now on." Wlodek had lists of René's assets on his desk—Charles had printed them off and handed them over. Tony nodded, not looking at Wlodek.

"Now," Wlodek went on, "we must deal with another death. Gavin knows of this already, as did René, but we held off telling Lissa because we knew it would upset her and destroy her focus, more so in light of recent events." Tony looked up at those words.

"What happened?" He was steeling himself for more bad news.

"Greg, Franklin's mate, has passed. He contracted pneumonia a month ago and the physicians could not find a way to combat the disease since he was already so ill. He slipped into a coma and died four days ago. Merrill and Franklin carried his ashes to New York—that is where Greg wished to be buried. They will return tomorrow and we must inform Lissa somehow."

"This will destroy her," Gavin muttered.

"I know you disagreed with my decision not to tell her, but she needed to focus her mind on what she was doing, instead of worrying over a sick friend. Now we must try to make her see the reason in this, or at least work to convince her to forgive and move past it." Wlodek steepled his fingers and gazed at the two vampires who sat before his desk.

"And we have the Annual Meeting in less than two weeks," Wlodek continued. "Lissa must be prepared to attend, Gavin, as I intend to make the announcement then. We have a Queen and she must hold her head up and go."

"Honored One, how many blows do you think she can take?" Gavin rose, pulling Tony up with him. Gavin gave Wlodek a curt nod and ushered his adopted child out of Wlodek's office.

~

"Thank you for taking us and bringing us back; I don't think I could have dealt with the lengthy plane rides," Merrill said. Griffin chose to drop Merrill and Franklin inside Merrill's kitchen. Greg's body had been cremated in England, but his ashes had been scattered in a designated place in New York.

"It was no trouble," Griffin replied. "When are you planning to tell Lissa?"

"As soon as she wakes," Merrill sighed. Franklin turned troubled eyes to his vampire father. "Child, would that compulsion still worked on her," Merrill offered. "I also know it will be a fresh blow to you. For that, I am sorry. We must find a way through this."

❦

"Lissa, Merrill has returned." Gavin had a bag of blood for me when I woke and pulled me inside his arms while I drank. I cleaned up and dressed afterward while he waited. Something was up—he hardly ever waited for me to finish dressing, doing my hair and brushing my teeth. He walked downstairs with me, too. Tony was already in the kitchen, waiting for us. As was Merrill.

"Lissa, we are all troubled by René's death," Merrill said, patting the barstool beside his. I settled there next to him. "But there is other news," he went on. "News that we did not give you earlier as we wanted to keep you focused on your assignment. We did not wish to distract you, causing you to worry over other things."

I was watching Merrill's face closely now and fear gripped my heart. Ever since Griffin told me it was beating again, I'd felt it pounding in my chest when I was frightened. It was pounding now—triple time.

"Lissa, if I could lighten this blow, I would," Merrill toyed with a scrap of paper in his hands. It looked like a note of some kind. "Greg contracted pneumonia a month ago. The antibiotics failed to control the disease and he slipped into a coma. He never woke and died five days ago. Franklin and I went to New York to scatter his ashes."

I was on my feet, shaking my head in disbelief. I was numb—completely numb. Greg had been ill and no one had told me. No wonder Merrill hadn't called, or cut off our conversations before I could ask questions. No wonder Gavin wouldn't lend me his laptop the last time I asked.

"Lissa, I was following orders," Gavin said from somewhere far away. That was an excuse and the poorest of excuses on top of that. Greg had been sick and all it would have taken was a plane ride from D.C. so I could see him. To see Greg, once before he died. Yet they'd deliberately kept the information from me. That hurt worse than I can say. It was one more betrayal in a long line of betrayals.

"There," I hissed out angrily, "is no excuse for this." I took a step toward Merrill, and he backed up. "No excuse, now or ever," my voice was rising. "You get what you want, every single time."

Claws formed on my fingers and Merrill backed up another step. "When will there come a time when you think of something other than what the fucking Council wants? Were you afraid your plans might be put on hold for a couple of days? Is that it? That Lissa wouldn't go out like a good little girl and do what she's told because somebody she loved was dying?" I was shouting by that time.

Merrill's kitchen island was ripped apart. The refrigerator was lifted and tossed through the back wall. I was screaming and crying the whole time I destroyed Merrill's kitchen, and somewhere inside me, a small voice wept pitifully, asking over and over why they hadn't told me. Eventually I turned to mist and flew right off Merrill's property. Yes, there wasn't a single soul there who could stop me. They should have thought about that before they decided to do what they did.

CHAPTER 14

"The Honored One isn't the only one with a temper." Charles examined the wrecked kitchen. He'd disagreed with Wlodek when he withheld information regarding Greg's illness and death, but knew better than to say anything.

Merrill was glad Franklin had been asleep—Griffin had placed him in a healing sleep at Merrill's request while Merrill took on the task of telling Lissa the news. Gavin was stunned at what had happened. He'd expected Lissa to weep uncontrollably. Somehow, though, they'd managed to push her over some sort of boundary, and uncontrollable anger had been the result instead. He knew the tears would come eventually, but now, none of them knew where she might be.

"I can set this to rights," Griffin appeared, examining the gaping hole in Merrill's kitchen wall with a deep sigh.

"The kitchen, perhaps," Merrill said with the tiniest bit of sarcasm.

"I told you it was a mistake," Griffin muttered. "You should have told her. She deserved the opportunity to see him before he passed."

"Maybe you should have pounded it into my head, instead," Merrill grumbled. Griffin snorted in reply.

"Where is she?" Wlodek demanded, walking in and surveying the damage. Gavin stood nearby, amazed when Griffin began using his power to put the kitchen back together.

"In a tree ten miles away, crying her eyes out," Griffin formed light around his hands and repaired the broken hinges on the refrigerator door before floating it back to its proper place.

"Will she return?" Gavin was now more frightened than before.

"No idea," Griffin grunted softly as he pulled broken bits of granite together with the ability that he held. The base of the island formed with a thought and a solid piece of granite flopped down on top of it. The hole in the wall came next; dust and tiny chunks lifted off the floor, reformed, then slapped against the wall. A broken beam was made whole again. Cracked tiles healed themselves. The light fixture was once again in one piece and shining over the island.

"If you'll tell me where she is, I'll go get her." Tony's voice was hesitant.

"I can go," Charles offered.

"I'll go, I'm her father," Griffin sighed. He'd been stalling by putting the kitchen back together. "Bear in mind, I will not intervene on your behalf." He looked at both Merrill and Wlodek. "Not this time. I did after she tried to kill herself, but those days are over. You have two weeks before your Annual Meeting. I suggest you try to smooth things out as well as you can between now and then." Griffin disappeared.

"What is he talking about?" Gavin growled.

"Griffin did something—healed something or planted a suggestion that you and I weren't her enemy or some such," Merrill raked a hand through his black hair and glanced at his kitchen—put together perfectly by Griffin's power. "She'd have tried to kill herself a second time, I think, if he hadn't done it."

"She loves you, Gavin, or you wouldn't have been able to hold onto her this long," Charles spoke up. "Although all this might have been handled with a bit more finesse and tact. Honored One, we only deal with males on assignments. You've never had a female to send out—not really. I've read Sarita's files. She chose her own targets and went after them. She accepted information from you but you didn't control her. Not like this." Charles blinked at Wlodek, surprised at his own outburst.

Wlodek glanced at Merrill before turning back to Charles. "Young Charles, I had not realized you'd gone through all the files. You are correct, but Sarita is not a subject to bring up with me."

"Of course not, Honored One." Charles hung his head in embarrassment.

"Sarita was never as gifted as Lissa." Gavin spoke again. "Are we still planning to make the announcement at the Annual Meeting, though Xenides is still out there?"

"I believe so. He must realize that he is going against a Queen. We have crippled him now, as he is turning to the Elemaiya for help with this instead of depending solely on vampires. We are backing him into a corner. The idea that she is still susceptible to compulsion has outlived its usefulness. We will send the message that she is strong—very strong—and willfully hunting him and any minions that remain." Wlodek nodded at Charles. "Come, Charles. We have work to do."

Gavin watched as Wlodek strode toward the doorway inside the pantry. Charles closed it behind him as they made their way down the stairs. "Lissa will be angry if she comes back at all." Gavin muttered.

"She'll come back—Franklin is still here," Tony observed. "I don't think she'll abandon him, even if she wants to leave the rest of us behind."

Rain dripped off dead leaves as I huddled against the oak's trunk, the icy drops falling down past my collar and making me shiver as I sat there. The sobs had quieted to hiccups now. My emotions had run from anger to sorrow to depression and back to anger. How could they do this? How? Were they so devoid of love or any other emotion that they didn't recognize it in other people? I failed to understand any of this. Right then, I think I hated all of them.

"Hate is a strong word." Griffin stood beneath my tree. "I know you don't truly hate Gavin. Or Tony. I can't say for sure about Merrill and Wlodek. Poor Charles has no choice but to obey—he is too young."

"They knew what would happen." My voice was sullen and angry.

"They knew—in a way. Their mistake was in thinking they might make it up to you afterward. That you are a child that can be placated with promises or the lure of possessions. You haven't believed in promises for a very long time, have you, little girl? As for possessions, those mean very little to you. They should have realized this by now."

Griffin had his face turned up to me. I wiped tears off my cheeks with my right hand while holding onto the trunk of the oak tree with my left. Why did I think I even needed that security? I could turn to mist if I fell. It comforted me, somehow, to have an arm wrapped around something solid.

"Lissa," Griffin went on, "you'll want to be at the Annual Meeting. Xenides is still out there and you must cooperate as much as you can with Wlodek and the others until he is eliminated. That seems to be your quest. After that, perhaps your decisions will be your own. I know that you will certainly have more leverage if you can take him down. Come back with me now. You don't have to talk to any of the others if that is what you want. Find a dress, hold your head up and go to the Annual Meeting. Find out where Xenides is and dispense justice. That is the only way to bring any semblance of peace to the vampire race on Earth. Come back with me, little girl. Franklin needs you."

His last statement was what got me out of the tree. I think I sobbed as I dropped out of it, too. Franklin. He'd lost his mate. Not just a close friend—a mate. How much pain had he suffered? Merrill and Wlodek had more than likely stopped him from communicating with me and that made me even angrier. He'd gone through this with support from Merrill only. Merrill was definitely on my shit list.

"I can get myself home." I didn't allow Griffin to touch my arm. I was still out of sorts with him—he'd manipulated my birth, after all. I was the answer, he'd said, to so many problems. Well, that didn't make me feel special. Not one little bitty bit.

"Very well," Griffin sighed and disappeared.

∼

"Don't bother trying to talk your way out of this," I flung out an arm at Gavin. Merrill was close behind him when I'd appeared in the kitchen after misting home. "Where's Franklin?" I asked, heading toward his suite.

"Sleeping," Merrill replied softly. "He'll wake in four hours."

"Good. I'll see him then. In the meantime, leave me the fuck alone." I walked away from all of them.

∼

"Father, we can't get through to her. None of us can." Charles placed a glass of wine in front of Flavio and sat beside him at the kitchen island.

"Child, this is not your fault," Flavio sipped his wine. "I was angry with father because he withheld the information that she was a Queen. He still has not informed the rest of the Council. They may be angry as well, although my sire believes his reasoning to be sound."

"The Council will never admit they're angry," Charles looked away.

"Of course not. It is the way we are taught—to be friends and enemies during our lengthy lives."

"I think Lissa has a right to be angry over this. She wanted to say goodbye." Charles still refused to look at his vampire sire.

"Child, while I agree with you on this, things of that nature are a luxury that we as vampires do not receive. I wish it could have been otherwise. We will need her in the coming days and we do not desire her enmity."

∼

234

"Frank?" I had a milkshake ready when he woke. Franklin raised a hand to his face, rubbing his eyes and sighing.

"Lissa?" Franklin blinked at me. There was such sadness in his eyes I almost started crying again.

"Frankie, I brought you a milkshake; it's strawberry—your favorite," I said. "How are you feeling?"

"Awful."

"I know, honey. I am so sorry." Franklin reached out to take my hand and surprised me by kissing it. I helped him sit up in bed before handing the shake over.

"He never woke after the first week," Franklin sighed and sipped his shake.

"Frankie, that's awful," I reached out and smoothed his hair back.

"Lissa, you're one of the few people who understands what that's like," Franklin ran a finger down the glass, wiping away a bit of condensation. "I know your husband was in a coma and on life support for a long time."

"Yeah. I know what that's like," I said, smoothing out Franklin's blanket. "I'm sorry I wasn't there for you. Or for Greg."

"Lissa, don't apologize, I know exactly why you weren't there. You would have been, if you'd known."

"Yeah."

"Try not to be too angry with Merrill, okay? He loves me."

"I know he does. That's why I destroyed the kitchen instead of him."

"Is my kitchen still destroyed?"

"No. I think Griffin put it back together."

"You won't call him father, will you?"

"So far he hasn't done much in the father department."

"Come here, Lissa, and lie down with me." Franklin set his glass down on the nightstand and scooted over. I lay down beside him and snuggled against his side. "This is good," he sighed over the top of my head and closed his eyes.

～

"This one," Charles said. Charles and Flavio had come to Paris with me. Franklin wasn't up to it. Frank wasn't up to much of anything, nowadays. I cooked for him as often as not, or he might not have eaten anything. Depression is an ugly word and one I understood all too well. I looked at the gown shown to us.

"It's white," I pointed out. There's nothing like being a fluorescent light bulb around a bunch of old, moth-eaten vampires.

"You look good in white." Charles bumped my shoulder with his. Flavio was standing nearby, allowing Charles and me to decide on my ball gown. If Griffin hadn't told me I ought to go, I would have given Wlodek and Merrill a rude gesture and refused outright.

I asked them to hold the white dress so I could try it on and went on to the rest that they had. I said no to the gold one, the yellow one and the red one. Not good colors for me. A dress made of aqua silk was brought out, which I loved, and another in black was set aside to try.

Charles liked the white, but fell in love with the aqua dress when I slipped it on. It was strapless and hugged every curve I had, falling to a full skirt that swirled around my feet. I thought about wearing the same shoes I'd worn last time, but Charles just shook his head. "Good memories, remember?" He tapped his head. Well, there was that.

The black dress looked good too, so Flavio tossed down his credit card and we walked out with all three, along with six pairs of shoes. We'd only come for the evening, so we loaded right back into Merrill's jet, which Brock had piloted for us.

Flavio drove us straight back to Merrill's after we landed in London, and I found Franklin moping around the kitchen. The Annual Meeting was in three days, and Franklin's depression hadn't improved. Of course, my anger hadn't improved, either, and I didn't see any way out of that, barring a lengthy passage of time. I went to the roof to spend what was left of the night—barely an hour, actually, after convincing Franklin to go to bed. He wasn't getting much sleep. The roof was where Gavin found me after going through lessons with Tony.

"Cara, are you going to be angry with me forever?" he asked as he settled beside me.

"Gavin, you knew and you didn't tell me." That hurt. Really.

"Cara, I know I told you it was dangerous to keep email information on your cell. And it is. Cell phones are easily lost. And I also know I told you that you could borrow my laptop so you wouldn't have to take yours along. I had no idea that things would go in the direction they did, I promise. We have protected ourselves over the years by doing as Wlodek and the Council instructed. I know this has hurt you. You have faced two losses whereas I have only faced one. Anthony has been damaged greatly by this as well."

"Gavin, would they have waited to tell you that René died if it happened while you were on assignment? Would they?" I looked up at him. His face was shuttered, just as Wlodek's usually was.

"Cara, I have been a vampire for a very long time. I have learned to control this."

"Is that what the problem is? I can't control my emotions? That you can't control my emotions? Gavin, listen to yourself."

"Cara, we were worried that the assignment would not be completed."

"Have I failed you or your precious Council, Gavin? Have I? Tell me when I didn't come through—for them or for you. Did I fall apart in that bar in Tampa when I saw you get burned to a crisp? Did I fall to the floor weeping, instead of taking care of Nyles Abernathy? Did I collapse in a heap when Glen was killed in New Mexico? Did I? If Tony hadn't called me back after I killed the vampire holding the First Lady in Washington, I'd have gone after Xenides and taken his ass out, right then and there." I was pissed. Really, really pissed. And shaking, too, I was so angry.

"Cara, I have seen you depressed and moping about the house. Tell me that was not the case when you learned six men were dying after receiving your blood." Gavin was giving me tit for tat, now.

"And I got sent off-world, right in the middle of all that. And I did what I was supposed to do there, too. Were we on some sort of time limit in Kansas City? Would it have been a big deal if we put it off for a day or two?"

I watched his face and drew in a breath. There *had* been a designated time and place. More than likely, it had been set up by Xenides himself, after he'd killed Don's brother, David. And, since Gavin and the others had the time and place, somebody knew that Tony would be there. He'd been the target in Kansas City, I was sure of it. Who might know he would come? Who?

Gavin looked away from me as soon as he knew I knew. They'd kept that away from me. That's why he'd asked me to go as mist—so Xenides or his minions wouldn't see me. That was just fucking wonderful. "Cara, you are young. So young, as a vampire. Yes, I know we have had this argument before and yes, I remember where that got us." Gavin held up a hand.

"Gavin, I can't help that. And I guarantee that no matter how old I get, I'll still be pissed."

"Lissa, I came up to make things right between us, not fight with you." He pinched the space between his eyebrows as if he had a headache or something.

"You sure as hell go about things strangely," I muttered. I missed Roff at times like this. If he were here, I'd have misted away and settled in bed beside him, I think. Gavin and I hadn't slept in the same bed since we'd come in from Kansas City.

"Lissa, what I'm trying to say is that I love you. Overlook my age and rigidity, I beg you." Gavin was attempting to pull me against him, his deep brown eyes begging me to allow his touch.

"I will if you'll overlook what you insist is youth," I muttered. "I can't help it, Gavin. I cry when I lose somebody. I get depressed if six people are dying because of me. Honestly, I don't know why you want me. We don't have that much in common."

Gavin lifted me into his lap and wrapped his arms around me. "I remember when I was introduced to you," he whispered against my hair. "I saw your perfect little mouth and I was lost. Forever lost. If it were possible to go back and revisit a time, ever, I would go back to that moment. I would hold your face in my hands, cara, and kiss you.

Your scent is an aphrodisiac to me—didn't you know? I thought I would have to contact Wlodek and ask him to get me away from you that first night."

"You would have killed me if he'd asked."

"And that would have killed me. I don't know how long I would have lasted, cara, if you'd died at my hand. Now, when I hold you, I can't say how fortunate I am—or how grateful. As if something precious was meant for someone else and it was handed to me by mistake. That's how I feel. Of all the important vampires in the world, the little Queen belongs to me. Wears my ring and sleeps in my bed. How many envy me already? How many more will envy me when they learn what I have?" He tipped my chin up and settled his mouth over mine. "Take us to bed, cara mia," he broke the kiss to whisper the words.

～

When I'd attended the last Annual Meeting, it had been on Merrill's arm at some location in Great Britain. This year it was held in France, and I couldn't help thinking of René as Gavin helped me out of the limousine we'd ridden in. Wlodek and Merrill had come separately, thank goodness. I wasn't in any mood to talk to either of them. And I hadn't talked to either of them. Not for days.

"Cara, you are lovely," Gavin kissed me lightly and tucked my hand inside his arm. We walked toward the entrance of an expansive chateau, with neatly trimmed grounds and gardens surrounding it.

Water tinkled in fountains, the scent of flowers floated past and hectares of land surrounded us as we walked toward the brightly lit structure. There wasn't another home, chateau or village anywhere in sight. Thank goodness, this chateau wasn't René's—that would have been sadness on top of sadness. For Gavin and me.

Wlodek insisted that Tony stay in England. He was too young, according to Wlodek, although Gavin thought highly of his fighting skills. Gavin informed me quietly that he imagined Wlodek would allow Tony to come next year, to help the Enforcers guard the meeting.

Vampire guards nodded respectfully to Gavin when we walked through the doors. After passing through a grand entry, Gavin led me into a huge ballroom, decorated in Louis XVI style. Russell, Radomir and Will were already stationed around the ballroom's perimeter, carefully watching the guests. I wanted to go to all three of them and say hello, but that wasn't acceptable. I was supposed to be more circumspect.

"Come this way," Merrill drifted silently beside us, leading Gavin and me toward a knot of vampires. It was the Council; I learned that quickly enough.

I had to be civil and respectful to Merrill, Wlodek and the others. I hated that I had to be there. Hated that I had to act as if I were enjoying myself. I wondered briefly how many others felt exactly the same.

The males were all dressed in expensive tuxedos, either white or black. A few had ventured into the fringe of fashion and worn a bowtie that wasn't black or white. Female companions dotted the floor like colorful snowflakes, fallen onto darker ground.

"Follow me," Radomir was there suddenly, Wlodek and Charles right behind him. Charles carried his laptop case, so there would be minutes taken. We were going to a meeting. All of us were led toward a doorway at the back of the ballroom, every other vampire present stepping aside to allow us passage. Most bowed to Wlodek as we passed.

The room was small, designed perhaps for more intimate gatherings. Still, it was large enough to hold all eight Council members, Wlodek, Merrill, Radomir, Gavin, Charles and me. Radomir closed the door behind us and stood guard there.

"Lissa, this is Montrose." Merrill was introducing me to the Council. Montrose lifted my hand and kissed it. "Ilaisaane." The Asian female that had voted against me. I schooled my face and muttered pleasantries. "Nestor. Cecil. Jarl." The three males who'd voted against me. Two of those were tainted, along with Ilaisaane.

Did I think anyone had paid attention to me when I'd said that before? Of course not. Jarl was the only exception. He was shorter than most vampires I'd met. "Oluwa," he actually smiled at me, his beautiful, white teeth a contrast to darker skin. His black eyes danced as he kissed my hand.

"Susila," the second female Council member. She didn't smile but her eyes sparkled. "And Flavio, of course," Merrill made the last of the introductions. Flavio kissed both cheeks in the European style. Still the handsomest male I'd ever met on Earth. I'm sure he knew it, too, although it didn't seem to affect him at all. Charles's laptop was set up and waiting before the introductions were ever completed.

"I called this meeting," Wlodek spoke for the first time, "to inform all of you that we have a Queen again." The only sound I heard after that announcement was Charles tapping on his computer. Wlodek cleared his throat. "Lissa is a Queen Vampire, and we will be sending her out quickly to hunt Xenides."

"She is susceptible to compulsion," Ilaisaane spat, breaking the silence. Well, she wasn't high on my list, either. None of them were. Gavin pinched my elbow to keep me from snapping at her.

"She is not. Even my compulsion cannot hold her," Wlodek admitted. Ilaisaane turned to him with a sneer. She might have opened her mouth to say something else, but the words were never spoken—I drew in a breath, a huge hole was blown into the side of the chateau and human companions were screaming in terror inside the ballroom.

No! I shouted mentally to Radomir, whose hand reached for the doorknob—he was ready to go out and do battle. That was a bad idea. Xenides had come to call, I was sure of it, and he'd probably brought friends. A lot of friends, unless I missed my guess.

"Well, bitch," I snarled at Ilaisaane, "you get to stay here. Everybody else is coming with me." Before Wlodek or Merrill could stop me, I turned everyone else in the room to mist, leaving Ilaisaane behind and cursing as I swooped through the ceiling.

My guess, sadly enough, turned out to be correct. An army surrounded the chateau; Xenides' troops were pouring through the newly blasted hole in the wall and either fighting or shooting the Aristocracy inside the ballroom.

I knew without a doubt that somebody had given secret information to Xenides, leaking information on the Annual Meeting. I smelled vampires, humans and Dark Elemaiya in the attacking army —Xenides had been busy collecting allies after we'd offed many of his vampires.

All of these were armed to the teeth, too; I saw weapons of all kinds, as well as armored vehicles (somebody had raided the army, looked like). And the humans? They'd all been given a little extra. I smelled vampire blood taint on all of them. Xenides had a disposable army of humans around him—they would all die—if not tonight then soon, from a terrible disease with no ready cure.

Lissa, take us to that hill toward the north. Merrill's mindspeech came through loud and clear when I hesitated over the battle in the ballroom below. *We will decide there what to do about this attack,* he added. Well, if we lived over this, Merrill and I might have a little chat. I'd tried to reach him before with mindspeech, and as he hadn't responded, I didn't think he could. Seems he had it all along, he'd just ignored me. There wasn't time to be more furious than I already was with him; there was a job to do and Xenides had stacked the deck in his favor.

Surprisingly enough, not a peep came from any Council member when I set them down on the designated hill. Located half a mile from the chateau, it was still within hearing distance as Xenides' army fought the Aristocracy and pounded away at the building; nearly half of it had been destroyed in their initial assault.

Screams filled the air—if anyone attempted to escape, they were taken down swiftly. Xenides' army was herding all vampires toward the ballroom; two outside walls were completely down and the room was visible to all of us from our hilltop perch. Wlodek cursed.

"We are formidable, but even our strength is no match for that many," Oluwa muttered. He was right—at least two thousand lay siege against the chateau.

"Agreed," Montrose sighed. "We might take out the perimeter, but we will perish if we attempt to make our way past that."

"We don't have enough here to properly surround them, or to fight our way out if Lissa returns us to the chateau," Flavio pointed out.

"And we still have no guarantee that Xenides is among them," Susila added. I jerked toward her—that statement frightened me. We all stood there, atop a grassy hillside, dressed for a ball while humans and vampires died below us. A horrified giggle threatened at the incongruity of the situation, even as my mind operated on another level, desperately searching for a solution to this problem.

"The humans have all been given vampire blood," I muttered. "What will that do for them?" I turned my eyes toward Wlodek. I wasn't speaking to Merrill.

"They will have enhanced strength—for perhaps half an hour. It depends upon how fresh the blood was when it was given," Wlodek growled. Great. Just what we needed—an army of super-strong humans.

"Honored One, command us," Montrose said softly, bowing slightly to Wlodek.

"We cannot leave the others like this—I choose to die with them, if that is to be their fate," Wlodek stripped off his jacket and let it fall to the ground. Radomir, Montrose and Flavio followed his example quickly.

"Wait," I held up a hand. "I have an idea." Would they listen to me? I was about to find out.

"What do you have, cara?" Gavin hadn't said a word until now.

"Gavin, how much of my blood did you take before, when we were checking to see if you had my talents after drinking from me?"

"No more than a mouthful, cara." Gavin's eyebrows were lifting. He knew where I was going with this.

"His temporary talents lasted an hour," I said. "All of you, take a little of my blood. That will allow you to hold every talent I do, for an hour." I searched every face there—they were blinking at me in shock. Wlodek hadn't been forthcoming, looked like.

Merrill might have plenty of compulsion to lay after this was over. If we survived, that is. "You'll be able to mist instantly, and only have your hands materialize," I began. "I suggest you fly through the army as mist, with only your hands and claws visible. Do a sweep and take heads. Bullets and bombs will go right through your mist." I watched all of them—Susila's eyes held interest and Oluwa's now held a bit of hope.

"You'll have mindspeech, too, so use it if you need it. Let the others know if you need help," I went on. "Fly swiftly. Cut quickly. Leave the dying behind you. If it is needed, gather friends away inside your mist. We can do this," I said.

"Lissa, this may weaken you," Merrill pointed out the obvious.

"I'll take that chance," I jerked my head, acknowledging his words. "Charles," Charles's head snapped up at the mention of his name, "will you gather up the human companions and take them to safety? You can gather them inside your mist and bring them here," I suggested.

Charles nodded at me, his eyes wide. He hadn't thought to be included in the onslaught, and he appreciated being included. "Gavin, make sure they only take what they should," I said, preparing to be bitten.

"Come. We will do this," Wlodek stepped forward. He was the first to take my blood.

"What is that?" Xenides' spy trembled as he watched his new master. Xenides held a small vial in his hands and worked to remove the cap.

"The last of its kind, until we capture our little princess," Xenides drank the contents of the vial quickly. He'd swallowed both doses of Lissa's blood and had perhaps an hour to search her out while his army worked to contain the others. They would all die—Xenides wanted that more than anything. He smiled grimly at his latest conscript before turning to mist and flying away.

I could see them all as we flew rapidly toward the chateau—a sea of attackers surged forward as they continued to bombard the building with rifles, rockets and bombs. I was terrified that none inside the ballroom might survive as we prepared for our attack.

Wlodek suggested we stay close together and destroy the attackers in swaths. I didn't care; I just wanted all of them dead. Russell was still inside the chateau, as was Will, Stephan, Brock and many others.

It infuriated me that human men and women were being targeted, when they had no defense against those coming against them. Yes, some of the human companions were males, and there wasn't any way they could fight off vampires, Dark Elemaiya or enhanced humans armed with rifles or rocket launchers. I hoped Charles reached them soon; I continued to hear screams emanating from the chateau.

Following Wlodek's suggestion, we descended upon the occupying army like a bomber squadron. Wlodek flew in the center, his mist a shining silver, Merrill to his right, Flavio and Radomir to his left. Gavin and I flew next to Merrill, with the others spread out on either side. Claws formed swiftly as we approached, and a hundred-foot swath of the enemy died in that first sweep alone.

e split up after half the army had been destroyed—
Susila and Montrose hadn't concentrated on taking
heads after a while, they'd lowered their claws and the screams from
dying enemies rent the night. Cut in half they died a cruel death, but it
sent a message to their companions—something was among them and
viciously destroying their numbers. Something they couldn't see to
kill. I could see the Council's mist easily enough, and soon the others
adopted Susila's tactics. It didn't matter how the enemy perished, it
only mattered that they did so.

Oluwa and Jarl went after those that began to run; most of those
were Dark Elemaiya. Xenides and his vampires had placed
compulsion on the humans so they wouldn't run, but either couldn't
or agreed not to do so with the Elemaiya. Those were now deserting
in droves. What still lived, anyway.

Radomir and Gavin misted toward the ballroom, prepared to fight
alongside those Enforcers left behind. Wlodek, Flavio and Merrill
were terrible to behold, slicing swifter than a blink through anything
they encountered.

I killed as I searched for Xenides, ignoring screams and flying blood. The ballroom was filled with vampire ash—many of the Aristocracy had died fighting off their attackers. Charles had done his duty, though; I only saw a few dead humans among piles of ash.

The hour was winding down, too, and I was counting off precious seconds as I continued my search for Xenides. Susila's words haunted me—what if he hadn't come? What if he were hiding somewhere, expecting his vampire, human and Elemaiyan army to accomplish this on its own? The army was nearing destruction—the Council had seen to that, with help from Gavin and Radomir.

❧

Xenides cursed mentally. He'd been searching for a single spot of mist, but he'd now counted thirteen. Those spots of mist ranged from bright gold to silver, copper, yellow, white, blue—he'd stopped listing the colors.

He had no idea which one might be his little princess, and he worried that his dose of her blood was wearing thin. He had to find her and quickly. His army was dying, killed by claws that formed from nothing and swiped easily through solid bodies.

The little princess was his hope of escaping and continuing his quest—he had to have her or all would be lost. Meanwhile, many of his were dying at the hands of three vampires who stood at the center of the ballroom floor, fighting off anything that attacked them. Xenides intended to destroy them and then continue his search for Lissa.

❧

Russell and Will were fighting in a triangle with Trevor, Wlodek's other Assassin, inside the ballroom. It would have been a pleasure to stay and watch them fight; nothing came close to them. And that's when I saw him. Xenides was mist.

He'd held back some of my stolen blood and was now searching for me—as red mist. But first, he planned to destroy Russell, Will and Trevor. Rushing toward them, he intended to materialize and take them by surprise. Unless I got there first, that is.

Xenides roared as he came back to corporeality—I'd snatched his three targets away at the last second. Xenides saw them disappear; he was just helpless to do anything about it.

I've spotted Xenides, I sent mindspeech to the others as I dropped my three on the floor and came back to myself in front of them. I should have looked behind me. I didn't. I should have expected what came next. I hadn't.

Charles had lifted a few vampires in his mist, along with their human companions. Now he, Gian Moretti and a few others were keeping companions calm and sitting on the grassy northern hill overlooking the battle below. Lissa's blood had given the Council the weapons they needed to combat Xenides' army, but Charles, whose vision was quite sharp, knew that many vampires had died fighting off their attackers.

While he'd been mist, Charles could see the others' mist. Now that he was corporeal again, he could only see the devastation they brought as human and vampire enemies fell, many of them cut in half by claws that formed from nothing.

Working to calm himself, Charles repeated silently that all would come right in the end. Until his skin began to itch. He attempted to ignore it at first, but then his flesh began to burn. Charles went to mist in a blink and blazed toward the battle.

Xenides' claws raked my shoulder before I could blink, and I screamed and misted away. His claws still out, he went after the three I'd just saved, their deaths clearly his intention. He hadn't meant to debilitate me—the rake he'd given was a warning. Still, the slashes were deep and I imagined they'd be bleeding when I came back to myself. Rushing forward, I formed claws, but Xenides was already poised to destroy Russell, who stood at the front of the triangle once more, lengthy claws out, ready to battle a nearly invisible Xenides.

"Hey!" I shouted, becoming corporeal ten feet away. Xenides misted in my direction. He'd opted for the more attractive target and now focused on me instead. When I misted again, he rushed right back to his intended targets. I tried to get there first, but Xenides had been closer.

"You will obey me!" he materialized and shouted at Russell, Will and Trevor. Oh, no. All three were now blinking and nodding at Xenides.

Merrill! I shouted mentally. *Xenides has Russell, Will and Trevor under compulsion!*

Coming, Merrill replied swiftly. Merrill was the only one who could remove Xenides' compulsion. Until then, Xenides had an elite fighting force at his command.

"Come out, little princess, or I tell them to destroy the others and then themselves," Xenides threatened, watching the air around him warily. "Come to me, or I will do much worse than that." Russell, Will and Trevor stood at Xenides' back, under his compulsion and blinking in confusion, waiting for their new master to command them.

"I'm here, you piece of shit," I materialized a few feet away and faced off with Xenides.

"You will not insult me for long," he offered a nasty smile. Dressed head to toe in black leather, Xenides was prepared for battle, his features displaying grim determination. More of Xenides' vampires came forward to join Russell, Will and Trevor. One of them I recognized. I hoped I lived long enough to see to his justice.

"Now, come." Xenides' voice held mind-breaking compulsion as he gestured for me to walk toward him.

What could I do? Xenides' compulsion held Russell and Will. I cared about them. I took a step forward.

"No!" Charles half-formed from mist and slashed Xenides across the back before going to mist again. That gave Merrill, Flavio and Wlodek an opening—they began to fight with the vampires at Xenides' back.

Xenides went to mist and I was about to follow him when he dropped to the ground ten feet away, barely keeping his balance as he fell. My blood he'd ingested had finally worn away. He was bleeding too; Charles had done quick and significant damage.

Xenides still believed me under his compulsion, however, and shouted for me to help him. The stupid fuck. When I didn't come as he commanded, he rushed me. I misted out of his way before becoming corporeal again. He rushed again, with the same results. Sounds of fighting came from behind me.

Pay it no mind; we have this, Flavio's voice floated into my mind as I faced off with Xenides once more. He was preparing to charge again. At least my blood still worked with the Council; I hadn't seen Charles again since his first attack against Xenides.

"You will disregard all former commands," Merrill's voice dripped compulsion behind me. Russell, Will and Trevor were now safe. Xenides snorted at this turn of events, a wounded bull about to charge again.

Charles's claws materialized and raked Xenides across the nape, just as he rushed toward me. Charles would have taken his head, too, if Xenides hadn't raced forward at that moment. Even so, his rapid momentum kept his head attached and propelled his body toward me. I misted away again, turning to face Xenides as he slid to a stop, panting on the other side.

"You will do my bidding," Xenides commanded when I materialized before him.

"Fuck you, shithead," I snapped. Charles dropped from the air beside me, and I heard similar sounds at my back. The Council's supply of my blood had just worn off.

Xenides was only now beginning to worry that his compulsion hadn't worked. Blinking dark eyes at me, he struggled to come to grips with reality.

"She is a Queen," Wlodek now stood at my left—Charles was at my right and glaring angrily at Xenides.

"She is not," Xenides attempted denial. "I will take you down, old man." Xenides pointed a lengthy claw at Wlodek's chest.

"I'll get this," Merrill stalked forward, claws forming on his fingers.

"No, I will." I'd been running through ways to kill Xenides in my mind, ever since Charles nearly killed him the second time. I didn't want any conventional death for this piece of crap.

Xenides' remaining vampires were held by the Council at my back, and I wanted them to see this. In fact, I wanted everyone to see this. I wanted them to know just what this Queen was capable of doing. Yeah, I was royally pissed, and a good mood was far off in the future for me. Plus, my arm still hurt and bled a little from Xenides' attack on top of all that.

"Lissa," Wlodek breathed beside me, "Show this animal that you are a Queen." He jerked his head toward Xenides.

"With pleasure," I growled.

Yes, I can turn to mist in a blink. And once I'm mist, I can mist through or inside anything. And once I mist inside something, I can blow my mist outward, making things explode. Xenides' brain was a tight space, but I got inside it anyway.

It's a good thing vampires turn to ash when they die. If they didn't, Wlodek and Merrill would have worn Xenides' blood the rest of the night. As it is, they wore the ash from his head when it exploded, and I wasn't about to pay any cleaning bills.

I'm not even going to ask about your mindspeech, I sent a private message to Merrill as I stalked away from him and Wlodek. I was angry, my arm hurt and I needed blood.

Your father's blood, came the terse reply. Well, I shouldn't have been surprised. Not even a little.

Vampires parted around me as I waded through them. More than half the Aristocracy was dead, if I were reading things right. The ones that remained, however, were going to their knees as I passed. Gavin, Charles, Russell, Will and Trevor fell in behind me, warning vampires away if they came too close. The Council, Wlodek included, followed in my wake.

❦

The grounds and gardens surrounding the chateau were destroyed, while abandoned vehicles and bits and pieces of human and Elemaiyan bodies littered the lawns. The scent of spilled blood was everywhere. Only one of the chateau's walls still stood; the rest was rubble and strewn everywhere.

Survivors had found candles and torches, and those were spaced here and there—mostly to provide a bit of comfort and to reassure human companions who'd been led back to the chateau by Moretti after the battle. Some of the companions were reunited with their vampires. Many were not.

Xenides and his minions had destroyed more than three hundred of the five hundred members of the Aristocracy. Charles was working nearby on his laptop, entering names of deceased vampires. I'd hugged him when we got a moment alone—Xenides might have done a lot more damage if Charles hadn't shown up when he did. If I had anything to say about it, Charles would be invited to join the Aristocracy. I didn't give a damn that he was barely three hundred years old as a vampire. He deserved that honor.

Someone found blood for me in an abandoned limousine, and I was drinking it as I settled wearily on a stone bench against a broken outside wall. Wlodek, Merrill and Flavio were sorting things out and assigning burial details to hide human and Elemaiyan bodies. If a spade couldn't be found, vampire claws were utilized to dig up earth and bodies were dumped in deep holes.

"You wanted this one?" Russell grinned as he and Will hauled Devlin to me.

"Yes. I want that one," I agreed, setting my bag of blood aside and staring at Devlin. "Did you intend to kill René?" I snapped at him. He was the one who'd sold all of us out. He'd given information on the

Annual Meeting to Xenides. I had a feeling I knew what his price had been in exchange for that information.

"No," he whimpered, struggling in Russell and Will's grip. "I wanted Hancock to die."

"Yeah, I figured that out," I muttered.

"Please don't kill me like you did Xenides."

"How do you want to die?" I asked indifferently. I had no patience for this one.

"I wish his death," Gavin stepped up beside me. "René was my kin and I claim Blood Vendetta."

"In a minute," I said, waving Gavin off. He stepped back. "Devlin, nobody else knows," I said. "Except you and me, that is. You made Aubrey. He wasn't René's. René only took him to keep you from dying. He gave you a gift, Devlin—René kept your head attached to your shoulders by claiming your child. Didn't he? You made Aubrey before you were old enough as a vampire. And how did you repay your sire?"

Devlin shuddered. "I didn't want him to die," he snapped, refusing to look at me.

"But he did die. You betrayed your sire and cost him his life. Over what?" I let my claws slide out.

"He was giving too much attention to Hancock," Devlin whined. It was an old song—sung by many. Killing over petty jealousy. It made me ill. "He's yours," I nodded to Gavin.

"No!" Devlin shouted, but Will and Russell had already stepped back and Gavin's claws were swift. That one word turned out to be Devlin's last. His body dropped before me and I watched in satisfaction as it flaked away.

"We have a Queen." Oluwa came, with Montrose and Susila behind him. And embarrassingly enough, they went to their knees before me. It was bad enough when the others did it; now the Council was doing it. I slapped a hand over my face.

"Yeah. A foul-mouthed, evil-tempered, bitch of a Queen," I grumped, hoping they'd get up soon.

"Xenides counted on your getting him away from here, my

daughter," Wlodek said softly, sitting down beside me. "The army was merely a distraction. Once he had you, he didn't need them." When had Wlodek arrived? The last I'd seen of him, he'd been yards away. "And we will have a discussion later about profanity."

"I'll look forward to it," I snapped. "By the way, Ilaisaane's dead." She was, I'd found the red silk dress she'd been wearing, amid a pile of ash. I'd walked right past it without a twinge of regret.

"Just as well, she was scheduled for termination anyway," Wlodek sighed. And that's when everything slowed. It was as if I was still moving at normal speed, but everyone and everything else began to move at a snail's pace. Words were so painfully drawn out they were unintelligible. Griffin appeared before me.

"Xenides is gone, your mission here is complete," he said. I already knew that, but I was thankful his speech wasn't so slow I couldn't understand it. "Now," Griffin went on, "I need your help. Desperately. If you do not come into the future with me, Lissa, many will die." Griffin had an odd, frightened expression on his normally handsome face.

"What do you mean, many will die?" I gave him a puzzled look. I had no idea what he meant.

"Dragon and the others—the Saa Thalarr. I can't give you any information other than that, baby, because it would be interfering. Please, come with me now. Please."

"But what about Gavin?" I turned to reach out toward Gavin, who wore a frightened expression on his face and the hand he held out had stopped in its momentum to reach me. I felt a chasm between us right then and wanted to stretch out my arm to bridge the gap between us. Wlodek, too, had reached out a hand, as if he could force Griffin away from me. That hand had also stopped, leaving unformed words of denial on Wlodek's lips.

"No, Lissa, you must come now." Griffin pulled my attention away from Gavin and Wlodek. He waved a hand and I was no longer dressed in the aqua gown that had cost so much and was now torn and spattered with blood. I had jeans and one of my T-shirts on, with athletic shoes.

"Lissa, come now. There is no time." Griffin begged. I stared around me. Everything was still and silent. Merrill, standing behind Russell and Will, seemed terrified. Griffin was his friend, why should he be scared? "Lissa, please," Griffin said, and his voice trembled slightly "they're outnumbered and they'll die." He truly was afraid.

"Fine," I muttered and stood up. Griffin and I disappeared.

The End